the Quelling

Barbara Barrow

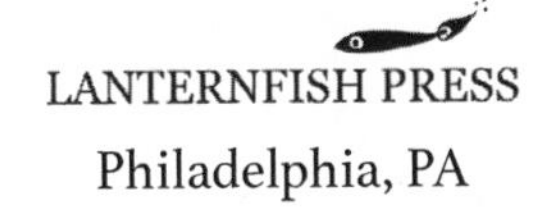

LANTERNFISH PRESS
Philadelphia, PA

THE QUELLING

LANTERNFISH PRESS
399 Market Street, Suite 360
Philadelphia, PA 19106
lanternfishpress.com

Cover Art
Image: "The Bride" by Alex Eckman-Lawn. Photography by Jason Chen. Design by Michael Norcross.

TRANSLATION
Excerpts from Lucretius, *De rerum natura*, are from the 1916 verse translation by William Ellery Leonard.

Printed in the United States of America.
Library of Congress Control Number: 2018942128
ISBN: 978-1-941360-18-7

Chapter 1

Dorian, Addie

Dorian

Some have jaws and fangs for the kill, and others have fast legs to escape. But every creature must chase or be chased. As children we were fascinated by these primal truths of the hunt: chimps screaming and pummeling their rivals, wolves piercing the necks of their prey. My sister and I gnawed each other in front of the television set. We sat alone in the house for days with the nature shows playing, and when the panthers came on, sleek and heaving, we dove and leapt at each other. At night, when the tree frogs came on, delicate and shining in the rain, we slept.

When they found the body they brought us to the police station and then to the private clinic outside Knoxville, where Dr. Lark and his nurses worked to make us harmless. They trimmed our nails, uncurled our fists, slid puffy black mittens on our hands, fitted helmets to our skulls. The same nature shows played and we still jumped at each other, thumping each other's helmets, chopping each other in the chest so that all the wind was knocked out. When we became teenagers he began to put some distance between us.

"Your bones won't heal so quickly now," he said. "You need to be apart."

Every night for months I waited in perfect silence outside the bathroom, listening to Addie pee and wash her hands and shuffle toward the locked door that separated us. When she emerged I threw myself against her as hard as I could, knocking her down, my fists battering her neck and cheeks, my fingers yanking her hair.

"It's a strange case, to be sure," Dr. Lark tells us. We are legally adults now, but he says we are still too unstable to leave the ward. And he is our primary specialist and runs the clinic, so everyone listens. "From what I can tell, it seems like you both lack a vital sense of security. You've never learned to attach to your caregivers properly. I'm not sure how to say this, but it seems as if you have never been quelled."

"Quelled?" Addie says. "Quelled? What does that mean?"

"Quelled," Dr. Lark says, trilling the L's. "It means you never learned that you are safe from attack. You strike first to protect yourselves. Some of this is about the murder. Some of this is about the abandonment. Some of this is about that early exposure to PBS *Nature* programming."

When he says this, the ward fades and I am back in the old house in Nashville with Addie, the colors from the television splashing across our skin, lions and cheetahs bounding and pouncing across the screen while the grandfather clock chimes and the oscillating fan twists its neck slowly back and forth.

"Quelled," Dr. Lark says again, almost to himself this time.

"What should we do?" my sister says. She is twenty, one year older than me, and delicately pretty apart from the misshapen jaw and nose that roll like waves in her face. "Does that mean we can't have our own families? Does that mean I can't have children?"

"I wouldn't go that far," Dr. Lark says. "It means you'll always have trouble forming bonds and attachments. But I've been working on a new approach to the cure that I think will help you and Dorian."

There will be many stages and sessions to this cure. "Think of it as a series of overlapping and repeating activities," he explains, gesturing with his clipboard while running his free hand through his peppery gray hair. His lab coat is a starched white wall and the lenses in his wire-rimmed glasses gather and reflect the light from the lamp in his office so that I cannot see the color or the expression of his eyes. "These activities will teach you new habits of empathy. Through proximity and closeness, through shared activities, you will learn not to attack but to attach instead."

At the first session we learn that we are to tend a tank of seahorses: this is supposed to show us the peace in nature. The delivery men set up the glass aquarium right in the center of the ward, next to the television in the common area, and Simon and Ellie fill it with algae-dusted rocks and red tree sponges and sea grass that sways and waves in the water. We are responsible for feeding the seahorses and cleaning their tank. The seahorses drift like dark hooks, like question marks. Like eardrums floating through the water. We watch them through the glass and our own reflections steal back to us softly. At night the tank is a beacon shining through the open door of our sleeping quarters.

During the sessions, we stand on opposite sides of the tank and watch the seahorses swim for half an hour or so while Dr. Lark and the nurses, Ellie and Simon, sit a few feet away with clipboards. Every few seconds we are supposed to narrate what is happening in the tank.

"You need to learn to work together, to see together," Dr. Lark says. "Tell me what you see, Addie. Speak loudly, so Dorian can hear you."

"I see two of them swimming," Addie says.

"Good, Addie," says Dr. Lark. "Now tell me something about the two of them, Dorian. The same two."

"I see them swimming," I say, "and dancing. They are swimming toward one another in the vines."

"Good," Dr. Lark says. "Now it's your turn, Addie. Tell me what Dorian said and then tell me what else you see."

Addie is silent. In the tank, two of the seahorses have broken off and are pursuing each other in a gliding, zigzagging pattern, up and down through the water.

"Tell me what Dorian said and then tell me what else you see," Dr. Lark says again.

Addie glares in the tank light. "They swam toward each other in the vines," she says stiffly. "Now they are mating together. The hen wants him to take the eggs."

"Good, Addie," Dr. Lark says, scribbling on his clipboard. Ellie leans over too and begins scribbling furiously. "Good. That's it for today. That's all."

Twenty minutes it took her to be able to say that. I want to punch through the glass at her and hold the mating seahorses right up to her eyes.

The day after the first session at the seahorse tank, he tells us we need to start living in close proximity at all times. We are strictly forbidden to attack each other, and Simon, who is restraint-trained, follows us everywhere to make sure that we don't. Over a series of several weeks I learn to spend every second within inches of my sister. Ellie moves our twin beds together and we read or watch TV while leaning on a shared pillow. If one of us goes to the bathroom, the other one comes in too and crouches next to the toilet and waits. We learn to share clementines and apples. We brush each other's hair. We sleep, wake, eat, shit, and tend the seahorses right next to each other, and strands of her blonde hair constantly brush my arm. Her skin stirs something violent in me. I can feel how warm she is at night and how the warmth slides off her body like steam slipping from the flat surface of an iron. I want to strike her but my wrists are bound and Simon watches from a chair near the doorway, ready to pounce on me the second I move. These nights are the worst nights. I watch between my bound hands as she sleeps and I see the sweat beading and slipping near her temples and my fists ache and I want to bring them down on top of her skull. In the mornings her skin is slick and clammy and gives off a humid scent.

"The goal of the sessions is to get you to cooperate, to exist together," Dr. Lark says in his office, sitting tall and straight, his muscular shoulders rounding out his white lab coat. Orbs of lamplight pool in his glasses. "If you two can do that, if you can begin to cooperate, then one day you will be able to remember and tell us what happened back in the house in Nashville. You will be able to know and speak about that memory. And that is the key to the cure."

He pronounces the last word like it is a prayer, in a reverent whisper. The Cure: the final end of the sessions, the culminating avalanche of memory that will free us.

There is nothing about that house that I want to know.

Addie

She will never be quelled. They will always have to sedate her and bind her fists at night to make her be calm. In the morning as we eat our breakfast from trays in the common area I watch Simon give her some toast and a knife to butter it with. Patiently, over and over, Simon takes the blunt knife away and shows her how to scrape the yellow pat of margarine across the crunchy surface of the bread. Then Dorian tries it, placated only for the moment, for just as long as Simon sits by her with his wiry tattooed arms ready to restrain her. No, they will never quell her or get her to hold still. She will wear herself out with punching first.

In the first session at the seahorse tank I stand across from Dorian and look at her face looming in the glass. Her hair, jet-black and longer than mine, hangs loose around her shoulders. The thick bolts of her scowling eyebrows wrench the skin above her nose into furrows.

"You need to learn to work together, to see together," Dr. Lark says. "Tell me what you see, Addie. Speak loudly, so Dorian can hear you."

In the tank the male seahorse floats up to the female like a mad little dragon. He has a pouch in his front and is beginning his courtship dance with her, a ritual that might take days, their bodies circling each other in looping designs, their tails linking around the same shared blade of grass. When the male is ready he will pump water through his little pouch to make room for the eggs of the hen. The nature shows have taught me how they mate, with their horsey heads parallel, gradually synchronizing their bodies through the meandering dance while a voiceover announces that the males, not the females, keep the eggs.

"I see two of them swimming," I say.

"Good, Addie," says Dr. Lark. "Now tell me something about the two of them, Dorian. The same two."

"I see them swimming," she says, "and dancing. They are swimming toward one another in the vines."

"Good," Dr. Lark says. "Now it's your turn, Addie. Tell me what Dorian said and tell me what else you see."

I stare into the tank. The hen lingers in the vines, dances

and hovers toward her mate, then twirls away airily, like a twig spinning on the current. To mate they will need to go down into the vines and the grass, where the male will puff out his pouch with the water. Then, when the hen's eggs are ready, they will both let go and drift upward, their snouts close, the female piercing him with her long, thin ovipositor, swelling his body with her eggs. In there, somehow, in that dance down in the grass, is the answer to the question.

"Tell me what Dorian said and then tell me what else you see," Dr. Lark says again.

"They swam toward each other in the vines," I announce. "Now they are mating together. The hen wants him to take the eggs."

"Good," Dr. Lark says, scribbling. "That's all for today."

Dorian backs away from her side of the tank, her reflected face slowly retreating out of the water. I know this about Dorian: she will never be quelled. And she will never respond to the cure. Dorian only knows the art of dumb blows, like a carnivore. Like a bear beating a fish with its claws. When she lunges for Simon after that first tank session, heaving and hitting, I slip away and follow Dr. Lark into the little office where he keeps his notes and files. He is sitting on a stool wearing his reading glasses, doing a crossword puzzle.

"You can forget about the cure," I say. "It won't work."

"You have to have faith, Addie," he says without looking up. "You have to believe the cure will work if you want it to help you."

"It's not me, it's Dorian. It will never work. It will be like the other cures."

He flinches.

"Addie," he says.

He takes his reading glasses off and looks at me. His eyes are brown and warm, set off by the gray traces around his temples and the folded white collar of his lab coat. He has faint laugh lines around his eyes and mouth that make his skin seem touchable. He looks long and deeply at me, and I stand and watch him back. Still, I can tell it is not my body he sees but my condition. My nose has been broken and reset several times. My jaw is woven into different shapes by dislocations, my lips have split and swelled, and my right shoulder has been knocked out of its socket so many times that it sits slightly lower than my left. I have a jigsaw figure, a young body battered and mended. It is like the first version of woman's body, blooming with defective newness when its Maker tore it out of a rib cage in haste.

Dr. Lark's diagnostic glance moves over me, looking deep into the story of my disorder, which is also Dorian's disorder. The small wrinkles around his temples deepen. I see my body in his eyes: the hips that have rounded and swelled, the skin at my collarbone where my scrubs fall open. I step forward.

"Addie," Dr. Lark says again, softly. "Addie, I'm a professional."

When I walk back through the ward Simon is trying to pry a broom away from Dorian. Dorian tries to raise it with both hands, to attack him in protest. She only knows about hitting in dumb fits of rage. Not the more delicate art of pinching, of squeezing new shades of color out of someone's skin. I see them up and down her forearms: bruises like the wings of tropical insects, large and colorful, peeking out from under her sleeve as she raises the broom again and again. She stops just long enough to watch me cross from Dr. Lark's office past the glowing tank and into our sleeping quarters. "The hen wants him to take the eggs," she hisses.

Dorian

Then they tell Addie and me to hold hands. "Concentrate on each other," Dr. Lark urges. "Try to think of what you know about each other, what you know that is not violent."

This is a new session of the remedy, of the cure that will teach us to bond. So Addie and I sit at a table and hold hands over the tabletop, like arm wrestlers. At first I want to lash out: her face is so close and her skin so slick and warm. But I make an effort. I concentrate. When I look at Addie this closely I cannot think of what is not physical, of what is not her body; what is her body is mine also, related to me or refracting me.

I see Addie's blonde hair and I see that it is the opposite of mine. I can tell whose it is when I see strands of it lying on the bathroom counter; I feel it tickle my arm at the seahorse tank. Her nose, dislocated, throws off the symmetry of her face, the spacing of her features. I picture all the organs in her body tilting off their axes: a heart askew, slanted lungs, ovaries rolling sideways. Blood splashing underneath her skin.

Addie's arms are not bruised as mine are bruised, broken vessels rising to just under the surface, like the inside of me made visible, my own blood glowing out in the open. Holding hands with her, I can tell she wants to squeeze. Her thumb and forefinger make hooks, begin to tense. Whenever this happens Simon darts forward and slaps her hand down and we start over. Dr. Lark scribbles.

One thing I know about Addie that is not violent is her desire to rear or care for another being. It is a desire that began in those heady days of early adolescence, in those confused afternoons of nature shows, when the energy to pinch and to attack suddenly gave way to some other impulse chattering beneath it. Some feeling that seemed in the moments of its greatest and most humiliating power to change the very structure of our bodies. Hips growing smooth and round like the sides of a honeydew melon. Alien curves to the waist. I first noticed this was also happening to Addie four years ago, when she began to lure Dr. Lark, who then had browner hair and less of a paunch in his belly, as he did his crosswords in the common area of the ward.

Dr. Lark often did these puzzles after lunch. That day he was obsessed with one clue he could not get, Seven Down. We were sitting on the couch watching a special program on the coywolf. On the screen, the lean gray coyote-wolf hybrid trotted up a long stretch of railroad tracks while a voiceover explained that the coywolf had made its way into urban areas by following the trains from city to city. Dr. Lark came out of his office with his yellow *Giant Crosswords* book tucked under his arm.

"Five letters," Dr. Lark said. "A primate native to Madagascar."

"Easy," Addie said. "A lemur."

"L-E-M-U-R. How did you know that?"

"*Discovery Africa*," Addie said. She stretched herself out on the sofa, long legs taut under flowered scrubs. "That puzzle is wrong, though. They aren't native to Madagascar. They came floating over on rafts of vegetation."

"No kidding," said Dr. Lark. Addie rose up on one elbow and looked at him beguilingly, crisscrossing her ankles. She was about to tell him some other bit of primate trivia, but then he said, "But dammit, if Seven Down is *lemur*, then how can Five Across be 'wolf-like omnivore'? *Jackal* doesn't start with an R. What starts with an R?"

He went back to his office. I started laughing. Addie glowered.

"That's okay," I said. "You can try again. But why would he want to do it to you in this place? He has plenty of women he can see on the outside."

Now Addie follows him straight into his office and closes the door, but she will not break him down. I can see it in her, this desire that is and is not violent, as she lies awake at night with her eyes lifted to the ceiling. At the tank sessions she stands across from me and answers all of his questions, staring into the water where his reflection floats and wavers in the seabed. I see the mating seahorses dance in the moon-like image of his face.

"That will never happen to you," I whisper to Addie over the bubbling jets of water. "Too many jolted bones."

ADDIE

"Concentrate on what you know that is not violent," Dr. Lark urges. But what is there that is not violent? The mating of the seahorses, the feel of Dorian's hair tickling my shoulder at night, Dr. Lark taking his glasses off and looking at me? They would say I was not stable enough to raise the child, if my body were indeed even strong enough to give birth to it. To him. Or to her. What comes before all that, the attraction and the seduction, is a matter for other women, women on the outside.

After we hold hands and after we gaze into the tank, Dr. Lark turns off the TV and tells us to read. "You need to form habits of reflection and of curiosity," he says. Ellie instructs us to go get books from the single shelf in the far corner marked LIBRARY. These books come from various places, from the nurses and their families or from schools and churches on the outside, and the shelf startles me with its variety and strangeness. The titles are all slanted like a row of toppled dominoes. A tattered, coffee-ringed copy of *How to Win Friends and Influence People* slumps next to an old Penguin edition of *Of Mice and Men*; an art book of Picasso paintings leans on a high school biology textbook with a sticker that reads SCIENTISTS SAY THAT EVOLUTION IS ONLY A THEORY. I find a crisp, unread copy of a poem by Lucretius, *On the Nature of the Universe*. "One ancient Roman poet's profound examination of the workings of the universe," reads the back cover; on the front is a fuzzy image of the cosmos. I go back to the couch in the common area and sit next to Dorian, whose head is bent over *The Call of the Wild*. I open the book to a chapter called "The Senses":

> *Yea, in the very moment of possessing,*
> *Surges the heat of lovers to and fro,*
> *Restive, uncertain; and they cannot fix*
> *On what to first enjoy with eyes and hands.*
> *The parts they sought for, those they squeeze so tight,*
> *And pain the creature's body, close their teeth*
> *Often against her lips, and smite with kiss*
> *Mouth into mouth,—because this same delight*
> *Is not unmixed; and underneath are stings*
> *Which goad a man to hurt the very thing,*
> *Whate'er it be, from whence arise for him*
> *Those germs of madness.*

The stings and pains that hurt the lovers remind me of the sensations I have when I am in the office with Dr. Lark, or when Simon hands me something and his hand brushes mine and his skin is warm and humid. Somewhere in those words lies the key to the cure. What was the feeling that caused the madness? What did the kissing lovers smite?

I look over at the drifting seahorse bodies in the tank, trying to remember the attraction rituals of the hens or the mating dances from nature shows. What are the traits of the most successful females? In tiny letters at the top of the lovers' passage I write out a list:

> *1. Initiation rites: a call or a dance*
> *2. Plumage*

I look at my body. I look at Dorian's body. We are thin; we have bruises on our calves; we look like boys in the baggy light-blue scrubs that play down our every curve. The nurses, men and women both, all wear the same blue scrubs that we do; we all resemble each other. They come and go at 6:00 a.m. and 6:00 p.m., entering and leaving in their bland, ghostly uniforms. Every day at shift change nurses pad lightly through the double doors, a parade in and out of the side kitchen and the nurses' station, stashing things in lockers: blue and red and black handbags, hair clips, cell phones, jangling keys. In and out they go.

Except for one, I realize, watching them go back and forth: one nurse who always comes padding in with glints of jewelry at her ears and neck and nose, dressed in a pair of scrub pants that's at least a size too small and clutches at her hips and a top that is, conversely, a size too large, so the V-neckline falls away and shows the little path between her breasts whenever she leans over. And then I know it. Ellie has *plumage*.

I study her while Dorian reads beside me. The main way Ellie has it is in her consciousness of her body. It is something essential, this consciousness, something that comes before the nose ring and the eyeliner and all the rest. She knows about her body and it makes the rest of us know about it too, creating a shared awareness of the way she stands and moves, of the curve of her hips, of the lean slope of her lower back. Whenever she walks she holds herself upright so that her shoulder blades pinch together and her breasts rise. She does little things throughout the day to keep herself neat and smooth: combs her hair in front of the little mirror that hangs in the nurses' station, applies ChapStick, rubs hand lotion over her knuckles and cuticles whenever she finishes washing her hands. I have noticed that Simon looks at her secretly whenever she bends over to get something from a lower drawer or when she disappears into the kitchenette with her waist swaying.

There is one other thing Ellie does. On weekend shifts she goes out straight after work, and she gets ready in the nurses' station. Off come the scrubs—there is always a tank top or a shell underneath, lacy black or pale pink—and Ellie sits on the bench, takes the clip out of her hair, leans so her head is bent over her knees, and brushes out her hair from the underside so that when she stands up it falls around her shoulders and gives her an air of studied carelessness. Then she touches up her makeup and adjusts her accents: a stud twinkling in her nose; a small barbell in her ear, high up at the tip, where the flesh is thin and the lobe folds over on itself like a tiny seashell.

Sometimes Dorian asks her about the concerts she goes to. “Why are you taking your rings out?” she asked once. It was a Friday night. Ellie had just finished signing off with the other nurses and was carefully unhooking the studs and barbells from her ears in front of the mirror. They made a tiny jangling sound as they collected in her palm.

“Because there’s a pit at the show.”

“Are you going to dance?”

“No. But I want to be careful.”

Ellie leaned into the mirror and began painting a smoky purple line along her eyelid, on the tender part just over the eyelashes.

“How can you do that? Doesn’t it get in your eye?”

“Actually, it’s very hard to poke yourself in your own eye. You’ll always blink, automatically.” Ellie turned to Dorian. “This plum shade would look good on you,” she said. “Dark tones to bring out the green in your eyes.”

Sometimes during these little primping sessions Ellie puts makeup on Dorian, too, just to show her how it works. Oddly, Dorian never lashes out during these sessions: too transfixed, perhaps, by the unfamiliar ritual of masquerade. The first time Ellie tried this she painted and combed until Dorian was nearly unrecognizable, her black hair parted on one side and falling smooth around her shoulders, the half-crescents of eyeliner and shadow making her irises more startling and green than ever. Ellie tugged at the bottom of Dorian's top so her cleavage would show just slightly and even powdered some of the bruises on her arms so that Dorian's skin tone became smooth and bare, as if those bright-winged tropical insects I gave her had, all at once, glided off of her.

Ellie and I stood back and looked at her. Outwardly Dorian was vampish and sultry, and my heart lurched a little when I saw how pretty my sister was. Under her familiar scrubs and ponytail a new body had developed, a slim, womanly, energetic frame that I had slept beside without ever really knowing it had grown that way.

But something was missing. What was it that marred the vision? It was as if there was some bleak little center in Dorian, something behind the cascading hair and the graceful height of her legs and her smile that was laughing at us, taunting us. I sensed that Ellie was trying to name it too.

"Something's off," Ellie wondered aloud. "What is it?"

Dorian beamed back at us, her grin as frozen and expressionless as a doll's.

"I don't know," I said.

Was it the sting lurking beneath? The pain that goads? I wonder about that quality as I sit with Dorian breathing over her book beside me and as I watch Ellie and think about where she might go and what she might do and who she might get close to when she is dancing or sitting around her apartment or going to the store. The trysts she might have, the passionate, disposable romances that happen in the times before she put the scrubs back on and pins her hair back up and returns to us in the morning. Shimmering back and forth across the boundary, to the outside.

Dorian

We are bound always by the walls of the ward, or by the fences and the hedges outside, the same way the creatures in the tank drift and scramble in their contained and tiny world. The ward is a square like the tank is a square, boxing us in with four white walls; the common area and the sofa and the sleeping quarters and the kitchenette and Dr. Lark's office are plastic castles for us to swim in and out of. We stand in front of the tank and watch the seahorses twist and drift in their enclosed space like proxy captives of our shared disorder. More creatures conscripted into the malady and the cure.

"Dorian, tell Addie what's on your mind," Dr. Lark says.

"I was thinking about the other side."

"The other side of what?"

"The other side of the ward."

"What about it?"

"Going there."

"With Addie?"

"If I must."

He scribbles.

Two days later he sits us down with Ellie in the common area and says he has arranged with the front desk for us to have a little garden plot in the grounds outside, on the east-facing side of the building, over where the low-risk patients live. "A new habit of cultivation," he says. "You two will learn to build something, to work on a project together."

"We don't know how to garden," Addie says.

"So learn," he says. "Ellie and Simon will go with you. Ellie knows how to garden."

On the following Sunday morning Ellie comes to work with a hangover, a wicker basket of seeds and trowels, a cardboard tray of seedlings, and a brace of shovels. She leads us past the intake desk, through the waiting room and the glass doors, and down the gravel path to the grounds alongside the building where the low-risk patients, in blue scrubs like our own, are talking their daily walks through winding hedgerows. I carry the seedlings and Addie clanks the shovels awkwardly along the garden path, Simon trailing emptyhanded behind us like a disaffected older brother. The garden area, with its tilled land and abandoned shed, is just at the bottom of a low hill. When we come to the rectangular plots, marked out with stakes and string and each running about the length and width of a coffin, Ellie drops the basket, takes a hoe from Addie, and begins to twist it into the earth.

"You need to turn over the soil first," she says.

Addie and I turn the soil like Ellie shows us, shoveling the dirt and then chopping it with the hoe to break apart the clods. The rich smell of loam fills my nostrils, a hearty smell, stronger and more vital than the sterile, aseptic smells of the ward.

Ellie kneels over her cardboard tray, wincing at the sunlight, the neckline of her scrubs falling away to reveal a lacy black bra, and begins to set out the seedlings: eggplants, basil, bell peppers, cherry tomatoes, each with its little identifying stake like a thermometer poking out of the soil. The bed shines in its little patch of sun. Addie scoops out shallow holes for each plant with a trowel and I place each seedling gently into the dirt. Then we pat more dirt around each stem. Ellie follows us down the row, giving instructions, making adjustments. When we get to the eggplants she leans over, frowning.

"See this?" she says, turning over a leaf to show us.

We lean in. Tiny red bugs trail along the underside of the leaf, over and between the little veins that run through it.

"Aphids," Ellie says. "Fuck."

She goes to her basket and comes back with a spray bottle of pesticide.

"Did you ever see *The Invisible World of Insects*?" I ask them. "Did you know that all aphids are female? That they reproduce asexually? Each aphid bears the seed of its daughter. The mother was once in the grandmother and the grandmother was once inside her mother."

"Really," Simon says.

"They reproduce asexually and matrilineally. But this makes them easier to kill, because they all have the same genetic makeup."

Ellie begins to spray the leaves of the plant. The damp aphids slow down in the rain of pesticide and freeze, a matrix of tiny dots, like seeds in a strawberry.

"It might be too late for this one," she says, caressing the plant. I can see more aphids trailing along the other leaves, untouched by the neighboring massacre. "You'll need to come out every day to water the plants and check on the aphid population. Twice a day, if it's hot. Take Simon if I'm not here."

She shows us what to take from her wicker basket: floppy sun hats and gardening gloves that we are supposed to put on before we come out to brandish the spray bottle at the little bugs. The twin housewives of the apocalypse.

On our walk back up the path to the ward Addie is quiet. We pass the grounds and the hedgerows and the benches where the nurses sit together, gossiping and proprietary, watching their patients like well-heeled parents looking out on a busy playground. I follow her eye to Simon loping ahead of us, his long legs taking one stride for Ellie's two, his shaved head bright and pale in the sunshine, beads of sweat twinkling on the back of his neck.

"Not him, certainly," I say. "Not desperate enough."

"Who's desperate? Me or him?"

"Both of you."

"Desperation's your great motivator. Not mine."

"What's yours, then?"

She searches for the word. "Rectifying. Setting to rights."

"Do you think this is about justice?"

She glowers at me. I can see her fingers clenching together at the tips, can see the little darts of freckles—which are also my freckles—stand out more starkly on the bridge of her nose.

"Setting to rights?" I say. "Are you serious? Do you think you will have a child and then somehow what you and I were will be different? What you and I are?"

She refuses to answer. Instead she stalks back along the path to our side of the ward, her blonde hair streaming.

Dr. Lark will ask me, again and again, to reflect on what I know about Addie that is not violent. On what she sees that I see. On what we share that is not the body, that is not our genetic makeup, that is not a habit of self-defense. But what I know, and what he will never know to ask, is that everything about Addie is about the violence of the body. And everything that is about Addie is also about me. Her every nerve my nerve, her strange yearnings all my own.

Addie

I think carefully about the garden. It is private. It is out on the grounds of the ward, half-hidden by a row of hedges. It is even romantic, with its view down the slope that leads to the security fences and, beyond that, into the firs and maples of the Tennessee wilderness, out into the swell of the mountains. I think about Simon, too, who is lean and tall and who always has a five-o'clock shadow and whose tattoos make colorful arabesques up and down his arms.

When he brings the evening meal into the common area and sets it down I say, "Why don't you feed it to me?"

"You can feed it to yourself," he says.

"No, I can't. I'm sick."

Simon hands me a fork and I lean so far over the potatoes that my top falls open a little, like Ellie's. I can sense him looking away, deliberately. No matter. I've planted the thought. Dorian sits next to me on the sofa, her lips clasped loosely around her straw, her face lit up by the television. In the seahorse tank the male's pouch is white and distended, swelling with the eggs; he lingers fatly in the sand where the stems and the roots of the plants are, perfectly still, bulging like an abandoned balloon with some of its air still left inside. Behind the tank the nurses are beginning to circulate through the ward in their shift-change dance, rattling their keys, calling out their hellos and goodbyes. Soon Simon will be among them. Six o'clock.

"Why don't you sit down and watch with us?" I say. I pat the sofa next to me with my hand.

"No, thanks. Eat your potatoes."

"Do you like cats?"

I use my fork to point at the TV. We are watching a Discovery Channel series about house cats, a documentary that follows the lives of three kittens from the same litter as they grow up in three different families. One of the families has a mouse in their cabinets, and for ten minutes the documentary cuts back and forth from the family discussing the mouse to the kitten, a tawny brown calico, batting it around.

"Sure, I like cats. But I don't want to watch a whole documentary about them."

"Look how it plays with the mouse," I say, "grabbing it and dropping it. Over and over again."

"That's not why cats do that," Dorian says suddenly. "Didn't you just hear what the expert said? They interviewed her and she said that the idea of cats playing with their mice is a popular misconception."

Simon and I both look at her. She has slouched so far into the sofa that her head is bent toward her chest and her legs are splayed out on the table. She talks around the straw in her mouth, her green eyes laughing at us.

"They don't do that because they want to play," she says. "They do that because their mothers never taught them to break a neck. That kitten's mother didn't, and so it doesn't know how to kill the mouse, and then when that kitten becomes a mother one day it won't teach its litter how to break a neck either. Cats born of housebroken cats don't learn the killing blows. It's a defect that comes from domestication."

Simon gathers up the empty trays and turns to leave.

"It's always charming," he says, "your dinner conversation."

"As is yours," Dorian shoots back. She raises her empty cup for him to take, like a petulant child. Just then I notice that Dr. Lark has come up in the corner of the common area, his omnipresent notepad out of his jacket pocket and his pen raised, scribbling it all down.

***

Dorian

She will not be able to do it. She has been thumped and ruined too much; she has not developed properly. She has less of a chance than the eggs in the swollen pouch of the male seahorse. Many in that brood of thousands will not fertilize; many will fall and crack. Those are Addie's.

But say that she does. Say first that she persuades a man to fertilize her. Or perhaps she threatens him. Say that out of wounded flesh a desperate, quavering life begins to form. What then?

Then the disorder that runs in us will be in the child, and then in the children of that child, so that our line will supply the ward with endless sisters and brothers. Addie will provide the next generations of doctors and nurses and specialists with their objects of study. Yet it will seem as if the cure has worked on her, worked *through* her. There could be no better evidence that the cure worked than her fostering the seed: letting a man that close; letting a being grow and form inside. And then the question: how will she learn to do it? She will not be able to get that close to a man without getting used to being close to me first. I am her testing ground and trainer; this is the reason she ceases to pinch.

We sit at the table and hold hands and I watch her straining, trembling to keep her hands and fingers flat at the alarming provocation of my skin. She is waiting for me to strike, I know, but I do not. It is what they all expect. But there is something else here, another possibility. The possibility is Dr. Lark. Or it is Simon. Isn't this the end goal of it all: the sessions, the hand-holding, the seahorse tank, the garden, the sitting close? To learn not to strike first? To be *quelled*?

The next time we go to the garden Ellie is hung over again and scolds us, marching back and forth, inspecting the tiny bulbs of eggplant, turning over and displaying the leaves, disappearing behind the shed to curse the wilting tomato blossoms. She barks out criticisms like a boot-camp drill sergeant addressing shambling new recruits.

"You were supposed to spray the aphids," she snaps. "Just like I showed you." She shows us the tiny holes that speckle the tender underside of a leaf. "They're going to spread to the other plants now and then you're going to have to spray them too. You have to use a lot of this because these organic sprays don't contain very effective pesticides. Also, you need to take care of those weeds. How did you let them grow in?"

Ellie sprays the garden in a raining huff of pesticide while Simon and Addie fall to pulling weeds with a dejected, obligatory air. I stand still, trowel in hand, and watch the grounds. Back and forth they go, the patients in blue, the nonsevere cases. The hedgerows come up to their waists and as they walk they crisscross into ever-new banks of hedges, as if wandering in an infinite green maze. I can hear faint strains of their conversations on the wind, a susurrus of unhurried voices under the angry plashing squirts of Ellie's bottle.

"Do you ever work with any of those people?" I say to

Simon. I point toward the hedgerows. He squints in the direction of my finger and shakes his head.

"Why not? Why do you always stay here with us?"

"Restraint training," he says, twisting a dead flower from the squash plant. "Some medics and nurses have it and some don't. They need the ones with restraint training back here. With the severe cases."

"Aren't there severe cases up there?"

"Yes, but they aren't violent."

"What are they like?"

He searches for the right word.

"Peaceful," he says. "Reserved. Quiet."

"Are they naturally peaceful, or does the medicine make them that way?"

"Sometimes they're peaceful because of the sedatives. Sometimes they're peaceful by disposition."

"Are we the way we are because of sedatives or disposition?" That is Addie, standing up with a handful of plucked clovers.

Simon looks at Ellie for help. But she has her back to him, her tanned lower back with its tribal tattoos creeping out under her scrub top as she leans over the seedlings.

"You are the way you are," he says carefully, "because of the way you were raised and because of the crime you committed, long ago. But no one is blaming you for the crime now. Everyone wants you to get better and everyone wants to make sure there will never be another crime. And there's no reason you can't get better now, because you have the best doctor in the world and because your environment is very different now from what it was then."

"Do you want us to change?" Addie again.

"I want you to be happier. And to be able to leave the ward one day and have a full life. So, yes, I want you to change. Parts of you to change. But not all of you. You'll always be who you are. Dorian and Addie."

"And who do you think needs to change more?" I say. "Me or Addie?"

"Shut up, Dorian," Addie says.

"I'll ask what I like."

"It's not about one person changing more than the other," Simon says. "It's about both of you working together. You have to get along and talk to each other in order for the sessions to work. You know that."

"You have to work together on your garden," Ellie cuts in. She hands the spray to Addie and turns to Simon. "Don't encourage them. They're just trying to antagonize you."

"On the contrary," I say, "we are working on a new habit of curiosity."

"Be curious later," Ellie says, "when you've finished the weeding."

We all fall back to the weeding, yanking up the clover, hoeing around the spiny roots. Addie and I pass the trowel silently back and forth. I feel the lashing impulses ebb and flow in me as her thigh touches mine. Beyond us, the other patients wade in the same hedgerows, floating to and fro like the drifting horses in the tank.

Addie

After the weeding session in the garden I go visit Dr. Lark in his office. He is sitting at his desk filling out a clipboard, surrounded by plaques and diplomas, giant medical encyclopedias, and piles and piles of notepads from his observations of Dorian and me, all heaped together in beams of afternoon sunshine. Souvenirs and relics of the malady.

"I want to talk to you about the garden," I say. "Does Ellie have to come with us? Can't it just be Simon?"

He sets down his clipboard, takes off his glasses, and motions for me to sit down.

"No, thanks," I say. "I'm covered in dirt."

"How is the garden?"

"Coming along."

"Does Dorian like it?"

"She doesn't hate it."

"I don't suppose you could get Dorian to try harder at the sessions."

"No, I don't suppose."

"You could invent a new habit. A habit of collaboration."

"You invent the habits. Not us."

"I beg to differ. New habits grow naturally, one right out of the other."

"Nothing is natural. You give us the habits and we complete them. When we've completed them to your satisfaction we graduate to other habits."

"They become natural as you complete them. Once you

complete and become accustomed to them, you graduate to other habits of greater duration and complexity. Some of them I suggest to you. But you will develop others on your own."

"So what you're telling me is that plucking weeds is supposed to make me develop a habit of affection for Dorian. Sitting next to her while I am taking a shit will create a bond of familiarity. Holding hands with her for minutes at a time while you take notes is supposed to make me think about all of the things that are not violent, with Dorian."

"No, that's not what I'm telling you. What I'm saying is that I want you to help Dorian start a habit that you have mastered but she has not. A habit of time out. Which is to say, a habit of calm reflection, of pausing to think. A habit of willed contemplation."

"How can it be a willed contemplation if I make her do it?"

"Try and get her to talk about the house," he says. "Those are memories that will come more easily if you have them together, without me. You have to remember the house and you have to think about the crime in order to get better. It will be better if you ask her. Just start by asking her about the house."

"If I do this, will you take Ellie off the garden?"

"Make some progress first," he says.

Back in the ward Dorian is stretched out flat, staring at the television. "Still trying to solve that puzzle?" she says. "What is Seven Down?"

"Just working on new habits," I say.

She slumps down even further on the couch and her thigh grazes mine and it is round and firm, the flesh packed tightly around the muscle. For an instant the other Dorian flashes before me, the beautiful young woman with eyeliner and with the indescribable unquelled thing inside, the mystery of her anger giving her a piquant and jagged allure. She is doing this deliberately, this smashing of her thigh to mine, but I look forward and I am calm, training myself, breath by slow breath, not to pinch.

Dorian

Then Ellie and Dr. Lark are arguing in his office and their argument drifts through the open door: her voice high and insistent; his low and brash, sometimes stopping for her voice, other times cutting into it, breaking it. From the couch in the common area I can just see half of her figure, one hip cocked, one hand gesturing with vigor, while he thunders and quells from the chair behind his desk.

"No matter what you think, they're grown women," she says, "and they can go out and plant things in a garden without me."

"Your job is to supervise them," Dr. Lark says. "You supervise them in the common area and you supervise them in the sleeping quarters and you supervise them in the kitchenette. Why can't you supervise them in the garden?"

"Because I have things to do in here. Preparing medicine. Preparing meals. Simon can take them out to the garden.

I don't like following their every step all the time. It's infantilizing."

"Are you suggesting you have a problem with the cure, the recovery plan? Last time I checked I was the doctor here. The last time I checked, I was the one giving orders and making recommendations."

They argue for a long time so that we are late getting the hand session started. In the tank, the male horse bobs amid swaying fronds of green sea grass. Their motion is like dozens of long hands waving goodbye.

Addie and I press our palms together across the table and Dr. Lark sits behind us and clears his throat. Addie looks back at him and then over at me. Our fingers, warm with sweat, twine around each other, and when she leans forward her pale hair slips forward over my knuckles.

"Try to think of one thing about the house," she says, suddenly.

"Since when are you in charge?"

"Dorian, answer Addie," Dr. Lark says.

"Just try and think of one object in the house," Addie urges. "See if I remember it too."

So I close my eyes and think back to the house—dim and shadowy, with flowing curtains that blocked out the sun, worn tan linoleum on the floors, the brown box of a TV with its rabbit ears stretching out, one silver antenna stretching high, the other falling to the side. At first, when I think of it, there are no sounds in the house and the room is cold and empty and still and evenly lit, like a display in a museum. I try to place myself in it, and to place Addie in it. And then I remember another object that looms above us in the family room, somewhere to the right of the television, like a dignified old butler with hands folded behind his back, watching, biding time, supervising. A boxy wooden frame long and slender as a grave, an active center ticking and swinging away a million seconds.

"I remember the grandfather clock," I say.

"Can you describe it to us?" Dr. Lark says.

"It was taller than Addie and me," I say. "It had carvings in the wood at the top and a glass clock and then the long pendulum that hung down. It was a brass pendulum. Our mother used to tell us a story about it."

"What kind of story?" Dr. Lark says.

I concentrate. All of the stories our mother told began with her legs and knees coming down off of the sofa, sometimes encased in long boots, other times in slacks or jeans; I can hardly remember her face except to know that she was blondish like Addie and, I think, had her same angular nose and cheekbones. We always sat on the floor facing her when she talked, and she leaned so far back on the couch that the primary image I have of her is exposed kneecaps facing my forehead. Was it because of those that I wanted to strike?

"It was a story about a boy she knew, a boy in her class, who climbed onto a big pendulum like the one in the grandfather clock," I say. "They were on a field trip to a science museum. In Washington, DC, where she grew up."

Our mother told us that this pendulum was at least fifteen feet long, golden, suspended from the ceiling, swinging back and forth, ringed off by a fence that the children stood on. She described how she stood next to her classmates and watched as the pivot creaked back and forth and the shining weight at the bottom swung up so close to the rail that you could have reached out and touched it, even though that was strictly forbidden. There were security guards positioned around the room with the pendulum and they came forward anytime someone—some entranced child, she said—would stretch a hand or foot through the rails.

But a boy in her class managed to get onto the pendulum. His friends had distracted the guards by hanging around in the corner and leaning too far over a magnet display, triggering the alarms, and when the guards went over to give them a warning the boy flung himself out onto the pendulum, wrapping his arms and legs around the pivot and resting his feet on the round weight. And there he stayed, going back and forth on the golden pendulum, his hair blowing, his eyes wide in horror.

"He probably thought the pendulum would slow to a stop," our mother said, "but he had overestimated his measly weight compared to the mass and force of the structure. And so, he was stuck."

A cadre of guards had arrived on the scene. The heads of the museum came, people in suits. Someone called the fire department and they spread out a net under the pendulum for the boy to fall into. The bottom floor of the museum, underneath the pendulum, was a food court, and all the museumgoers and the staff and the fry cooks and the baristas and the cashiers from the gift shop gathered there to watch the boy swing back and forth. From where my mother stood, she said, his figure looked frail and tiny; he clung desperately to the pivot, afraid to let go. One of his friends told the firefighters his name and they began to call out words of encouragement. Soon the crowd joined in: "It's okay, John! Come down. You're safe!" At last the boy slipped off the pendulum and fell into the net, screaming. The crowd burst into applause.

That night our mother saw him on the local news, being interviewed. "How did it feel to be on the pendulum?" the anchorwoman asked, and stuck her microphone under his chin.

"Like, scary at first," the boy said. "But then it was peaceful." He described being horrified by the height and motion of the great weight upon which he rode and then lulled into drowsiness by the oscillation, yielding to the graceful back-and-forth motion, knowing he could not stop the pendulum.

And it was the same way with our pendulum, our mother had said, gesturing to the grandfather clock in our living room. It showed us that our lives were passing. Every day, a little more went by. That endless, indifferent march and sway of time.

"And do you remember what the moral of that story was?" Addie says.

"'Go with the flow,'" I say. "'Let life carry you where it will.'"

"No." Addie shakes her head. "It was: 'Don't overestimate your own influence.'"

"That's impossible," I say. "Why would there have been two different morals? Maybe your moral went with a different story."

"Maybe she told the story twice," Addie says, "once to you alone, and once to me alone."

Dr. Lark clears his throat.

"Have you thought, Dorian, about going back to look at that clock?" he says. "Of taking the pendulum?"

"What would I want with it?"

But the second I say that I realize I do want the pendulum. In some way it still seems to sway back and forth from the house to the ward, connecting both places through its interminable oscillation. I try to picture it back in the living room, moving in my peripheral vision as I stared straight ahead at the television. Was it still swinging there, in that same living room, its sound ghosting through the empty house? Whose moral did it underwrite?

"Maybe seeing it again will help you remember," he says. "You will remember the moral that was intended for you."

After the session Addie and I go back to the common area to watch the Discovery Channel and I stretch out long on the sofa, taking in the ward, all of it. The bobbing seahorses. The aseptic smell. And, next to me, her slender shoulder grazing mine, is Addie. Addie and Dorian. Dorian and Addie. The sessions. The cure. We will be like clocks and sundials coming slowly into harmony with each other, pea vines linking their tendrils in the garden.

Addie

The next time Simon brings the dinner and hands me the spoon, I hold on to his hand a second longer than is necessary. I am sitting on the couch and he is standing above me so that his waist is at the height of my head and I can just sense the contour of muscle where his hips join to his legs. His brown eyes look down, surprised, into mine. His palm is warm from carrying the steamy tray and I can see the flushed veins standing out in his wrist.

"Addie," he says. "Your spoon."

"I don't want the spoon," I say. "I want to hold your hand."

"Excuse me?"

"A habit of closeness. Just like in the sessions."

"I have work to do, Addie."

"It will only take a minute."

So Simon sits next to me on the sofa and holds my hand, delicately, as if he were handling some expensive object in a store, cradling the back of my hand in his palm as if he were a fortune-teller. I concentrate. It is like holding Dorian and yet not like holding Dorian: the heat of the body is the same, but his hand is larger, weightier, darker—less like my own hand. If this is the weight of the hand then what is the weight of the arm? Of the torso? Of the whole body?

Then Simon does a strange thing. He picks up a clementine off the dinner tray with his other hand, gently removes his fingers from mine, and begins to peel the fruit for me, handing me the individual sections as he frees them from the rind, pulling the webby pith off and placing it on the table. When he withdraws his hand it is like the removal of a warm compress, a sudden deflation of temperature. I accept the little orange crescents from his fingers and they, too, seem drenched in the heat of his body. Simon does not look at me directly while he does this; instead he keeps his eyes trained on the fruit and our fingers. He seems as puzzled as I am. It is as if he were about to embark on a routine task and then suddenly received, before his departure, some new and unexpected set of instructions.

"There you go, Addie," he says when I have swallowed the last wedge. He rises and goes back to the kitchenette.

All night I am confused. Does the weight of the hand and the peeling of the fruit mean what I think it means? Is it like the slinking dance of the seahorses in the tank or of the bobbing, chattering birds in the nature shows? Like the force of the crushing and kissing lovers in Lucretius?

If so, then why does he still look at Ellie? The day after the clementine, a Sunday, we are all sitting in the common area having breakfast and Dorian is asking Ellie about a concert she went to down in the Knoxville old town. Ellie is wearing liquid eyeliner that makes a little curl right outside of her eye and her ponytail is pulled high to show off her ear piercings, the ones that are high up on the tender, thin part of the ear.

I feel my stomach lurch at her plumage, at the way Simon's eyes train on that exposed curve of her neck.

"It was in an old church," she says, "and all the steps were steep and we all sat in the pews. The band was down front at the altar, where the priest would be."

Dorian douses her potatoes in salt. "Did you dance?"

"There wasn't enough space," she says. "Since it was a church, not a big public venue, there was only one bathroom for the women, one for the men. There were three stalls in the ladies'. But there were tons of women waiting, maybe thirty. So they had pee-patrol ladies working there. They went down the line and asked what you wanted to do in the bathroom and you had to say if you were going to do number one or number two."

"Which one did you have to do?" Dorian says.

"Both," Ellie says, without embarrassment, with her nurse's frank approach toward the vile processes of the body. Dorian listens with eager interest. "If it was number two you had to step aside and wait to be called. If it was number one they assigned you a booth and when it was your turn you had forty seconds. If you took longer than thirty seconds to pee, they started knocking. 'Hurry it up,' they said. 'Got folks waiting.'"

"I couldn't do that," Simon says. "Too much pressure."

"How long did it take you, Ellie?" Dorian says.

"Two minutes, tops," she says. "I shit and get. You know what I mean?"

"I know what you mean," I say, munching on a piece of

celery. "You mean, you're fast."

Ellie's expression changes and she sets her water bottle down on the table, too hard. "Why don't you girls watch TV while you finish up," she says. She passes Simon the remote and saunters back to the kitchenette, scrubs tightening and relaxing against her hips as she walks. Simon looks after her and then stares hard back at me, and in his eyes is that same look from the day before, that expression of hearing some bewildering command.

When he gathers the trays and leaves Dorian says, "Why do you always say stuff like that to her? Why do you have to be so puritanical?"

"It's not my fault if she wants to whore herself out at concerts," I say. "How many concerts does she go to every weekend? How many men does she take home?"

"No more than you would, if anyone would have you."

I watch Simon go his rounds, dumping the trays, slouching around the kitchenette. "On the contrary," I say, "I only favor the one."

"Slim pickings," she says.

When we eat, when we sleep, when we bathe, I stay close to her body and try to imagine the weight of that other absent body, the larger limbs, the warm press of the skin. The arms stretching across. The rough stubble on the cheeks and the neck. The muscles that grip themselves around the hip. Dorian submits, remains close, does not strike. We breathe into each other at night, curled up side by side and facing each other, our inhalations and exhalations mingling in the air between our faces, our kneecaps touching. Her body is like a bridge to his body, a skin that yields to a second skin. A heat that opens out onto vistas of other heats, other sensations.

Dorian

She will not be able to do it now because of her cycle. I know because my cycle is her cycle, because we share the same rhythms of the body. We are always due together, in unwilled, dutiful harmony, a dumb biological rhythm, eggs going in slow sync through their death patterns. The women on the other side of the ward must get it at the same time too, must wake up cursing like us, sticky, our blood all responding to the same trick of the tides. A coven of egg-wasters. But maybe she will try.

We sit at the table and hold hands and Addie asks me to think of another memory we both know. This time it is not an object in the house but rather a holiday, a celebration, something we did as a family. I concentrate. I think they want a Christmas or a Thanksgiving, something with dinner tables and alcoholic punch and extended family where everything is appropriately strained and Oedipal, but what comes to mind is Halloween.

"I remember the first haunted house," I say.

"Describe it, Dorian," Dr. Lark says.

"We must have been five or six. Our parents took us."

"What did they look like then?"

"All legs and shadow," I say.

Addie was a princess and I was a witch. The haunted house was in a neighbor's house filled with black light and glowing plastic jack-o'-lanterns and other children squealing up ahead of us. There were pots of spaghetti made to look like brains on the floor and a bunch of cardboard headstones that made a little graveyard. Plastic bats hung from the ceiling. There was a strobe light pulsing and an EXIT sign lit up over a door at the very end. Addie and I tiptoed forward toward the EXIT sign, holding hands. The strobe made each of our movements seem to jump in time. We advanced by imperceptible leaps.

Our mother and father followed closely behind us, her leading, him shambling after her as always, still in his mechanic's uniform, looking absently around. The skin under his eyes was worn and tired. Our mother lectured us as she walked and from time to time he would nod and agree, his nods also coming in the slowed-down time of the strobe light, so that her voice came clear and unbroken to us in the dark while his murmurs, his nodding head, were like long echoes of approbation trailing on the tails of our mother's words.

"In a haunted house there are going to be surprises," she was saying. "There are creepy things and people leaping out and you have to learn to expect that and to govern your reaction. You have to be prepared for the unexpected."

Addie's thumb presses mine as I recall the rest:

At the end of the hall a man in a skeleton costume leapt

out at us. "GAAH!" he screamed. He was a blur of black suit and glowing white bone; the rows of ribs in his abdomen flashed fiercely at us. We launched at him, Addie and I: she tackled his waist and I went for his throat.

"Addie! Dorian!" our mother was shouting. "Let go RIGHT NOW!"

I felt my father's hands pull me away from the skeleton just as I was going to sink my teeth into his shoulder. We had knocked him onto the floor and he lay on his side with Addie clinging to his waist in a death grip. Our father removed her, delicately, as if he were uncurling the tentacles of a rare octopus from a mollusk, Addie screeching all the while in her rumpled princess dress.

"I'm so sorry, Mr. Wayne," our mother told the skeleton, over and over.

"It's okay," the skeleton said. "Jesus." He picked himself up off the floor for what must have seemed like a long time in the strobe light but was in actuality only a few seconds. As he straightened up I saw a rip at his waist where we had torn his costume. The skeleton looked down at us from a great height, his mask askew. Under the mask, around his chin, was a little patch of stubble.

"Happy Halloween," he said.

In the car on the way home she lectured us. "There are two kinds of fear," our mother said. "There is a fear that scares and there is a fear that thrills. Out in a street, out in the wild, that would be a fear that scares. Then, you pounce. But Halloween is a fear that thrills. Being scared is part of the fun."

But it wasn't fear, I wanted to tell her. What was it? Reflexes? Instinct? I never knew the word. Addie and I tried, the next evening, and the next, to practice the difference. One of us waited in the hall to scare the other; one of us was always taken aback, always pounced and fought back. How I hated it, this dull repetitious hilarity! This rehearsal of a fear that thrills! Now the ward is suffused with that same flushed sense of expectation, that sense of a leaping-out any minute. Maybe we will wear ourselves out with sessions first. But the question we are all asking ourselves is: When?

"What is the difference between wearing out and healing?" Dr. Lark says.

"It's the same as with the fear," I say. "The difference between dread and enjoyment."

Dr. Lark scribbles for a moment. Then he says, "What would you think about actually returning to the house? Of confronting the 'dread and enjoyment'?"

I do not look at Addie, but her palm presses into mine as if she is pressing a door that she wants to open, and the tops of her knees graze the tops of mine under the table. "I will take it under consideration," I say.

Addie

Then Dorian agrees to go back to the house with Ellie to get the pendulum. "Simon and I will take care of the garden," I say. It is a Sunday afternoon and Ellie is hung over in the nurses' station again. Outside, the rhythms of the patients on the other side are different. On weekdays the nonsevere cases walk the endless mazes of the hedgerows, but on weekend afternoons there are games and activities; movies; visitors driving in from Chattanooga and Charlotte and Atlanta, their tires rolling over the gravel lot out front, where they emerge with care boxes and blankets and mementos and paperwork for the patients to sign. The sun splashes over our little plot and the garden is kissing itself into bloom, small purple eggplants and yellow squash and green fronds of broccoli beginning to group together into florets.

This time I take Simon's hand without asking, just when he sets down the basket of garden tools. I pull it to my waist and I am surprised again at the shock that runs through me when I feel its weight and its warmth. Is this the fear that thrills?

He tenses but does not take his hand away. This time he looks at me directly, his brown eyes turned down to mine. There is another warmth and sharpness there like what I find in the heat of his palms, and it is hard to look back.

"Addie," he says, softly. "I work here. I'm your nurse."

"That doesn't matter," I say.

For a moment we are perfectly still. Then his hand moves down and circles the thorn of my hip and relaxes. In a moment he reaches the other hand onto my other hip and pulls me close. I concentrate. What do I know about Simon that is not violent? Right now all of Simon is violent: the stubbly chin that scratches the top of my forehead, the surface of his skin gliding over mine, his lips on the underside of my jaw. We press together and it is like the image of snakes shedding a skin to get at another, deeper skin beneath. The lovers crushing as they kiss.

When I come back in from the garden, my basket filled with vegetables, Dr. Lark follows me into the kitchenette. He is not wearing his ward coat, only a pair of carpenter jeans and a black polo shirt and no glasses, so that he looks a little younger and less like a specialist and more like a weekend bachelor, like the men that gather to sit at the bar and watch sporting games in the background on the *America's Best Watering Holes* shows that are always playing on the cooking channels. He stands close to me at the counter and I am suddenly afraid that he can sense the residue of Simon on me, feel the lingering heat of his hands and the moisture they produced from somewhere deep within my body.

"Dorian is doing well with the sessions," he says.

"Do you think so? Maybe she's just playing along."

"She's remembering the house without being prompted to, and that is doing well. Don't you think?"

"If she was so keen to remember everything in the first place, she would have done so alone by now."

"That's the logic of repeating the sessions," he says. "Sometimes they have to fail before you can make them work."

He gestures at the counter where I am laying down, one by one, a few florets of broccoli, a series of radishes, and two golden squash flecked with soil, like a dutiful housewife coming home from the market.

"Maybe when Dorian returns from the house and when the seahorse has its fry we can have a celebration of your progress," he says. "Harvest the garden. Make something new. Send Simon out for bagels. We can do it at the morning shift change so that everyone can come."

I look across the ward to the tank, where the male is swelling day by day under the bubbling jets of water. "A habit of sociability," I say.

"Exactly," he says.

Dorian

Back in the house everything is coated with a thin layer of dust, but the furniture and curtains are exactly as they were. Walking through this house must be like walking through one of the museums our mother used to tell us about, where she saw everything in curated displays. The blankets we used to sit on in front of the television are still there, musty and trampled into the carpet. Our old clothes, little girls' clothes, lie folded in the dresser drawers of the bedroom that still holds our bunk bed. In our parents' old bedroom the same jewelry box perches on the vanity, and the mirror reflects the burgundy headboard and the white coverlet that I remember. When I lift a pair of earrings from the jewelry box, cobwebs fall away from them. I look up and see the same cobwebs clouding the ceiling, a thin matrix of gray clinging there, fine and light as strands of hair.

Ellie brushes some of the web off my scrubs. She is

wearing her street clothes, tight skinny jeans that cling to her contours and a baggy, oversized white top that slouches off one bare shoulder. "Why is it so musty here?" I demand. "Doesn't Stella still come?"

"What do I know about Stella?" she snaps. "Call her and ask her yourself."

She points at the kitchen counter where an old rotary phone sits like a relic on a little stand in the corner, its cords coiled up neatly around it, disconnected. So she has given up the phone, I think. But there is still evidence that she has been here: the kitchen towels piled up on the counter are crisp and folded and whiter than anything else, as if they have been washed recently; on the counter by the sink is a fresh bottle of dishwashing soap. I look in the garbage and see a pizza box folded and crumpled into the bin, a little heap of orange peels. Stella.

Stella will not give up the house. And who can blame her? The house was their mother's before it descended to them, two sisters linked by the house, as Addie and I are linked by it. But Stella won't live in it, for which no one can blame her either, and no matter how many times she comes to vacuum, to freshen up, to pound out the trash cans, maybe even to sit down and have dinner and watch a little TV, she cannot beat back the desolation of this house, clean out its unlivedness. I open the back door, the one off the kitchen, and see a pile of *Watchtower*, the Jehovah magazine, clomped against the doorframe, stiff and faded from the rain. So she's forgotten to check in the back. I picture streams of Jehovahs advancing on the neglected house in their neat dresses and ties, rapping on the doors, peering through the silty windows.

The last time we lived in this house was the time we made the body, when our mother said goodbye to us from the light in the doorway. We were sitting in front of the television and nature shows were playing and our father was sleeping on the couch and our mother said she was going around the corner for milk. I can just barely remember her standing there, dim, shadowy, and—I think now—criminal; she told us to start counting and said she'd be back by the time we got to two hundred. "Stay right where you are," she said. We attacked each other eagerly at first, thrilled at doing something we were always told not to do, then slowly, wearily, the colors from the television splashing across our tired bodies.

When the mailman found us here our father was still sleeping and we had stopped counting and we were howling and pouncing. Stella was the first person they called. I still remember her coming for us at the police station, her face tear-stained, a distant version of our mother's face with the same hazel eyes and the same brown hair slipping out of its ponytail into windswept, frazzled strands. She pulled us close to her. She drove us back to her studio apartment in Chattanooga, right around the corner from the big aquarium, and fixed us hot chocolate and gave us a bath and tucked us into bed on the foldout couch in the living area, where I slept fitfully next to Addie as I sleep next to her now, listening to the huffing sounds of semis barreling down the highway. I remember that for three days we lived with Stella. But how could she keep us? We smashed everything. We threw our food on the floor. When she reached out for us we struck at her. We were a danger to Stella and ourselves. So then it became Addie and me in the ward and Stella in visiting hours, on the weekends: every weekend at first, then every other weekend, and now mostly on holidays and over the phone, sometimes not even that. Understandable. We are grown now, and no woman should be made to suffer forever for her sister's mistakes.

Ellie crouches in front of the grandfather clock in the living room and opens the long display window. Inside, the brass pendulum still swings back and forth, flashing in the afternoon light that pours in through the slats in the miniblinds. I reach my hand inside, but Ellie stops me and yanks my arm away.

"Wait," she says. "Put these on." She digs in her purse and withdraws a pair of blue latex gloves, the disposable kind she always wears when she is cleaning the kitchen. "The oil from your hands," she explains. "It can get onto the brass and make it discolor."

I slip the rubbery gloves on like a doctor going into a surgery and reach in and stop the pendulum and unhook it from its suspension spring. Ellie puts on another pair of gloves and helps me wrap the pendulum: first in plastic bubble wrap, then in a set of pillowcases she has taken from the closet in the bathroom. Together we wrap the pendulum like an ancient relic, a talisman exuding its twin morals of submission and humility.

Addie

Soon Simon and I begin a habit of accumulation in the garden. The next time we go to water the plants he takes me to the far edge of the garden, behind the shed, and pulls me close. He holds me, his warm forearms pressing against my lower back, his hands roaming under my scrubs to touch my stomach, my thighs. The hose trickles at our feet. Far past the hedges and the hills I hear the swoosh of highway traffic. I close my eyes and concentrate on the press of Simon against me.

"What does it feel like?" he says.

"Like being in a bath."

He steps back and looks at me.

"Am I sweaty?"

"No," I say, and pull his arms back around me. Like being in a bath where the warm water submerges most of me, I want to say, but where the air against my body, against my neck and shoulders, feels different and ticklish. The parts of me that are not touching Simon feel exposed. The parts of me that are touching Simon are damp with him, drowsy with him, a languor in the skin. I can feel him stiffen against me and I push myself closer into his body as if I am slipping deeper into the water.

"I want to," I say.

"Not now. I don't have anything with me."

"You don't need anything. I told you. I can't have babies. Too much hitting."

He steps back and squints at me in the sun.

"I'm serious," I tell him. "Want to go ask the doctor?"

"We won't have much time," he says. "You'll need to make yourself ready, the next time."

"How?"

"Touch yourself the way I touch you."

"There's no way for me to be alone."

"Try just thinking about it, then."

That night after Dorian falls asleep beside me and the ward is flushed with shadows I lie on my side in bed and try to think about it, about that press of Simon's body in the garden and the cool, tickling sensation of the hose water slipping by our toes. I reach my fingertips down under my waistband like Simon does, and I try to focus on him and the garden, but sometimes I think of Dr. Lark too, and the way he takes off his glasses when he looks at me. It is hard to feel alone; at any moment I feel like Dr. Lark could walk by, jotting on his clipboard. What habit was this? The habit of fantasy? Of the kissing, crushing lovers?

Dorian

At the next session Addie and I hold hands and Dr. Lark asks me what it was like to go back to the house and get the pendulum. I tell him about the memory I had when I was looking up at the webs, and when I was sitting in the quiet living room with its sheen of dust and the afternoon light slatting through the blinds.

It is a memory of one time in the house when I was sitting still and a voice was speaking to me, our mother, but she was speaking as if from offstage. Or the voice of our mother was speaking but she was taking care to stay out of the way, to make us focus on the words themselves and not on her face or her body.

"The voice told me that I should stand very still and try not to look down or around or to get scared at what the voice was going to tell me," I say. "And what it told me was that I needed to go over to the mirror, and that I needed to go look because there was something on my shoulder I needed to remove, and that I wouldn't be able to see it if I twisted my head to look.

"'There is a spider on your shoulder,' the voice told me. 'Remember I said not to be afraid.'

"I didn't want to disappoint the voice so I tried to stay very still, to not panic, to not look. I walked over to the mirror as the voice had told me. I saw a tiny black spider just a few inches away from my neck, and when I saw it I realized that its legs were tickling my skin.

"'You see, what he did,' the voice went on, 'is he was letting himself down from the ceiling on his thread, and he came down and landed on your shoulder.'

"I remember taking it for granted that the spider was a he, that the voice would know for sure if it was a she or a he. 'You're going to have to lift it off your shoulder and take it back outside where it belongs,' the voice said. 'Do you think you can do that? Do you think you can do that without getting scared? Are you afraid that the spider is poisonous?'

"'I can't tell,' I cried. I didn't know. But the voice told me that I must know the answer. How would I know where the poison was? Was it in the legs or the thread?

"'Do you think I would let you have a poisonous spider on your shoulder and have you remove it yourself? Do you think I would let you be in that sort of danger?'

"'I don't know,' I said. I guess I was crying. I remember thinking that the voice would be angry if I cried, but I couldn't help myself.

"The voice was silent, and then it said, 'Pick up the spider by the leg and take it out.'

"So I took the spider out."

Addie's index finger and thumb pinch together a little in my hand when I say this, as if she were remembering the spider too, the feel of its slender leg. "I took him out onto the lawn and put him in the grass. His thread clung to me and I brushed it off so the voice wouldn't be angry. I remember thinking that the voice was cross that it had to tell me what to do. I should have known how to pick the spider up, how to take it out. I had done okay with staying calm, I had not panicked, but I failed once I got to the second part, the part at the mirror, the part with the leg and the thread."

Addie says, "Do you remember the moral of that story?"

I remember the voice coming from far away, the calm orderliness of it.

"Know the people you trust," I say. "Know who wants to help you and who wants to do you harm."

Addie and I sit in the pale, oval circle of light and wait out the session, answer his questions. Who are the people to trust? Dr. Lark? Simon? Ellie? Do Addie and I trust the same people? Her palm is like a gateway into something else, different sensations of being and thinking. The door has opened in her hand and beyond her skin there is another, new Addie, a different woman who presses back.

Addie

We always have to start with whatever we did last; there is so little time, no time to let things mount and build, so that stepping close to him in the garden becomes a shock of the body, a heat so sudden that my senses recoil and it is only afterward that the languor begins to creep through me, the aliveness to pleasure.

I worry that it will show afterwards, some responding dampness against the light-blue linen of the scrubs. But no one says anything. They are busy with Dorian and her memories, the cure slowly forming itself out of the living room and the sleeping body and the swinging pendulum, like the purple and white crocuses in the garden that open their petals in the early morning, their buds uncurling and spreading as wide as a dozen opening hands.

Every week in the garden Simon and I lay down beside each other on the far side of the eggplants, the fat lumps of vegetables shining in the sun, the soil parched and dry. The hose trickles into the garden bed and makes little sockets of mud. Usually Simon sneaks a towel from the ward bathroom into the basket of garden supplies and spreads it awkwardly on the ground beside me, tucking it under my thigh. Then he coaches me to guide him inside, bit by bit.

"Come down just a little, whenever you're ready," he says. I inch down and feel a press against my skin inside, a pushing or a compression. It is like the compression of my upper arm once a year when the medical transport van takes us down to the hospital for our physical and blood tests, the rubber tie wrapped above my elbow, the blood gathering in my veins and spilling into the syringe. I come down a little more and it gives way suddenly, sharply, a raw upward driving. Our faces are suddenly close together and the round curves of the tomatoes and eggplants loom above us. He puts his hands on my waist and moves me back and forth, against the grazing touch of fruit, in the flood of warm sunlight on my back, until his face contorts and I look away above his head through the tangle of plants until I can just make out the shapes of the mountains, their curving slopes like the backs of a dozen arching cats.

Afterwards there is moisture on Simon and there is moisture on me and sometimes he goes to wipe my skin with the edge of the towel. "Leave it," I tell him. Back in the ward I picture that little evaporating patch of dampness shared between Simon and me, as he leaves me and the garden tools just inside the door and goes off to do his rounds.

At the tank Dorian eyes me through the water, black hair streaming, her face aglow in the light. Inside the tank the seahorses are still making their needling little arcs up and through the water, and the male hen is more swollen and distended than ever.

"Dorian, tell me what you see," Dr. Lark says.

"The male hen is guarding his fry."

"Good. Addie, tell me what Dorian said and tell me what you see."

"The male hen is guarding his fry," I say promptly. "His belly is swollen and distended. Soon the eggs will split."

"Good, Addie," Dr. Lark says. "Now, Dorian—"

But Dorian interrupts him. "Soon the eggs will hatch," she says, "and release the fry upward where they will fend for themselves or die. They get all their comfort in the incubation. Next morning, the male hen is ready again. Same thing. Incessant cycle of life and birth."

There is a restlessness in Dorian that makes her impatient with these questions, that sends her reeling back to the couch in the common area or to bed, where she tosses back and forth in endless irritation. She cannot stand to be asked and not to ask herself, to be the subject of so much scrutiny and not, in turn, to scrutinize, to demand.

That evening when we are waiting for our food trays in

front of the television Dorian stops Dr. Lark as he is making his way to the nurses in the kitchenette. She says, "When will you know how to fix us?"

He comes over to the couch and sits down a few feet away from us and takes his glasses off and looks at Dorian. Underneath the frames his eyes are tired and bright. "We just keep trying every day, Dorian," he says. "We learn from you as much as you learn from us."

She tips her face up toward him so that her hair slips off her shoulders and exposes the dim patchwork of fading bruises on her neck, her eyes very large and dark and hostile. She looks at him for so long that Dr. Lark stops smiling at her and looks away, over at the television.

Then Dorian asks him the same thing, but in a different way. "Have other doctors ever tried to fix this malady before?" she says. "In other places like this place?"

"Doctors have tried to cure it before," he says. "There was a remedy called holding therapy. That was the first cure. But things were different then. It used to be that they would try to match you, blow for blow. When you hit, the doctors would hit back, harder. To try and subdue the patients, to show them they were stronger."

"It didn't work?" Dorian asks.

"No, Dorian," he says. "It didn't work. Patients died this way. Doctors died this way too."

"How long have you been looking for a new cure?"

This time Dr. Lark laughs to himself, softly. It is a sad, angry laugh, and when he laughs this way Ellie and Simon stop serving the trays and the drinks and look at him in surprise. I look at him too.

"I have been working on a cure since I was very young, in many different places like this one," he says. "I have been working on it since before you were born."

"And, Dr. Lark," Dorian insists, sitting up on the sofa, "when you first started working on it, in other places like this one, did you try the other kind of cure? The first kind?"

Suddenly the air in the ward feels thick and the loping, thundering bison on the screen seem tinny and small. We are all looking at Dr. Lark, Dorian and Ellie and Simon and me, waiting.

"Yes, Dorian," he says finally. "I have tried the first kind of cure. I have tried every kind of cure."

Dorian looks straight at Dr. Lark, her hands folded in front of her, her hair hanging loose in her face, waiting.

"It has to fail before we know how to make it work," he says. She nods, her jaw set. She turns back to the screen. It is as if a door has just been opened on a hot room and a stream of cool air has rushed in. Ellie and Simon begin serving again. Dr. Lark goes to the nurses' station, picks up a clipboard, begins to read.

What are the things that fail before they work? The sessions? The afternoons in the garden with Simon? The new proximity of our lives, our bathroom routines, our bedroom routines? Behind the cracked-open door of the sleeping quarters the beds appear rumpled and undone, piled high with clean linen, like giant pieces from a checkers game, regal and misshapen. In the tank the male is all pouch, enormous, a ridged head and eyes atop a giant swollen ball of skin; it is impossible to see his tail. He is battered with his fry, sinking, tortured in his fecundity.

Dorian

The eggs break early on a Tuesday morning, the fry rising to bob in the currents of the tank with desperate squiggling motions. We watch them move helplessly against the flow of the water, pushed this way and that, their eyes struggling to stay open. Our shoulders touch in front of the tank. From the high window near the ceiling, the sunlight filters in and makes the tank awash in a pool of beams. The fry drift into the currents, tiny pink hooks, vulnerable, slight, lost forever to the notice of the male and his hen, who will begin, almost immediately, another dance of mating. The fry crowd the waters with their desperate irrelevance. The ward is a riot of scents: fresh coffee, vegetables from the garden. The excited chatter of the morning nurses coming onto their shifts energizes the air. We stand for so long, shoulder by shoulder, that Ellie nudges us away from the tank and toward the bathroom.

"Come on, you two," she says. "Time to get the morning started."

When I get out of the shower two small drops of blood darken the mat I stand on to dry myself off. I go over to the supply cabinet and look back at Addie expectantly.

She shrugs.

ADDIE

Then Ellie is standing with us in the bathroom and she has an endless series of questions. "What do you mean, you have it and she doesn't?" she demands, looking at Dorian. "When did you get yours?"

"Tuesday."

"You're telling me you got yours on Tuesday and now it is Friday and she hasn't had hers?" She turns to me. "Addie, is that true?"

Dorian starts to break in but Ellie puts her hand up.

"Dorian, let Addie answer for herself," she says.

"Yes," I say.

"Addie, look at me." Her eyes are digging straight into mine. She steps closer and I hold my place and look back at her. "Did you go to bed with someone?"

I do not know how to answer, so I look back down at the shaggy bath mat. Outside the bathroom door the morning noises of the lab are coming alive: the clash of dishes in the kitchenette, the flurry of shift change.

"It has nothing to do with them," Dorian breaks in.

"Dorian, I'm talking to Addie."

"It has nothing to do with them," Dorian insists, her voice climbing. "It doesn't matter about them because I helped her do it. I helped her do it with the cure."

"What are you saying? Are you saying that you covered up for Addie?"

"No," Dorian says. "She couldn't have done it without

me. They didn't help her with it, I did. So, it isn't theirs. It's mine."

Dorian gestures to include me.

"Ours," she says.

Chapter 2

Dr. Lark

Dorian and Addie. Addie and Dorian. They are like a group of cells dividing. One cell uncurls itself and pulls away; another follows, swelling and trembling.

Sometimes Dorian and Addie ask me about when I knew that I wanted to work with patients like them. I tell them that it started when I was fifteen: awkward, solitary, sitting in the back of a biology class watching a video about cell division. Before me, the split screen showed two different kinds of cells under a microscope. On the left: a clear purple orb, perfectly round. On the right: the misshapen twin of the healthy cell, crooked where the other was straight, foggy where the other was clear.

The healthy cell divided in a slow predictable cadence, the new membranes peeling off slowly from the parent cell, the way skin rises and unsticks when you pull off a Band-Aid. But on the left the sick cell divided and multiplied itself in a manic hothouse rhythm, membranes rapidly splitting, the parent spitting out daughter cells in a furious, diagonal pattern.

The new unhealthy cells blossomed into a misshapen, poisonous catacomb, built toxic cities in the body of the host. I couldn't stop watching them. Their deadly speed reminded me of a black widow spider I had once watched in our basement as it pulled sticky threads from its own abdomen, creating a treacherous maze out of its body. I filled in the worksheet and handed it to my teacher, who glanced at my answers, paused, and looked down at me.

"Jimmy, these are the traits of a sick cell," she said. "I asked you to define the traits of a healthy cell."

Thirty years later, that feeling hit me again as I stood in the foyer of the lab on the day Stella, apologetic and tearful, brought the girls for intake. Fresh from murder. One blonde and one brunette. Addie, with the wide blue eyes (how was it possible for two sisters to have such different eyes, such different hair?): two of her teeth missing, cheeks bruised, her childish face twisted discordantly. Her face was shaped by dislocations, the shadows and contours of her sister's rage. And Dorian, glaring up from a frame of dark hair, eyes like twin thunderstorms, holding her sister's tiny hand in a death grip. They reminded me of wrestlers parted just after the bell, still panting, their muscles still holding the tension of those last, desperate clutches.

Ever since I have been haunted by that grim ballet of the sick cells, by the deathly cadences of their multiplication.

***

To create order you must first understand the sprawling content of the sickness. Every disorder is different. The disorder that is Dorian and Addie's, the attachment disorder, requires a unique clinical intervention, a harmony of reiterated patterns and structures. Underneath these patterns and structures is the balance of power. You have to show the patients that you can overmaster them. They are the violent rumples and glitches and you are the smoothing, necessarily harsh locus of regularity and order.

"What is attachment?" Dorian used to ask when she was younger, breaking the long, enigmatic word into two in the middle: Attach Meant. Her dark eyes glittering under the helmet.

"Attaching means that someone or something is connected to someone or something else," I said. "Like my thumb is attached to my palm. See my thumb and my palm?" I showed them my hand. "If a person is attached to another person, like a child is attached to a parent, it means that they feel very close and together. It means that they have a bond."

"And we are here because we don't have a bond?" Dorian said.

"That's correct. You are here because you never learned to attach yourself to another person, to a caregiver."

"Why does it matter?"

"Because human relationships work through attachment," I said. "You have to be able to attach in order to have happy bonds with other people. To become nonviolent. To learn other ways of coping. Like animals in the wild who stay near their parents to learn about the world and to be protected. You have to learn to take comfort in other people, and to be comforted yourself. To be soothed. To be *quelled*."

She is not satisfied with this answer, I can tell, but she knows what *quelled* means and she will not ask the question again. This is how the vocabulary of the treatment works. It is a treatment based on the outing of rage and the reassertion of adult control over that rage. On this model it is not the past relationships that matter, or the present environment of the children; it is the battle for power between the adult and the child. The child is violent and resistant because of the inner rage. You have to get it out of them and at the same time show them that you are in control. You have to show them that you will not be manipulated or coerced. In order to do this you have to set the terms, get them to see manipulation and coercion differently. To be coerced is to be quelled, but it is a thing that only the doctor can do to the patient. To Dorian and Addie it is *quelled*; to the rest of the medical world, the doctors at conferences and workshops, it is *coerced*.

My mother was a sick cell. But her sickness was of a different sort, more private and interior. Not a thing of fists and bruises, like Addie and Dorian's. It was a quiet, meticulous, and visual disorder, a lunacy of images and pictures.

It was because of her that the locals used to refer to our house as the Bone House. Our house was halfway up the third peak of the Smoky Ridges. Not the first peak, with its antique shops and its cider-bottling houses that the tourists saw as they drove in from Knoxville, nor the second, higher peak with its hiking trails and protected campgrounds. We were on the peak where the workers used to sleep in their one-story houses before they traveled down the foothills to work in the coal mine. Now the houses are in shambles, most of them unoccupied. Some are intermittently filled with squatters, who ride up to drink beer on the porches and wash clothes in the stream that chuckles down from the peaks and meanders over the terrain like a lost, panicked animal.

My mother was a jewelry artist and used to work part-time in a little gift shop over at the bottom of the first peak, selling long beaded necklaces and dangly oval earrings to the weekend tourists who drove up from Atlanta. When my father, a truck driver, moved out to go live with a diner waitress in Chattanooga, my mother quit the jewelry shop and went back to school to train as a radiologist. "A practical profession," she said. She was in her late thirties then, and slender. She wore her hair in that voluminous seventies way, windswept and frozen into place with blow dryers and hairspray, brunette bangs winging out on either side of her forehead. She still wore the chunky bracelets and flashing brooches from the jewelry store, so the accents at her throat and neck and wrists would flash out and shine as she turned to set a bowl of cereal or a glass of juice on the table for me at breakfast. She would sit and read the paper while I finished eating, and then she would put on her white lab coat, drop me off at school, and drive to the hospital, where she instructed patients how to don the lead vest and sit in the machine. All day she made X-rays (she used to call it "Xeroxing") of their jaws and lungs and bones, muttering to herself as she padded back and forth through the hallways, hanging up those ghostly images of people's skeletons.

One day, when I was about twelve, my mother was instructed to destroy some expired patient files. There were several boxes of old manila envelopes filled with the medical records and X-rays of patients the office had seen fifteen, twenty, even thirty years earlier. My mother destroyed the records at work. But she pulled the X-rays out of the envelopes and took them home. At night, after dinner, she sat in the kitchen with a glass of wine and colored them in. She traced contour lines around the edges of bones. She drew designs inside of lungs, images that were symmetrical on both sides: pyramids, cubes, refracting geometrical shapes. She filled in wombs, craniums, and stomach cavities with different patterns of shade. She drew roses inside of teeth and colorful tattoos down the blazing white arms of those forgotten bodies. If there was a blight in the X-ray, a patch of tumor, a shade where there should have been no shade, she turned it into something else: the tiny funnel inside of a lily, the fool's hat of a jester. When she had finished she got a ball of twine and strung a line across the middle of the kitchen windows. Then she attached each X-ray to it with a paper clip so they made a banner. These windows looked to the west, and every evening when the sun set the orange glow made those bones and joints and kidneys blaze, garish disarranged parts of a body that had been lodged in the mountain so long it took on the color of the twilights and the sunsets that bathed it.

They frightened me, these images. At night, when the porch lights came on, they shone through the X-rays from behind, scattering grisly shapes all over the kitchen floor. My mother washed dishes and read magazines in the infernal light of these glowing bones. I was terrified that the old patients would know, somehow: that they would come staggering up the mountain in search of those private copies of their insides, their desecrated organs and bones.

The week after my mother began this project a tall, pretty girl who sat behind me in math class poked me in the back and asked me what it was like to live in the Bone House.

"The Bone House?" I said.

"Yeah, the Bone House," she said, tossing her hair over her shoulder. "That's what we call it."

"It's fine," I said. "It's just a house, like any other house."

"That's not what we heard," the girl said.

"What did you hear?"

"We heard that you have a crazy mom," she said, matter-of-factly, "and that you aren't allowed to go out anywhere and that you have to help her in and out of bed and that she has to take medicine or she goes even crazier."

"That's a lie," I said.

She shrugged. "Prove it, then."

"Come over and see for yourself."

"*I'm* not going over there," the girl said. "Not to that crazy house."

That was the first time I had ever heard the word *crazy* and connected it to my mother, the first time I linked the private cocoon of my mother's daily movements, her flashing bracelets and her inky hands, to the malignant public world of gossip and curiosity. It was true that she was not like the other women who came to pick up their children from class and who dropped their sons and daughters off at school dances. Those women were clipped and polished and eager; they knew one another; one of them would sit smoking in her car while another would stand outside it and they would exchange greetings and pleasantries, inquire about husbands, praise the hair and figures of each other's daughters. My mother would sit shyly in her car with the engine off and her eyes searching the crowded school grounds for me; when she saw me she would wave, too eagerly, her gaze drinking me in as I shambled awkwardly across the grounds and got in the passenger side and stared straight ahead without speaking to her.

I was smothered by my mother's ardent intensity, by the way she would put down her newspaper and look across to me at the breakfast table, her eyes seeking approval, reciprocation. I was smothered by her hum, by the way she closed her lips and sent her voice through her nose in a low, cloying music as she drank her wine and shaded in the bones at night. When it was time for bed I would carry the empty wineglass and the bottle over to the sink and I would help her out of her chair and into bed where, still humming, she would lie quietly as I pulled the glinting bracelets from her arms and slipped the rings from her fingers and unwound the coils of beads and pendants from her neck.

Once, when I was in the secretary's office handing in an excuse for being late—my mother sometimes stayed in bed, one arm flung over her forehead, staring at the ceiling with a blank, suffocating expression long after it was time for us to leave for school—I overheard my history teacher saying to the principal, in a low and earnest voice, that Mrs. Lark was a little *disordered*. Like *crazy*, this word had that public, invasive air about it, that resounding cadence of verdict and judgment, but there was something softer in it too. It had a lilt of tact and politeness, the tone of a dinner party host discreetly defusing the boorish comments of a drunken guest. *Disordered*. Like a slight rumple in a tablecloth or a mis-shelved library book that disrupts the neat, linear procession of call numbers. The flashing jewelry, the eager gaze, the Bone House, all of it just a tiny, easily remedied glitch in a world structured by benign, orderly patterns.

When I was a senior in high school my mother began seeing a security guard named Ronald. He was fiftyish, with a pink head shaved bald and a beard and a bulky body and a heavy tread; the whole kitchen floor creaked when he moved around. They had met when she Xeroxed his lungs to check for possible tumors, and I used to wonder if she thought of that grainy photograph of his chest cavity when she touched him or when they sat across from each other at the table drinking wine—whether she peered through his shirt and remembered the flushed and spongy organs, the concave slopes of his ventricles. When Ronald came over, the uncolored X-rays and the art supplies went away, and my mother sat in the colorful shadows of bones and talked, eagerly, about everything that had happened to her at work. Each interaction, no matter how small, was remembered and described with vivid emotion. A gentle reminder from her boss, a back-and-forth with a patient about a slight adjustment of the jaw in the X-ray machine, a misunderstanding about filing with the receptionist: each of these brought forth a burst of fervent and minutely detailed narrative.

In those stories I glimpsed a world of social interaction very different from any I had ever experienced. There were two layers: one the layer of everyday conversations and requests, the other a smothered and broiling world of veiled hints and threats and sinister implication, where latent dislike or persecution could rear its ugly head in the subtlest gesture. My mother began her stories on the first layer and quickly sank to the submerged universe. Each body in her day played a symphony of unspoken communication. Compliments from her coworkers were immediately undermined by their glances; even the ordering of lunch was charged with subtle manifestations of power.

Ron acknowledged all this with intervals of patient grunting, sometimes reaching out for her hand, other times refilling their glasses and nodding while she talked. Sometimes when the bottle was empty he went out to his truck and came back with a few cans of beer dangling off a plastic six-pack holder. He'd crack them open and let the trapped air inside hiss out resoundingly, as if to announce a new program, a turn in the conversation, but always she returned, embellishing and scrutinizing, finding subtle new details to dissect, reordering and refining her daily catalogue of irritations. Sometimes her voice rose urgently over the crack and hiss of the cans; other times it sank low and broke as she leaned on Ronald's arm and cried. It was in those moments that I hated the beseeching quality of my mother's voice the most: the audible equivalent of her thirsty, desperate gaze from the car outside of school.

Ron must have felt it too, because a few weeks after the initiation of these little routines, his truck stopped appearing in our driveway. After he stopped coming by there were a few tearful late-night calls from the rotary phone in the hallway, then a few angrier ones, and finally the X-rays and markers came out of the hallway closet again and she sat at the table in the evenings coloring and humming with her lips pressed tightly closed. Now it was I who listened to the stories, only instead of crying on my shoulder my mother punctuated her narratives with an impatient wave of one hand, as if to banish the memory of the shoulder and the thick chest packed with its heaving, grunting lungs. My mother had dated Ronald for only a few months, as far as I can recall, but she spoke of it as a tempestuous affair, one that had irrevocably altered our lives and left behind a trail of compromises and rearrangements. "I'm relieved, really," she said once, while squinting down at her markers and hunting for the right color, "that there will be no disruption, that you will be able to stay here and focus on your classes with no conflicts or changes at home." I was to begin classes at the local community college in the fall. I heard these pronouncements with a passive, mild surprise: I had feared no looming changes on the horizon for me, as there had never been a possibility that I would be leaving our home, or that anyone new would settle into it.

My former mentor, Dr. Rachel Coe, once told me that there are the textbook cases and then there are the exceptions. And it is, frequently, the exceptions that will lead you to the cure. Dorian is textbook, beautifully regular in her dances and tantrums. She is like the single bee that always flies, in its chancel patterns, back to the honeycomb, that classic bee that aims before it stings. The bee that dies so that it can kill. But Addie is the exception, the one that hovers and sticks in its honey, the one that moves more slowly and gives you more time to examine it.

She is an exception in the way she comes to me now, unsummoned, walking straight into my office with her hair around her shoulders and her top pulled to the side to expose her collarbone (broken and reset) and her skin (bruised purple), presenting herself to me and waiting, patiently, for me to notice the shape of her hips (perpetually dislocated) and the swell of her lips (still split from a punch). When I do not respond she comes a little closer and takes the journal I am reading from my hands and sets it down. When I still do not react she puts her hands on either side of my face and unhooks my glasses and takes them off, gingerly, with a delicate fanfare, like a jeweler removing a necklace from a display case and presenting it to a customer.

"You can forget about the new cure," she says. "It will never work."

"You have to have faith in cures and solutions in order for them to work," I say. "In order for the treatment to help you, you have to believe that it will help you."

"It's not me, it's Dorian," she says. "It will never work on her. It will be like the other cures."

"Why do you think that, Addie?"

"She'll never do it. You'll never get her to build a nest or to sit through the sessions or to do anything without hitting."

This is a test, an experimental strategy. A battle for authority over Dorian and what is best for Dorian and who knows Dorian better.

"I don't know about that," I say. "You might be selling her short. You're more thoughtful than Dorian, but Dorian is more adventurous. She's more of a risk-taker."

"Is that what will make your cure work? Risk-taking?"

"That. Among other things."

"Is that what made it work in the past?"

This is another test, an intrusion. A grab for weakness.

"There is no past," I say.

She does not know how to respond to this, so she tries the question again in a different way.

"Is that how it was treated in the other records? In the medical history?"

"There are no records. There is no history."

She is frustrated. She takes a step toward me and fumbles, clumsy in her seduction. Her body, now grown from an adolescent's into a woman's, is awkward and unpracticed in its new role. She is like an apprentice carpenter picking up a new tool, timid, waiting for instruction. I pause, as always, before I offer it.

"Addie," I say. "Please remember that I am a professional."

To be a professional, too, is to be a man without a past. A man without history.

A man without history: this is the life that appeals most to me in those moments, mid-shift, when I am watching Dorian through the one-way observation window in my office—flailing and kicking, hair storming around her face, wild legs pumping. Simon comes up from behind and grips her arms and hugs her to the floor; when he is behind her this way and she is sobbing it is so violent and so intimate at once, like a man spooning a distraught girlfriend after a fight, that I have to struggle not to look away, not to give them privacy.

They come back from the garden in an intimate little trio, Simon and Addie and Dorian, like friends just coming in from a drink, except that Addie and Dorian are covered in dirt and Simon is slouching behind them with his aura of wiry lax authority, suddenly stiffening his posture and prodding them along through the doors into the lab when he sees me, so that whatever seemed relaxed or natural about the entry hardens and now it is like a policeman bringing late at night to a man's home his drunk and weeping teenaged daughters. I call Addie back into my office.

"How is the garden?" I ask.

She looks back at me, pale and sullen, but her hips are already arching forward and she pulls her shoulders back into a more attractive posture. I pretend, momentarily, not to notice.

"Coming along," she says.

"Does Dorian like it?"

"She doesn't hate it."

"I don't suppose you could get Dorian to work on building a nest."

Here she tilts her head, stares. "No, I don't suppose."

"You could invent a new habit. A habit of collaboration."

"You invent the habits. Not us."

"I beg to differ. New habits grow naturally, one right out of the other."

"Nothing is natural. You give us the habits and we complete them. When we have completed them to your satisfaction we graduate to other habits."

"Is that right?"

I let my eyes roam the curving half-crescent of skin that emerges above her waistband, its round, soft, womanly fat. I trace its imaginary bends upward past her navel and around the fleshy undersides of her breasts, climbing toward the uneven collarbone that parts in the little hollow beneath her throat. She looks straight back at me and in her eyes there is something like fear and disgust and arousal all mingling at once.

"The last time I checked, I was the one in charge of assessing your progress. Some of the habits are suggested to you. But you will develop others on your own. Maybe start by just talking to Dorian during the sessions. Maybe you can ask some of the questions, instead of me."

I lift my eyes to hers but there are traces of my gaze all over her body, new pathways on her skin where it has roamed and searched and prodded, and she feels this and stiffens and holds still. When she speaks, it is not in the same defiant voice and mien as before but rather in the tone of a question, the tone of someone who has stopped to ask directions of a stranger, with the ends of the sentences lilting up, searching. Her voice protects her voice, the way one instinctively covers with a hand that area where one hates to be tickled.

"If I do that," she says, "will you take Ellie off garden duty?"

"I'll think about it," I say.

She waits, so I release her with my eyes, letting my gaze fall back down to the reports on my desk. She hesitates for a moment and then turns to go, her back and hips still held stiff and straight for me, for that event of my looking, for the raising of that unasked question. We will split the sessions into two, create new habits of mutual attention and exchange. Between the two of them they will divide the sickness and the recovery, lob it back and forth like a ball.

***

When I graduated from college, I entered a program in clinical psychology and began to work in a child development unit that was attached to the general hospital in Knoxville. This was a bare white building, with sliding doors that whispered open and bins of toys in the waiting room and posters on the walls of grinning, happy children hugging their caregivers. The doctor who supervised my training was Rachel Coe, a woman in her thirties who had already begun to establish her reputation as a national expert on attachment disorders. She was petite and professional, with long, curly hair that she wore loose around the shoulders of her white coat and wire-rimmed glasses that she sometimes slipped back onto her head when she was reading. When she stood at the observation window next to me, she kept her back perfectly straight and her shoulders back, a clipboard anchored to her side. She wore no wedding rings and never mentioned any family or children; one got the sense that there was nothing slippery in her life, no sick, doddering mother or unreliable lover hovering at the periphery of her career or disturbing the quiet sanctity of her rare evenings off. Standing next to her, I felt as if some of her pert stability was communicating itself to my muscles and bones. Self-conscious, I held myself straighter.

"The ones with severe attachment disorders have anger on a deep, almost primal level," she said. "The rage has to be let out. Until catharsis, they will continue to lash out and fail to attach. The first thing you have to do is overmaster it. You have to show the patient that you are the absolute authority and that lashing out will not work. Then you can begin to initiate different treatments. Watch Jenna with Andy."

I looked back through the two-way mirror into the play area. This was a long rectangular room with a pale-blue carpet, pastel area rugs, and large cushions propped against the walls. There was no solid furniture, only cloth: a brown cloth footstool, child-sized armchairs made of cloth, large reading pillows propped up in the corners of the room. High up on the walls—too high for the children to reach or to break—were framed posters of animals: monkeys scaling trees, giraffes reaching for the highest leaf, with slogans like *Perseverance* and *Motivation*. Below these posters, tumbling on the carpets, were five children between the ages of two and nine, playing with toys from a locked wooden chest in the corner, each supervised by an intern dressed in scrubs. The children and the interns seemed a little faded and distant through the window, as if they were farther away than they really were.

The child-intern pair Rachel was pointing to were off by themselves in one corner playing with blocks. Jenna was a healthy-looking blonde intern. Andy seemed to be the oldest of the children, with bowl-cut hair and a splash of freckles across his face, freckles of so many different sizes and distances that they seemed to form a small galaxy. He wore, in addition to the regulation animal-patterned scrubs of the center, a black bicycle helmet with a red racing stripe along the side and large yellow oven mitts on his hands. The mitts created the odd impression of a small gourmand rather than a child in a psychiatric ward.

"Andy has a severe case of reactive attachment disorder," Rachel said. "He was taken from a home where he was abused and neglected by his biological mother. His foster mother noticed his behavioral problems and brought him to us. He's been with us for three months and we've had him in holding therapy, with sessions of enforced closeness and enforced eye contact. He's shown a little progress."

Together, we watched the intern hand two small wooden blocks to Andy, slowly, as if she were passing him a hot or delicate object. He looked down at them and clumsily, first with one huge mitt and then the other, took them into his hands. He began to clap them together. At first he clapped them slowly, experimentally; then harder and faster; then in a blunt violent staccato that made his cheeks under his freckles turn bright red. Jenna placed her hands over his, closed both mitts over both blocks, and held them tightly shut, the slender muscles in her wrists and triceps rippling. Andy looked up at her. Color flushed over his neck and forehead.

"Now watch how he escalates, and how she defuses it," Rachel said.

Andy sprang at Jenna, raising his mitted hands with the blocks, launching his body toward hers. The helmet gave him an adventurous, outdoorsy look, as if he were merely a boy springing off his bicycle to jump into a pile of leaves, which made it seem all the more terrifying and violent when Jenna used her own tanned, slender arms to pin his behind him, and when she turned him around so that he was facing us and dug her knee into the small of his back. Andy's helmet had slipped so far over his face that his eyes were hidden and all I could see of his face was the angry rash of his skin. His small body struggled so energetically, and so vainly, against his captor that the veins in his neck stood out like tiny snakes. I looked away.

"Is that the only way to handle the extreme cases?"

"It's the *first* way to handle extreme cases," Rachel said. "For the most part, the child's protest is a form of resistance and manipulation. You have to get them to experience catharsis though holding therapy and, eventually, rebirthing. Then they can begin to form attachments again."

This is how it is with Addie: she is defiant and coy but underneath that defiance and that coyness is a living rage that needs to be expressed and laid quiet. Dorian is the closer one, the one inching into recovery, hovering around its periphery. Dorian is a perpetual state of catharsis, a constant, trembling expression of that primal urge to hit. But Addie approaches recovery obliquely, elliptically, with strange lurches and drives in the body, as if she is learning a new series of dance steps and repeating them, clumsily.

When I first started working the long shifts with Andy, I moved out of our house on the mountain and into a one-bedroom apartment in a large complex four blocks from the hospital. All night long I heard the shrieking wails of ambulances climbing the highways. In the evenings, nurses and technicians in scrubs returned home with takeout containers and brown bags from the package store, their keys jangling, and slipped into each private, carpeted, anonymous unit, where soon the tinny sounds and iridescent flashes of their televisions leaked through the cracks in the blinds. My neighbors and I all shared the antisocial hours of the medical profession, rising and eating and going to bed at strange and irregular times, grocery shopping on Friday nights or having a post-shift drink by the pool at ten in the morning. In place of the ghostly shadows and colors of the Bone House on the mountain were boxy white balconies and neat, symmetrical hedgerows, each meticulously shorn to the same height by the sunglassed maintenance men who wandered daily around the complex brandishing their hedge trimmers like swords.

There were times when I sat on my balcony in the evenings and hated to think of her alone in that house coloring the bones, or of my aunt driving over from Pigeon Forge to take her to her doctor's visits. But once I started to study the cure and to work with Andy, it seemed that there were limits to the human ties I could keep connected to me all at once. Human bonds became a branching spider's web: the silky octagons at the center were the strongest and the ones that were farthest away became stretched and distant, easily snapped by their lateral connections to the others. And so my mother and I went in opposite directions. She retreated into the shadows of the Bone House while I went forward into the clean lights and bright empty spaces of the cure, where the patients were young and their lives stretched before them, full of threatening, abundant possibility.

I became obsessed with Andy's recovery. Every shift, I stood before the two-way mirror and watched him; each time it was the same. The helmet and the mitts, the clapping and the rage, and the moment of the putting down, when Jenna would lean in or flip him around and pin him to the ground in a chokehold. Always the flush of red rising through his constellations of freckles, always the features screwed up in rage, always that moment of desperate subdual: the limbs fighting and straining and then going slack, his small body tensing and then relaxing, fitfully, resignedly, against her. It was like the moment after giving blood when you let go of the rubber ball you've been squeezing and the veins stop pulsing and filling and recede back under the tender skin of the wrists. Something vital went out of Andy in those moments. He came every day to playtime hoping to attain it, that vitality: I saw it in the defiant way he came in, faced Jenna or Rachel, and accepted the blocks. But every day they found it—sometimes sooner, sometimes later—and pressed it down out of him, and he went off afterward to lie in his bed with his mitted fists clenched together, trying to get the blood, that vital thing, to fill up in him again.

When I first started watching Andy I hated to witness these moments. They looked so savage in the context of that cheerful room with all its pastels and its posters and its cushions and its other children playing in various states of rage and placation. It was always the same lashing out and the same smothering response, so that I dreaded the predictability and the repetition of the violence all the more.

Over time, though, I almost came to relish it and to wish for it, as one wishes for the righteous slaying of the villain in a movie one has seen many times. I had a hard time explaining this feeling to myself. It was almost a physical feeling, leaping in me when I saw Andy lash out; a troubled, uneasy calm stole over me once his cheek was pressed to the ground and his arms pinned behind him. At peace. But was it peace? Didn't the anger steal back again, creep around his body like an exoskeleton that every day he had to shed and reclaim?

I tried to describe this feeling to Rachel.

"It's like a feeling of relief when it happens," I said, "but it isn't relief. I don't like to see him be violent, but I don't like to see him restrained, either."

"It's hard because it's a child who has to go through it," she said.

"He doesn't look like a child when it happens," I said. "He looks like a grotesque."

I began to think about ways of calming him that would not be violent. I studied his movements when Jenna or Rachel put him in the hold, looking for some moment of transition from rage to whatever feelings followed the rage. (Quiet humiliation? The feeling of being overmastered? Quelled?) Always, when he was bent forward in the hold, there was a moment of struggle and a moment of surrender. But what happened right before the surrender? There seemed to be a split second each time where he almost relaxed into the hold. It was like the second right before a glass teeters and falls, when the darting hand is not sure if it will crash. An edge-balancing, a moment of catastrophic possibility. What came before that moment? Was it always a struggle?

My mother took an interest in Andy's disorder. Before my evening shifts I used to sometimes call and tell her about the symptoms and cases I was researching, the different patients we learned about in class, the controversial treatments and therapies. She listened—I could picture her sitting by the old rotary at our hallway table, pressing the receiver to her ear and twining the cord around her long, slender fingers—and threw in a little "mm" or "hah" every now and then. An inveterate hypochondriac, she was especially interested in the clues and the warning signs, the little details that led on gradually to the discovery of the malady, the rousing drama of convalescence.

"Some doctors have had success with a treatment called rebirthing," I told her once. "They re-enact the psychological birth of the child again, so that the angry child inside can fade away and the new, attached child can be born."

"Re-enacting a childbirth?" she said. "Like in a hospital?"

"No, in a clinical session," I said. "Sometimes they use sheets and blankets to simulate a womb and the child crawls inside. Then the doctors hold the blankets down and they talk to the child and try to get it to agree to be born again."

"Does it work?"

"Sometimes," I said. "But some children have been injured this way. There was a case in Denver where a girl was held under the blankets too long and she suffocated."

"The doctors suffocated her? To death?"

"They didn't mean to. She called for help and to get out. But they thought she was being manipulative."

"Hmm," she said. "But you said it usually helps to cure them."

"It has worked for the patients in our lab."

"Well," she said, tentatively. "Maybe you have to fail before you know how to make it work."

Once, when I was just getting off of a late-night shift, my aunt called from the law office where she worked as a receptionist. I could hear the trill of other phones, of keyboards tapping somewhere behind her. "Your mother talks about nothing but you," she said. "She's so proud that you're getting a doctorate."

"Yes," I said.

"She says all the time how busy you are with the work and the observations. It's why you never come to see her, she says. She makes so many excuses for you. It's not an excuse for me. There's no reason why you shouldn't go see your ma more often."

"You're right," I said.

Rachel passed me on the way to the vending machine just as I was hanging up. "Everything okay?"

"Everything's fine," I said. "Just a family situation."

"Ah," she said sympathetically, unwrapping a cereal bar. "Is your family here in Knoxville?"

"No," I said. "They're in Farragut."

The lie came off my tongue without me even searching for it; it was an automatic response, one that seemed to become true as I said the words. My mother faded, reassuringly, into the faraway vistas of Farragut, a town I had never seen, and our house faded with her, receding into the distance with its X-rays fluttering like white flags of surrender.

My chance to work with Andy came when Jenna had finished her internship and left the center for a residency in Atlanta. The day after her last shift the attendants brought Andy in and he sat, out of his restraints, seething. Rachel kept her place before the two-way mirror and looked over at me. "You go," she said, nodding toward the window.

My heart began to beat faster. I looked at the mitted, helmeted boy on the carpet, at the rise and fall of the panting breath in his chest.

"Won't it disturb his routine? He's used to you now."

"It won't disturb his routine. He needs to know that he can't strike, with anyone. Period."

I hesitated.

"It's only hard the first time," she said. "Go on."

In the common area the other interns raised their eyebrows when they saw me instead of Rachel, but Andy seemed not to notice my entrance. Up close he was paler than he had seemed in the tint of the two-way mirror, his skin peaked behind the scattering of freckles, his yellow shirt and red shorts more vivid. It was like suddenly seeing a neighbor in the stairwell the morning after you have overheard him having a bitter, intimate fight. I went to the box, pulled out two blocks, and handed them to Andy as I had seen Jenna and Rachel do a dozen times before. He put out his mitted hands in a spiritless way, like a desultory baker accepting a delivery.

"Where's Jenna?" he said.

"Jenna's not coming today."

"Where's Dr. Coe?"

"Dr. Coe's not coming today either. You've got me instead. I'm Jimmy."

I reached out my hand but Andy kept his mitts clutched around the blocks, his right leg jiggling up and down.

"If you're here, then that means Dr. Coe must be in there," Andy said, pointing at the two-way mirror. "And that means that when Dr. Coe is out here, you must be the one in there."

"Let's focus on the blocks for now. Don't worry about that window. Why don't you tell me what you did this morning?"

"You're here, and she's there," Andy said suddenly, with an unchildlike pensiveness. "Why is that?"

He gestured toward the mirror again, so forcefully that I turned my head to look at it, without thinking. The blow came so fast that I just barely got my hands up in time. Andy managed to clock my jaw with the blocks just once before I grabbed his arms and pinned him down. His body was warm and frail, warmer and frailer and more yielding than I expected, and I slackened up almost immediately. I got behind him and pulled him to my waist with my arms pressing his arms to his sides. At first he thrashed wildly, but then he went slack against me and his shoulders began to shake.

I felt something wet drop on my forearm and realized suddenly that he was crying. He cried in a quaking, violent way, sobs rattling his bones. His tears frightened me. I had never seen him cry with Jenna or Dr. Coe, and I was unsure how to react. I stayed completely still and held him; I was afraid to move or to wipe his snot and tears from my arms. He sobbed. It seemed like ages, that sobbing, an eternity in which we were both as still as statues except for the movements of his face and shoulders. Eventually he quieted down and one of the other interns led him away with the rest of the children, his face flushed bright beneath the helmet.

"He was humiliated," Rachel said afterwards, in the observation room.

"He was vulnerable," I said. "He opened up. He let something go."

"He was approaching catharsis," Rachel said. "It might be time to start thinking about a rebirthing therapy session. We'll see how he does."

The next day's session in the common area was even worse: leaping, lashing out, screaming at Rachel. He demanded, loudly, to see me; he said he would kill me. He managed to get onto Rachel's knees and very nearly clocked her with his blocks too before she pinned him back down. Even after he was pinned, he continued to yell out for me, sometimes turning to face me in the observation window, making lewd gestures, screaming that he would find me.

Once he broke loose and ran up to the two-way mirror and pressed his face against it, glaring in at my invisible figure. The effect was strange; he knew I could see him, but he didn't know where to position himself on the glass, so one moment he was yelling into a void beside me or beyond me and the next moment he got it right, by some uncanny chance, his face against the mirror only inches from mine. He thumped the shatterproof glass with all his might; I believed he would break it, and that he would leap in to strangle me and I would die by his hands on a floor littered with shards of glass. At night I dreamed of Andy shrieking at me through the window. I dreamed that he escaped and that I awoke to see his face peering through the windowpanes of my bedroom, or that he was waiting for me outside when I left the house.

After three more sessions like this one, Rachel called me back to the observation window, her face red, her forehead misting with sweat. "We can't go on this way. You need to see him. You need to show him that he can't bully you. He needs to break," she said, almost to herself. "When will he break?"

"Won't it make him worse to see me?"

"It might make him better. He knows you're there behind the window; it's all he ever talks about. He's ready. We'll schedule the rebirthing session."

Together we looked through the window at the crying, screaming child in the helmet, and through him to that new child waiting to be born.

Watching Addie through the two-way mirror in my office is like watching Andy playing on his own, in those rare moments when the interns used to let him wander off into the corner and sit sullenly, clapping his blocks, almost forgetting that he was being watched. I watch Addie come in beaming from the garden, lean her rake against the wall, and obediently reach out to drink the pills from the little cup that Ellie hands her. What is it that makes her want to come back and sit in stillness and solitude in the sleeping quarters, to wrap her arms around her knees and smile to herself like a teenaged suburban girl sitting on a bed, to reach for Simon's hand when he delivers her dinner as if he is a gentleman in livery helping her down from a carriage and she is the heroine of a Victorian costume drama? It is the alchemy of touch she is experiencing, the transformation implicit in one warm patch of skin grazing another.

"The hen wants him to take the eggs," Dorian says to me one day after they have returned from the garden. I turn and see her standing in the doorway of my office. She has rolled her scrubs up over her knees and over her shoulders and her skin is growing rosy and tan, browning itself in those daily sessions of sunlight. She is looking straight at me and her eyes are laughing, but the corners of her lips are still.

"Why don't you work with Addie?" I say. "Instead of

splitting off from her, try and be close with her. Take an interest in the things she takes an interest in."

"Oh, I'm interested," she says rapidly, her eyes never leaving my face. "And so is Simon, and so are you."

"Get interested in the cure," I urge. "Think about going back to the house. Try to remember what happened, Dorian. It will only work if you believe it will work."

Instead of answering she disappears from the doorway, and a moment later I see her through the window as she crosses the lab and throws herself on the sofa, picking up the remote. In the fluorescent light, with her tan shoulders and tousled hair and dirty knees, Dorian fades from the assertive woman who stood in my doorway to a rumpled teenager and all the way back to her first life as an innocent and gaping child. Somewhere in that child is the smoldering center, the raging and blazing core.

The week before Andy's rebirthing, my mother passed away suddenly from a brain aneurysm. My aunt gave me the news on the phone just as I was coming off a shift with Andy one evening.

"It's such an irony," she said. "She was so worried about getting cancer from the X-ray machine that she never worried about her brain."

"I'll make the arrangements."

"There's no need," she said. "We were the only people she had. She didn't have anyone else. She wanted to be cremated and scattered over the mountain. I know that." Her voice broke as she whispered, "I'm so sorry."

"Not your fault," I said.

Working and living around hospitals and doctors, hearing nurses confer in whispers about their patients' mortal conditions, and eating lunch almost every day in a cafeteria where the spouses and family members of sick people gathered to ruminate had all made me immune to news of death and tragedy, or at the very least unsurprised by its sudden proximity to me. It was like the ending of a story or a movie that you hadn't anticipated but that, when you looked back, you could see building up all along: it had the aura of the inevitable. In a strange way I suppose the news gave me a sense of relief: there was no more needling question of care homes and weekend visitations, of my mother coloring her strange pictures at a table with other decrepit people, eating Jell-O and croissants out of separate compartments of plastic trays, receiving little cocktails of pills in the mornings and the evenings. That vision faded, and I was left with boxes of my mother's trinkets and X-ray art and the little one-story house on the mountain, which I sold to a newly married couple who both worked in medical billing.

My aunt arranged for the cremation and we divided the ashes in half. She tossed hers over the little stream that wandered fitfully down the mountain behind the old house, and I took mine home to the apartment complex in a little black urn that I placed on the mantel of the fake, bricked-in fireplace in the living room. Next to the urn I put a small photograph of her standing in front of our house, back when she was younger and still worked at the jewelry shop. In the picture she is beaming in a teal dress with see-through sleeves and a matching teal hat slouched diagonally on her forehead, like a moll in an old gangster film. Next to this picture and the little urn I placed a vase full of petunias that I refreshed every week at the flower shop in the hospital.

Then one night I noticed the date I brought home—a receptionist, I think she was, redheaded and chesty—leaning in to squint at the picture and the urn and frowning while I went to mix her a cocktail. The following weekend I saw another date, a woman from the escort service, make a similar frown at the little display. The next morning I removed the urn and the picture. I took the petunias out of the vase and threw them in the garbage and put the empty vase back on the mantel. I put the urn and the picture in the top shelf of the hall closet next to the boxes of X-rays and some old camping equipment, where, in time, I forgot about them.

In my memory the death and the rebirth converge in a strange way, as if some of my mother's sickness went out at her death and was absorbed through Andy during his cure: as if the morbid imagination; the taut, trembling wire of the high-pitched voice; and the eager, drinking gaze all converged in his frail, helmeted body, making his frailness a shadow of her frailness, his disorder a shadow of her disorder. I did not tell Rachel about the death. I had already lied about being from Farragut, and to explain the lie or the death or the house now seemed like yanking a thread that would cause the rest of the threads that bound me together to unravel. So I went forth into the clinic and prepared for that new child to be reborn as a healthy cell, a human being free of pain and distress and violence.

For the rebirthing session Rachel had dimmed the lights and cleared the play area. The toy chest and cushions were pushed into one corner of the room. In the middle was a large mound of blankets, regulation hospital blue, arranged so that their corners were neat and exact and matching like a stack of papers. Rachel was to lead the rebirthing session; I would assist her. She was already in the room when I arrived, kneeling to one side of the blankets, holding what looked to be a script. She handed a second copy to me.

"Here's the transcript," she said. "We'll try to ask questions in the order they appear here. We can revise as we go along if necessary. Jimmy, I'd like you to take the lead on this."

"Why me?"

"Because he responds to you emotionally more than to anyone else. I'll be right here if anything happens. You ask the questions and I'll play the role of Andy's mother."

She waved at the observation window and a few moments later the door to the play area crept open. Two interns came in, each leading Andy by a hand. As soon as he saw the two of us kneeling there with the stack of blankets, he stopped in his tracks. I saw his hair for the first time: red and cowlicked, scarlet strands swirling around to peak in little tufts on the back and sides of his head. Without the helmet his face seemed broader and paler; he seemed less like a patient and more like any other child you would see on a playground or walking with his mother at the mall. It was if he had been deflated.

"What is this?" he demanded.

"Andy, this is a rebirthing session," I told him. "Today we are going to have you come under the blankets and then you will come out and be born again. Do you want to be born?"

"No," Andy said.

"Andy, I am your mother," Rachel said sternly, "and I love you and I want you to get well. The only way for you to get well is to be born again as a good child and to get rid of the bad child. I'm going to ask you again. Don't you want to be born?"

"I don't know," Andy said. A tremor had crept into his voice and his brow furrowed.

"Andy, come here and get under the blanket," I commanded.

He seemed to come willingly, slipping his small body under the thick blanket that Rachel held open for him. Once he was fully seated under the blanket he shifted around so much that the surface of the blanket resembled the surface of a pond with carp swimming in it, little ripples emerging here and there, the top of the blanket absorbing the tension of his fidgets. Rachel and I held down the blanket on either side of his moving body, pulled this way and that by his movements, like two rowers trying to stay afloat on turbulent waters.

"Andy, can you hear my voice?" Rachel said.

"Yes," came the muffled, petulant reply.

"Andy, I am your mother and you are hearing my voice from your place deep inside my womb," Rachel said. "My voice sounds happy because I am going to have a baby. I'm so excited. I can't wait for my baby to be born and I can't wait to see him in real life, outside of my body."

"Andy, do you hear what your mother is saying? She's saying she can't wait for you to be born," I read. "How does that make you feel?"

There was a long silence.

"Happy," came the soft voice, up from within the cloth.

"Do you want to come out of the womb and see your mother?"

"Yes."

"Then you need to be born. But you said a moment ago that you didn't want to be born," I said, improvising now. "Have you changed your mind?"

Silence. He began to fight under the blankets, lashing out his legs and fists. I pinned his kicking legs, more tightly, with my body.

"All the kicking," Rachel said. "I can feel the contractions."

"How do I get born?" Andy said, his voice climbing into a panicky register. "Where do I get out? I want to get out. Let me out!"

"You have to fight to get out," I said, returning to the transcript. "It's not easy to get out. You have to struggle to be human. You have to split yourself in half and come out a good boy and leave the bad boy behind. If you come out you can't lash and hit like you are trying to do now. If you come out you have to trust the people you will see. Can you do that, Andy?"

Silence again. Then, from under the blankets, I heard the stifled sound of choking sobs, a cathartic flood of weeping. My heart swelled. I pictured Andy as a changeling child, regressing back to his primal life as a sick cell to multiply himself out of his sickness, to sink back into his cells and divide them anew. Then the vision of the cells vanished and I saw the ghostly X-ray of Andy's body posted high on the windows of my mother's house, with the porch light shining through. My mother had colored in part of his abdomen a bright, flaming red. That was where the bad child was, the flourishing tumor of his disorder, and as I watched the red patch seemed to fade and grow smaller, shrinking until it was just a red point in his stomach cavity, surrounded by bones and organs that winked peacefully like stars.

As the blooming patch of red shrunk away Andy's sobs began to recede, growing quieter and coming at longer intervals, with short bursts of hiccups in between. Rachel nodded at the transcript.

"You have to be bold to live a human life," I read out. "You have to accept and trust others. You have to be calm and not hit. Do you think you can do that, Andy? Are you ready to be born?"

"Yes," Andy said.

Together Rachel and I loosened our grip. Clumsily, head-first, Andy scrambled out of the blankets and kicked them away with his feet, his scrubs rumpled and his eyes a bright red. His sweaty cowlicks had all been plastered down. On his sleeves I saw the damp patches of snot where he had wiped his nose and my heart lurched for him, involuntarily. The first thing he focused on when he emerged was me. As he looked at me, blinking sleepily in the sudden pouring in of light, he looked not like a patient or a sick cell but like a young suburban boy in a house, any house, waking up and rubbing his eyes after a long nap.

Then he pounced.

I do not remember what part of my body he seized and bit first, or how he managed to get his tiny hands halfway around my neck and squeeze so that his thumbs pressed into the hollow at my throat. I felt his anger choking in his hands, hardening them like steel traps around my neck; it seemed as if someone could rip him from me and his hands would remain, still smothering, still clutching, a severed instinctual hatred. With a tremendous effort I tore his hands from my skin and tried to press them down against his sides, but he broke free and sank his teeth into my shoulder and dug his thumbs into my eyes. I saw behind my eyelids a firework of shifting colors, twin kaleidoscopes of pain. He thrashed. I felt the rash dance of the disorder in my arms. Rachel pulled and I pushed until we had loosened his limbs and his teeth from me, until we had wrestled him to the ground and held him with his cheek turned against the floor, his face as red as an apple, still fighting and thrashing, my blood on his teeth.

By the time we got him onto the ground, two of the interns watching through the observation window had rushed to our aid. Together the four of us swaddled Andy in a blanket like a newborn child and the two interns bore him away. He was still sobbing.

"Are you okay?" Rachel said. She reached out, suddenly, for my hand. I was surprised at her gentle touch after the angry thrashing of the boy but I wrapped my fingers around hers as well.

"I'm okay," I said.

"Don't let it get to you," she said. "You did well. He just wasn't ready. Maybe it wasn't his time. Maybe it's not the best cure for him. It's not an exact science. It's a young disorder. It's a new process of recovery."

"I know," I said.

Rachel is the only one I ever talk to now about the failed rebirthing, some nights on the phone when we are both wide awake after our shifts and drinking, or in the afternoons when we grab lunch down at the hospital. When I finished my internship I stayed on for a few years with Rachel as my supervisor until I was asked to direct the psychiatric center up on the hill, the intensive laboratory with its surrounding mountains and winding paths of gravel. Those were hard days, in the beginning. All of the patients brought to me had the disorder—at first, they were all referred by Rachel—and we struggled very much with resources and funding. Wealthy donors and foundations like to donate to something with a public face, something with name recognition: the most notorious and heartbreaking cancers, the most dramatic epidemiological maladies. They do not pull out their checkbooks for the unlovely: the old, the pocked and sullen young, the abandoned children who suffer from ungovernable, unheard-of psychic maladies. But we persisted; I kept up the long shifts, we had a flow of new patients from Rachel's center, and she and I cowrote so many articles and presented at so many conferences that soon my reputation grew. I started taking referrals from Chattanooga, from Atlanta, from Charlotte, even from as far away as Baltimore and Washington, DC.

I never worked with Andy again after the rebirthing session. That was a mutual decision between Rachel and me. "It's too much for him," she said. "There was something about you that incited his rage, but we could not quell it." But I followed his case, recognized him as the patient disguised by pseudonyms in the scholarly articles Rachel wrote, kept track of the small advances and the persistent setbacks of the recovery. Andy, now cast as "Theodore," never fully recovered and never lived independently of care centers and psychologists. He was eventually able to work shifts of up to five or six hours in the cafeteria and to care for a tank of fish that stood in the waiting room of the adult care center. Rachel used the case of Theodore to argue for a more compassionate rebirthing process, one in which the child is talked through the difficult pathway out of the womb. "Healthy attachment is based in trust and encouragement," she wrote. "Once the child has achieved a cathartic release of rage he or she should be gently encouraged to shed that anger and emerge into a new world of trusting and fulfilling relationships with others, relationships that include human touch and contact as well as mutual conversations and respect."

So, yes, I often think of Andy when I am watching Simon grapple with Dorian through the screen of the two-way mirror in my office, or when Addie comes straight in from her work in the garden, perspiring and fragrant with pesticide. I think of him when she steps in close, for the umpteenth time, her blonde hair pouring over my shoulder. When her jaw, angular and misshapen, presses against my neck as she touches her lips to my ear and I let her. When she reaches her hand, inexpertly, for my zipper, and I let her do that too.

"You have to fail before you can make it work," my mother had said, sitting in the light of those sheer holograms of bones.

Did I fail Addie? Yes.

But what did it mean that she could come to me in that way? What did it mean that she could touch me and whisper those things? That she could use that language of desire? What did it mean that she let me touch her, run my fingers along her battered skin, along the soft downy hair that covered the back of her neck? What did it mean that she could give herself to me?

It meant that my cure had *worked.*

CHAPTER 3

Ellie

They are like a pair of magnets, the one making the other quiver: Dorian and Addie, Addie and Dorian. One girl fidgeting sends the other girl into shivers of fidgets. They stand in the bathroom swaddled in towels, one around each of their bodies and another wrapped turban-style around each of their heads. Both girls wear their limber adolescent bodies like shells: hard outer layers hiding bruised and battered cores. With the different shades of their hair hidden it is harder to tell their faces apart at first glance, but the one who is speaking excitedly, the emotive one, is Dorian.

"I have it and she doesn't," she says. For the second time that morning.

"What do you mean, you have it and she doesn't?" I demand. "When did you get yours?"

"Tuesday."

"Today is Friday. You haven't seen it at all?"

Dorian shakes her head even though it is Addie I am

addressing now, Addie who stands bemused and dejected behind Dorian like the silent, dour puppeteer of the marionette.

"Dorian, let Addie answer for herself."

"No?" Addie says, as if it is a question.

"When did you have it last?"

"Last month. The same time as Dorian."

"Have you ever had it at a different time than Dorian?"

"No."

"Addie, I want you to look at me," I say. Instantly she lifts her head, but then her eyes falter and she looks down at the bathroom mat, and the towel on her head slips down her shoulders so that her wet blonde hair is visible again. The expression and the way the hair cascades around her bare shoulders make her look younger, like a child, not a grown woman who has somehow gotten herself knocked up under my supervision. "Listen carefully. Have you been to bed with someone?"

Addie keeps her head tilted up, her eyes cast down, and shakes her head.

"It's not like that," she says. "It's not theirs."

"Addie, answer me when I talk to you. Did you or did you not go to bed with someone?"

"That's not what she means," Dorian says. "She means that it doesn't matter about them because I helped her do it. It has nothing to do with them."

"What are you saying? You covered up for Addie. Is that it?"

"No," Dorian says.

They exchange looks and there is another episode of fidgeting, shifting back and forth.

"It means they didn't help her with it, I did. So, it isn't theirs. It's mine. Ours."

"You can't have it," I say immediately.

"So what can we do?" says Addie. "They'll take it away from us."

"What if it was yours?" Dorian says. "And someone had helped you with it. Wouldn't you want to keep it?"

Now they are both children again: artless, with questioning faces.

"I don't know," I sigh. "Let me think."

What if it was mine? Would I want it? Some of my friends had them. I almost had one, once. My lover was not upstanding; the procedure was not thorough at such an early stage; there were follow-ups, grave apologies, a specialist from somewhere within the clinic, corrections. "It's going to feel like I'm opening you up to heaven," said the specialist, laughing gently and sympathetically, tugging the stirrups wider. There was a picture on the ceiling of a woman standing in a blurry field, holding a parasol. There was a month of bleeding. I slept on his floor—he had no proper bed, he was in between places, he said, and he doubled over some comforters for me. We watched basketball and drank whiskey from a plastic cup and I got up every hour or so to change out the pad, the whole time wondering how it was possible to lose a thing that I could not see. Was it life? Life is not visible at its smallest level; there are tiny aphids in the garden which are life, many lives trammeled out in a second, in one holocaust of a shoe, one blast of the mower. It is not necessary to see life to know it exists. But must it be so fragile, so delicate? Are there not forms of life that insist, like the dark shoots struggling out of the garden plot, that battle their way through tangled vines and choking weeds and fight their way into bloom? And if that unseen life wanted to be visible, wouldn't it have insisted? Why else would it have been so easy to stamp out and trample?

I never told Mel. I could have stayed in her intake room at the women's charity, raising the child in the same corridors, around the same giant jets of water where I had played as a young girl. I could have become the spokeswoman, the darling of the brochures, the one who showed that Mel gave as good as she got. That she would take anyone. Smiling together over my little girl or my little boy in the sanctuary of the megachurch, that hallowed mother that welcomes back all its stray and broken children.

Instead I went on three months of benders. I went back and forth between the Knoxville bars and the tabernacle where the traveling acts used to play. I drank whiskey with the man on his doubled-over blankets and when we finished I went back to the tabernacle, into the bathroom stalls with those insistent hustling attendants outside, and drank ketamine from the bottle that one of the attendants always kept full inside a fake plant on the back of the toilet. You just had to slip the money in her hand and she would tell you what stall you had to go into. The bottle was smudged with the lips of the other women who came and went before you, their lip gloss blurring on the cheap plastic rim like detonated kisses. When I came back out into the tabernacle, the steepness of the stairs and the quick slope down to the stage made me dizzy and my stomach lurched. One night I vomited into the pew before me—no one was there, but as my sickness ran down along the seat the restroom attendant saw me and rushed me outside—"That's enough, honey"—and I lay flat on the grass, the music still thrumming from somewhere inside. I looked up at the sky and hung my jaw open to try and air that soapy taste out of my mouth and I thought, it's enough. It's time. The whole night lying in the grass surrounded by dropped tickets and cigarette butts, with my mouth and my dizzy eyes gaping upward. Opened to heaven.

When I returned full-time to work the sessions had started, and so had the garden. I liked the garden. Our mother, before she died, had been a landscape designer. She planted all the hedgerows and shrubs outside of the megachurch and the beds of hostas and carnations that flanked the benches in front of the giant fountain and the cross. Before she got too sick to work she used to call me out into the garden to help her, and she used to keep me amused with stories about the caterpillars and aphids and other bugs we saw when we were tending the flowers.

"Did you know that aphids are asexual?" she said to me once, on a Saturday afternoon, before the big weekly service. The aphids were coursing down the underside of a giant hosta leaf, like a dozen tiny red beads of dew. "They reproduce out of themselves. They don't need mates. But that makes them easier to kill, because they all have the same genetic makeup. One coming out of the other."

Later I heard that from Dorian and Addie.

"Did you know," Dorian said, "that all aphids are female? That they reproduce asexually? Each aphid bears the seed of its daughter. The mother was once in the grandmother and the grandmother was once inside her mother."

We were in the garden and the girls were looking at me, blinking sleepily in the sun, Simon looming behind them with a bag of potting soil. That rich smell of peat and loam drifted up to our nostrils.

"So there aren't any male aphids?" said Simon.

"Only female. It's an entirely female species. But that makes them easier to destroy," Dorian said. Together we looked down at that tiny community where like was like, whole sequences of identical daughters.

And now they are doing it. Somehow. Like the daughter cells emerging from the parent cell and splitting themselves again in a dancing twoness. A community of life that will never insist itself into being, that will only retreat and crumple and weaken before the violent grace of its mothers.

One blonde and one brunette. Girls. Women. With soft

shoulders and hips like women. And hands and fists and mouths like something else. I am here to tend the parts of them that are women. I leave my mark in the caretaking and the primping: the pill and the painted eye. The men do the rest: the diagnoses, the restraint. The cure.

It was obvious what Dr. Lark wanted from me when he hired me over dozens of other, more qualified applicants. I was straight out of nursing school, rooming with girls from the megachurch, when he called me into his office. He glanced hurriedly at my resume on his desk, looked up, paused, then looked at me more closely. I noted the wrinkled bachelor polo under his lab coat; the unringed left hand; the beach tan; the musculature of the shoulders, firm and defined against the slouching reaper of middle age.

We went through the preliminaries. My background. His background. The background of the ward. And then he said, abruptly, "In most situations you would be working a rotation, visiting many different patients. Here, there would be only two."

"I would like that. I like working one-on-one with patients."

"It's not just that. It's an unusual situation." He sighed. "The two young women we treat here have never lived anywhere else. And they're teenagers. They need someone who can take care of their daily routine and their meds, but they also need someone they can relate to on the level of women's experience. You see, we have a lot of female nurses here, but none who are really close to their age. And they're curious about those things. Growing up, you know. What can you say about"—here he stalled for a moment, then recovered—"the lives of women?"

"The lives of women?"

He fumbled with a paper clip, then dropped it. "The day-to-day needs of young women. Young women who haven't seen much of the world."

"I've lived with a lot of women their age. I work well with women."

"And where was this?"

I told him about Mel's charity at the megachurch and his eyebrows lifted. He set my resume down. Three days later I started the new position. And since then, every day, I have taken care of Dorian and Addie: Dorian and Addie watching television, Dorian and Addie getting haircuts, Dorian and Addie holding hands through the different sessions, Dorian and Addie sleeping close to each other, their light and dark hair mingling like the water of rivers.

I grew used to them very quickly. Still, it made me feel weird, knowing I could leave and they couldn't. Standing behind those women at the mirror over the bathroom counter, being myself a woman who could do her own eye makeup, fix her own meals, go out at night. Strange to be a woman who can go home with a man, who answers to no one.

It made me despise my own vitality a little, watching them.

***

The megachurch is a giant structure that looms like one of the seven wonders of the world. It's so big that it has its own exit off the main highway, Interstate 40, and a parking lot the size of a football field. The church itself is brick and traditional, with a steeple and pews and red carpet, but attached to it like a bigger animal carting its prey is a more modern glass-and-concrete building that contains the set where the actual filming is done. There, every Sunday, women in print dresses and hats with gauzy veils and men in ties and sport coats arrive from Gatlinburg and from Johnson City and even from as far away as Asheville, caravans of Buicks and Hondas jamming up the highway, crawling obediently off the exit into the lot where the local police gesture and beckon and blow out commands with their whistles. They park and unpack themselves and hike up the lot to the megachurch, streaming through the security line where officers aim flashlights into their pockets and beige purses. They take their seats in long curving rows that flow around the great stage decked in red velvet. The stage is flanked by two enormous monitors, where Christ in his agony twists his face up to the vaulted ceiling. A red-robed choir sings "Say a Prayer" as they enter.

When everyone is seated our father comes out, in his black suit and blue tie with the microphone on his lapel, a shock of gray hair rising imperiously over his forehead, and he begins to preach. His voice rises and sways in peaks of *hallelujah*; he paces the stage in a fervent, stomping rhythm; the monitors send his face, caked with concealer and crumpled, trembling, in devotion, out to his brethren sitting before their televisions in Tennessee and North Carolina and Georgia. He calls out *Amen?* and the congregation swells with one answer, canes banging, hands coming alive with dances of thankfulness and praise.

Meanwhile, if you're out in the parking lot, his voice still shoots to you like an arrow from loudspeakers beside the decorative lake, reverberating against the enormous white cross that towers over the interstate. This cross is surrounded by underlit fountains, their jets of water yearning toward its spread arms, and also by benches where more worshippers gather. These brethren are less well-dressed: rumpled all-night men holding drinks in brown paper bags, ashamed fugitive mothers who wander over from Mel's charity and sit hunched on the benches as if they want to dissolve themselves and their transgressions into the wood, as if they want to vanish under the terrible grace of this gospel.

I go around to the service entrance and knock loudly so that Mel can hear me. She answers the door in a blue robe, her hair loose around her shoulders, her eyes wide and startled behind her wire-rimmed glasses. "Ellie?" she says. She whispers, so as not to disturb the sleeping women. "It's after lights-out. What are you doing here?"

"It's about a patient. I need your advice."

"Hold on." She closes the door for a second and I hear her footfalls retreat down the long dark hallway inside where the women sleep, all of them in various stages of pregnancy:

round bellies, swelling ankles, hands resting lightly over their abdomens or, I imagine, wrapped around one of the little velvet crosses Mel gives out at intake, with the logo of a child's hand wrapped in a mother's hand and underneath it, in looping cursive, the words *I Stand 4 Life*.

When she reappears she is dressed in her work clothes: tan, high-waisted khakis that are tight around the ankles and baggy around her midsection and bottom, as if to mask any possible signs of sexuality, and a T-shirt with the *I Stand 4 Life* logo right across her breasts. She leads me to a bench just outside of the main entrance, in front of the fountains and the cross.

"What is it, Ell?" She has pushed her glasses up onto her forehead and her brown eyes are dark and worried. Her eyes the color of my eyes.

She is quiet while I explain Addie's secret. Then she says, looking out over the water, "Who else knows?"

"Just me."

"And Dr. Lark?"

"I haven't told him either. I haven't told anyone. I wanted to talk to you first."

"Okay." She blows a breath out of her nostrils and drums her fingers on her knee, thinking. "What is the scenario with Dr. Lark? What will happen when he finds out?"

"He'll force her to have an abortion. He'll say she isn't fit to raise a child. She's too sick."

"What about the father? Who is he?"

"She wouldn't say. Another patient, maybe. Although I

don't know how they would have had a chance to be alone together."

"If he isn't fit to raise a child, either, then that makes it more difficult. We couldn't sue for him to take custody. What about adoption?"

"They'll say she's too sick to even carry the child."

"Is she?"

"Maybe. Yes. No. I don't know. She's gotten better. They both have."

"What does she want?"

"Both she and the other girl want to have it. I think they want to try and raise it themselves. They think it belongs to the two of them. Not to anyone else."

We are both quiet then, staring into the brightly lit jets of the fountain.

"Give me some time," she says at last. "Let me think about what to do." We stand up together and she points at the main entrance door, where the spectators line up in their dark suits and flowered linen dresses on Sundays. "Have you been inside lately?" she says. "Dad's redone the whole interior."

"Don't push your luck," I say. "It's bad enough that I came to you."

It is strange to think about the divergence of sisters. All the possible and unlikely combinations. Take the two of us: my sister, fifteen years older than me and running a right-to-life charity, and me, working as a nurse and companion in the ward. Or the two of them: Addie with her hand already resting on her flat stomach (why do they always pick up that gesture so quickly, these women?) and Dorian standing next to her at the counter, one arm wrapped protectively around Addie's shoulder, like a concerned father. We have five minutes, tops. The bathroom has become our retreat and our meeting place, the only space where we can be sure to be alone and undisturbed.

"I might be able to help you," I say, "but I don't know. I need more information."

"What information?" says Dorian.

"First, I need to know for sure that you're pregnant." I set the package, still in the plastic bag, on the counter. "I need you to use that. You won't be able to do it today. We'll be out of time. We'll do it in the morning, first thing. I'll hide this up in the supply cabinet and I want you to follow the instructions and take the stick and place it back in the box and put it back up in the cabinet and call me. I'll get it back out."

"Okay," Addie says.

"And I need you to tell me who the father is. Right now."

"We don't think the father matters," Dorian says. "Like we said before."

"It matters a great deal. There are legal reasons why it matters, first of all. And, second, once the news gets out everyone will demand to know."

"Fine."

Addie whispers to Dorian, who leans into my ear and whispers a name, gently. Then she steps back and pronounces another word, more distinctly.

"*Probably*," I say. "What do you mean, 'probably'?"

"I mean because it is the most likely scenario," says Addie.

"How often did you meet him?"

Addie whispers again to Dorian, who whispers a number in my ear that makes me recoil. Still, in that moment of shock, I am surprised to notice myself noticing how well they have internalized the logic of the sessions. Learning to speak together, to see together.

"Thirteen times? In the *garden*?" I yell at Simon. "What were you thinking?"

"It's not like you think," he pleads. "She started the whole thing. It was her idea."

"It was her idea? She's sick, Simon! Are you crazy?"

"Please, Ellie, lower your voice," he begs.

We are seated in my car in the gravel parking lot outside of the ward. The other off-shift nurses glance over at us, curious, as they cross the lot with keys in hand, cardigans slung over their forearms, cell phones at their ears. Simon is in his street clothes, loping and delectable in a vaguely distasteful way like a drink that's too strong, with a light thatch of brown stubble on his chin and a detached, faraway look in his eyes.

"It's not like you think," he says again. "It happened as part of the sessions. We spent a lot of time together. She pursued me relentlessly. Mostly I did my job and just ignored her. But she kept asking me questions, asking to hold my hand, touching me. Over time, we grew close."

"You grew *close*? To a nineteen-year-old patient in a locked ward? How does that even happen?"

Then Simon tells me a story. It is a confused and winding story, one that he mutters at indistinct intervals and that I have to piece together. It is a story about a conspiracy of touch. It starts with a brush of the hand. A lingering press of skin on skin, downcast eyes turned away, blond hair tickling the knuckles. Another time, the exchange of a spoon. The passing of the utensil and the gripping of the wrist, this time a glance that goes straight into the eye, slender fingers wrapping around that crease at the bottom of the hand. From there, a graduation. Pressing limbs together in the garden behind the shed, bare feet squelching in the mud, the hose gurgling and trickling, the thump and press of one heartbeat against another. All the touches work that way, by increments. They become part of the sessions and the treatment. A habit of stolen intimacy. Increments working by accumulation. Eventually, the touches take their natural course.

"I know it sounds crazy, but what made it easy was how angry I was for her," he finishes. "For them."

"Angry?"

"Why should they be denied everything?" he says. "A life outside, a family, friends, a home, a proper education—because of a crime from years and years ago? Because of the way they were born and raised? If they want to be close and intimate with someone, why shouldn't they be able to have that, like anyone else? Just to have sex, like you or I or anyone could? Why can't they have things too, even being the way they are?"

"So you fucked her out of pity?"

"No," he says, his voice low and solemn. "Out of solidarity."

The thing is this: I am not a right-to-lifer. I don't believe that every fetus is a living being. I despise the scare tactics: Mel and her protestors outside the Chattanooga Planned Parenthood shrieking and holding baskets with little dried peaches meant to represent the life inside the body. Mel and her protestors walking eagerly by the sides of the frightened young girls, themselves escorted by policeman, crossing the parking lot to the building in a dismal procession. All the yelling. *God wants you to have*, et cetera. *The Lord has given you a gift. A precious gift.*

I have never thought life was precious: not when I did my hospital rounds in nursing school, giving morphine injections to young children struck by cars or beloved family members seized by terminal disease, nor when I slowed to a crawl on the interstate while passing ambulances and those bulging white figures on stretchers, those cars so crumpled and bent they looked like discarded aluminum foil tossed onto the freeway. I never thought it was precious when our mother's doctor found a cancer so cruelly advanced that there was no part of her ovarian X-ray that was not a tumor, or when we let the last gray dusting of her ashes go fluttering over the megachurch's lake while, yards away, young children gurgled and shrieked in their water wings. And I never thought it was precious when yet another sobbing pregnant woman showed up at Mel's charity after hours, her lips beaten into a gruesome plum-colored pulp, the skin around her eyes blackened and smashed, and Mel would call me while I was at dinner or in a bar and beg me to come over with my supply bag and my bandages. I never thought life was precious even when I saw Dorian and Addie brighten at the sight of the things they grew in their little plot: that garden, slumping now with its own abundance, the unplucked eggplants and tomatoes weighing down stems, the ground tangled with desperate rotting blossoms. But the life that is in Addie, the life that the girls have grown, is precious to me. Why?

Because, watching them, I see a new form of cooperation grow, some new collaboration made possible by the life that they lead now. Together. Standing before the tank, watching those small drifting fry twirling through the grass, narrating the story of what they see together. They are on the same side now—Dorian next to Addie, Addie next to Dorian, their reflections glowing in the water, their strong, coltish limbs grazing each other. Flushed and young in their expectation. They are like an excited couple attending a Lamaze class or picking out diapers and onesies in a department store. They make Simon's words make sense to me, echo and resound in me. Why shouldn't they have what they want to have? Even being what they were? What they are?

***

"The test had a plus," Dorian says.

"Show it to me."

She leads me back into the bathroom, stands up on tiptoe, and retrieves the little white wand from the top of the supply cabinet. Together we look at the foggy cross in the viewing window.

"What do we do now?" Dorian says.

"Sit tight. Let me talk to the doctor. In the meantime, make sure Addie gets lots of rest. If anything seems funny, you come to me first. No one else."

"But what will the doctor do? Will he be angry?"

"Probably, yes."

"Will he let us have it?"

"Just let me talk to him."

She tilts her face up to me: alert, freckled, flushed.

"You will help us?" she says. "Promise?"

"I can't promise anything, Dorian," I say. "You know that."

"Then promise to try."

"I promise."

Dr. Lark's office is getting worse. As the sessions have advanced, it has declined. Files are strewn across the desk. The garbage can is overflowing with takeout cups and Styrofoam lunch containers. The window blind is askew. The books on the tall shelf are all turned on their sides, like row after row of tumbled dominoes.

As the sessions have advanced Dr. Lark has declined too, becoming unkempt and unshaven, his face a patchy lawn of brown and silver stubble, purple crescents of exhaustion under his eyes. His white lab coat is rumpled and there is a large brown coffee stain near his waist. Underneath, his unbelted khakis sag to reveal a glimpse of the curly trail of hair on his soft abdomen. He is standing near a bookshelf, squinting so hard at his clipboard that he doesn't notice me in the doorway until the second time I knock, hard.

"Ellie," he says. He takes off his glasses and sets them on the desk, on top of the clipboard. "What's going on?"

I shut the door and move closer to his desk.

"We need to talk," I say.

"Is this about the garden?"

"No. Well, sort of. It's Addie."

"Is she hurt?"

"No. No. It's just that she's"—here I find I cannot find the right word for I want to say. *Expecting? With child? Pregnant?* Which is the least severe word, or the most alarming and impersonal? In the end I simply retrieve the white wand from my pocket and lay it face up on his desk.

I expect that he will be upset. But I do not expect him to be this upset. He stares at the window with its blurry little cross. His eyes widen, then close, then open again, blinking. His fist crumples atop his clipboard. The skin around his eyes furrows and he does not breathe. He seems to forget that I am here.

We both stare at the cross and suddenly I have a crazy vision of the thundering white cross of the megachurch, with its aura of crucifixion and fury, rising out of the box, bolstered with the life that is stirring in Addie's body. I start talking, nervously, quickly: providing details, information.

"She's only in her first trimester as far as I can tell. She missed her first period last week. Addie and Dorian are being cooperative. They came to me first and they wanted me to tell you. Simon has already admitted that he is the father. He is cooperative and he wants the best for Addie."

At this last admission Dr. Lark's eyes stop blinking and fix on the foggy cross. The hand on the clipboard uncurls, the fingers straightening, the joints making a little cracking sound. He tilts his head to the side. Like a birdwatcher listening to something, a rare call, low in the bushes. To something that I am not saying.

"If I might just offer my opinion, I think there might be ways to let her keep it and to cede custody to Simon," I say, rushing again, "but there will be things we need to prepare. Addie needs to see a doctor, right away. Simon will need to take a paternity test."

"Oh," Dr. Lark says, loudly. "That won't be necessary."

"No?" I say, surprised.

"No. Let me talk to Simon."

Dr. Lark walks over to the window with his back to me and looks out over the grounds, over the gravel lot with the shining cars gathering heat and light in the noonday sun. I cannot see his lips or his face and his voice seems to emanate from the bath of sunbeams at the window.

"No, a test won't be necessary," he says again, in a gently remonstrative tone, as if he were reminding me of a task he had already several times asked me to complete. "I'll handle Simon. There will be no pregnancy. It's impossible. She's not fit for it."

"But she and Dorian, in the sessions—"

"The most important thing is the treatment," he says, still with his back to me, looking out at the mountains spiking upward like accusing fingers. "We need to keep up the sessions. We can't get sidetracked by mistakes. She's not fit for pregnancy. We need to take care of it. There are ways. It doesn't have to be invasive. They make pills you can swallow. It's very easy, now."

"Dr. Lark, I don't know. I know it's not my place, but shouldn't we talk to them first? Maybe take them to see an ob-gyn? It just seems like Addie should have a say."

"Ellie, we aren't dealing with a typical, healthy young woman," he says, his voice drifting again from within that strange bath of sunshine. "She's not fit to judge for herself. I understand your concern. But please leave this to me."

After this he says nothing, his back cold and flat in the light, and so I turn to leave, my rage caught in my throat. But then he calls me back into the office and turns around to face me, standing straight: all tall authority again. Commanding. Diagnostic. Like a judge coming in to deliver the verdict, the courtroom standing expectantly, the judge waving them down with his hand.

"Ellie, one thing you can do," he says. "Tell Addie. Make the news gentle. Help her get used to the idea. Help her remember the cure."

***

"He wants me to talk to Addie, to give her the news," I say to Mel in the common room after the evening prayer. The overhead lights are out and the room is lit by standing lamps in the corners. The women with round bellies are sitting in a cirele talking amongst themselves, wearing long flannel nightgowns like young girls at a sleepover party. Some of them look strained, with their faces pinched and their cheeks swollen and their stomachs so painfully large that they cannot stand up without assistance, not without great distortions of the body; others have merely a gentle rounding under the clothing, a curve like the groundswell around the trunk of a great tree that strikes its roots deep into the unwitting soil.

"When?"

"Friday. Friday he wants me to explain it to her and to give her the Mifepristone first and then the next day the Misoprostol. He doesn't want to delay. He doesn't want there to be too much time. He wants it to be in the morning when I give her the other pills. Just like any pill. Like an antibiotic for an infection, he said."

"What time on Friday?"

"There's a doctor coming at 8:30 to give Addie a checkup and to deliver the pills. Just to make sure there's no problem with her other medicine. Also, she has to have an ultrasound."

"What doctor?"

"Nora something." I dig in my bag for the little triangle of paper. "Nora Sumner. She's an obstetrician."

"Where?"

"She's driving up from Atlanta on Thursday. I don't know why exactly. I think Dr. Lark didn't want any people around who would know us, know the ward."

"What's the space around the ward like?" Mel says abruptly.

"Why?"

"Just wondering. I have a hard time picturing it."

I describe the gravel parking lot, the short rows of hedges that zigzag around the back, the rippling waves of foothills. Mel listens, breaking in every now and then with a question about dimensions, where the different entrances are, the number of cars that fit in the lot. Then she takes the folded paper I've given her and stands up, surveying the room, her handiwork: the coven of pregnancies, the growth of unresisted life. The women as waddling and unstable as penguins.

"Okay," she says. "Give me some time."

I prepare a speech for Addie. We have something to discuss. Only your best interests. Doctor arriving this morning. And all that. Every time I think of the right order of the sentences I falter. There is no good sequence for the words I have to say, no arrangement that will calm and soothe her and Dorian. There is only an official-sounding delivery of medical news in a bath of fluorescent light and the innocent, terrified eyes looking back, the hand resting on the helpless belly.

I rehearse and reorder the arrangement as I drive to work the next morning, ready to arrive in time for the 6:00 a.m. shift change, speaking the words aloud to myself in the quiet car as I pass by the mountains. But I am unprepared for what I see when I turn off the exit.

Surrounding the ward, standing, chanting, screaming, are hundreds and hundreds of protestors, male and female, old and young, dressed in jeans and khakis and T-shirts against the gently warming dawn, all of them chanting, hiking high signs that read *Save Addie's Baby* and *We Stand For Life* and *Abortion Kills* and *Stop Child-Murder.* Their voices ring out over the mountains. They crowd together and they are like an advancing army, like a phalanx of soldiers swarming the gates of an ancient city, their faces angry and contorted, fists beating the air in practiced solidarity.

At the large window in the front corridor of the ward, the side with the nonsevere cases, the patients peer between the black security bars that fence them in, their faces dilated with curiosity and terror. Before the main entrance, the two off-duty policemen who work our security clearance are pacing distractedly in their black uniforms, speaking into their walkie-talkies, stopping the protestors who stray too close to the entrance. Through the sliding double doors in the waiting room, the nurses and the family members who have come to visit patients are all looking out at the crowd, and I picture Addie and Dorian somewhere inside, maybe in Dr. Lark's office, peering through the blinds at the great consternation that their bodies have caused.

The street that turns into the lot is filled with news vans from the local Channel Seven Voice of Knoxville and from some of the right-wing AM stations and even from the National Public Radio service in Atlanta. There is no room to park in the flurry of reporters, so I have to turn back around and park in the grass on the side of the road and walk back up through the gravel lot. Immediately a reporter spots my nurse's uniform and hastens over with her cameraman.

"I see you work here," she says, holding her microphone like a weapon. "May I ask you a few questions?"

"No comment," says a deep voice behind me.

I turn to see Dr. Lark approaching us from his gleaming white Lexus, freshly shaved and dressed in a tan sport jacket and tie. He puts his arm protectively around my shoulder and steers me past the reporter. "Please let us through."

"Can you confirm that there is a doctor arriving this morning to perform a mandatory termination on an unwilling young female patient in your ward? Name of Addie Glens?"

"I said no comment at this time."

The reporters fade away behind us and Dr. Lark wrestles me ahead of him through the throng of protestors, ducking under the dance of signs. When they see the two of us together as we fight our way toward the lab, when they realize who I am and guess who he might be, they roar even louder. Some of them try to block our path; others spit in his face; others start up a new chant: *The Doctor Is a Mur-der-er*, breaking the syllables across their raised fists.

"Jesus," Dr. Lark says, when we have finally made our way

to the security guards at the entrance. We both turn to take a final look before we slip through the doors into the safety of the ward. "Where did they all come from?"

"I don't know," I say.

Then I spot Mel. She is holding a megaphone and standing before a big circle of her women, all of them clad in the maroon sweatshirts with the *I Stand 4 Life* logo, some of them clutching babies to their hips or holding the hands of children who twine bewilderedly around their legs. All of them bow their heads respectfully when Mel begins to speak, her voice electric through the megaphone. She is graceful and righteous; her hair streams out behind her; her eyes are set heavenward; she is an angel of God's will.

"Today we are on a mission to save one of the Lord's children," she says. "Let us pray."

Chapter 4

Simon

The doctor from Atlanta has vanished outside. She parked her silver Jaguar off the side of the road on the patchy grass, where two Knoxville policemen came to meet her. She linked arms with them and they came slowly toward the crowd, like a Red Rover game in slow motion: the police burly in their blue uniforms, weapons at their hips, and she in her khaki slacks and oxfords and no-nonsense white blouse, her expression practiced and unsurprised. They came past the news vans toward the entrance and had just made it onto the gravel lot when the throng descended, the angry riot of chanters encircling them. Now the circle has closed on her and she and the policemen are lost to our sight. The backup patrol cars from Knoxville have not arrived yet, and Dr. Lark has gone outside to talk to the security guards.

The lot is filled with a fervent, terrible chanting, like an apocalyptic chorus. They are a band of witch hunters united under the direction of the one calling into the megaphone, the one in the maroon sweatshirt with the wire-rimmed glasses and the waist-high jeans and the streaming hair, her face contorted with a terrible purpose and majesty. Like the woman clothed with the sun, I think suddenly, that voluptuous, celestial figure of the vision in Revelations with her body made of light, and then the thought fades and I am once more looking at a throng of pro-life protestors blocking an abortion doctor outside a private mental health ward in rural Tennessee.

We are standing at the window in Dr. Lark's office, that morning's session forgotten. Dorian and Addie are peering out and holding hands instinctively, still dressed in their standard-issue blue pajamas with the button-down fronts, their hair loose around their shoulders.

"But why are they here?" Addie says again.

"I told you already," Ellie says. "They're here for you."

"For me?" Addie says. Her free hand goes up to her belly, protectively.

And for me, I think.

When Ellie gave me the news my heart had dropped into my stomach and it was all I could do to restrain myself from tearing the car door open and marching back inside, finding Addie, and seizing her by the arm. "It can't be," I said. "She told me it was impossible."

"Why would it be impossible?"

"Because of all the punching. She said she could never have one and Dorian could never have one either."

Ellie let out a short, scornful laugh at this. "That's what she told you?" she said. "That neither of them could conceive?"

It is what she told me, I reflect, thinking back to the garden, of the moment when we were first lying side by side with the tangled vines tickling our backs like playful fingers and the afternoon sunshine beating down its warmth, pooling in that pale curve just along her waist, the one that curved into her body like a hollow *c*, the one that trembled a little under the weight of my hand. Despite what she'd told me the week before, I had brought a condom, but she waved it away. She said, again, that it was impossible—which seemed to make sense because of all the fighting, but then she said something else, too, another word. *Infertile.* Was that it? I think of that moment again and the word does not seem right in Addie's mouth. It is too clinical; it does not have her characteristic air of childish, vaguely malevolent fantasy. *Immaculate*, I thought. That's what she said. That she was immaculate.

"What are you going to do if it gets back to your ex?"

"It can't get back to her," I said immediately. "She'd use it to get custody of Sandy."

"But what if it does?"

"Then I have to try and tell her the truth. That I made a huge mistake. That Addie lied. That she is manipulative and damaged."

"'Bitch is crazy?' That's going to be your excuse?" Ellie said. "'Bitch is crazy' only works when you talk to your guy friends at the bar. Not when you're explaining things to your wife."

"I guess not," I said.

We both looked back at the main entrance to the ward, at the flurry of the shift change with the nurses meeting in little groups at the door and scattering out to their Hondas and Jettas, heading back home to their boyfriends and girlfriends and spouses and children. Throwing their bags in the passenger seat, adjusting mirrors, starting engines. The tinny sounds of music and talk radio floated out of their half-cracked windows. That is the worst thing about this sort of news, I thought: the benign indifference of the rest of the world, the complacent trail of coworkers who will go home and change clothes and eat dinner and watch television with their husbands and wives and small children. Meanwhile, I will go home to a shitty rented apartment three streets over from the university, where the faucet leaks and spotted trails of mold are forming in the bathroom, and where the sidewalks and yards on game nights are filled with slurring UT undergraduates stumbling around the neighborhood with red Solo cups, like bad actors in a low-budget zombie flick. I will unlock the door and sit on the Salvation Army couch and crack open a Busch and think about how when Nora finds out she will get not only the house but everything else. Everyone else.

Ellie tapped the screen on her smartphone, looked at the time, set it down again in the cup holder, and stretched her legs out under the steering wheel. "I need to get back," she announced.

"Does Dr. Lark know anything?"

"Not yet," she said.

"When are you going to tell him?"

"I don't know," she said. "Just be ready."

Now I am ready, have been ready every day, have waited anxiously for the axe to fall, have watched this young woman bearing my child roam back and forth across the ward. It is lunchtime and the doctor has turned away, defeated, crawled back into her Jaguar and headed away toward the metropolis. The throng of protestors has only grown thicker and stronger and more unified, new vanfuls arriving from Nashville and Atlanta and Charlotte every hour to assemble under the golden-voiced woman with the megaphone. Dr. Lark is outside with the security people again and Ellie and I are in the kitchenette making lunch. Dorian and Addie are staring gape-faced at the local television broadcast that announces why this, their ward, is the center of a hot regional controversy. The news anchor says that the Board of Directors stands behind the doctor; that they have issued a public statement in his support. The news channel cuts first to the reporters in front of the ward and then back to the studio, where doctors are giving interviews about attachment disorders and the ethics of abortion. Their faces appear in little boxes on the screen parallel to the reporter who is interviewing them. First the doctors blink and nod while the interviewer asks a question and then the interviewer blinks and nods while the doctor answers, sometimes interrupting them to press another question.

"It's a very uncommon disorder," one of the doctors on television is saying, "and it has been the subject of many controversial and fashionable cures."

I slide down the wall of the kitchenette and stare at my knees. The truth. The end of everything. A second stint of unwitting, unwilling fatherhood. The accidental perpetuation of life. The male hen guarding his fry—or the black widow devouring her mate. From the stovetop comes the sound of bubbling water, the homey, starchy smell of pasta boiling. Ellie is stirring the pot with a large wooden spoon, a stiff white apron over her uniform, her full hips swinging maternally as she paces from the fridge to the counter to the stove and back again, her hair piled high on her head in a frazzled ponytail that reveals the Chinese symbol for "water" tattooed on the back of her neck. She turns to the spice rack and sees me as she takes one of the little bottles down.

"Simon, it's going to be okay," she says, and sets the wooden spoon down on the counter. She comes to join me on the floor, settles next to me. Our knees touch. She reaches out her fist to me, uncurls her manicured red fingertips, raises her palm to my lips. I think at first that she is bringing a palmful of spices to my nose, pinches of dried basil and oregano and rosemary, and so I am startled when her lifted palm reveals to me, dead pale in its fleshy center, a single white pill.

***

On my first day at work in the ward, two years before, Ellie was the one who showed me that cabinet.

"This is the kitchenette," she announced, without fanfare or interest.

She produced a jangling bunch of keys from somewhere inside the loose pockets of her uniform and unlocked the door—it was one of those split doors where the top half could swing open while the bottom stayed shut, a dispensary window with a flat shelf for beverages and pills. Like a snack bar at a neighborhood pool. Inside, everything was secure. Locked blue cabinets over a bare blue countertop. Sharp knives and dishwasher-streaked silverware in a locked box next to a shining, empty sink. Pill bottles, each with a child safety cap, nestled next to bottles of chives and oregano in a wooden spice rack on the wall. They made an odd impression on me, these bottles in the rack, recalling memories of hospitals on the one hand and family holidays and dinners on the other: Valium and tarragon, opioids and basil, beta blockers mixed with the inviting smell of cumin and dried peppers.

It was that spice rack that first came between Nora and me.

Or maybe it was that Nora and I had the big problem first

and then the problem with the spice rack began.

I only know that I had been up for thirty-six hours, first for a double shift in the ward and then the next night with Nora in one of our hysterical fights. She came home late, in a slinky dress and dangling earrings, and as with all of her fights this one started with something small, something about our cable bill, which she had just brought in from the mailbox. Then it became tangled with everything else: my long hours at the ward, and her trying to keep the house together while she was back in school again, and whether we were being good parents to Sandy when Sandy was always having to stay at Nora's mother's house.

It was the kind of fight that moves in cycles, that would start to die down and then regenerate itself from some fresh, just-remembered injustice—the kind of fight that begins to incorporate all previous injustices into itself, tying together sexual proclivities and bad domestic habits and intimate details and feelings that only a partner could know until it becomes a complicated web that tangles all of your history together. It was the kind of fight where you follow each other around while you're brushing your teeth or undressing, where you ambush each other with fresh provocations, where you fill the most intimate, private spaces with the argument. It was a vintage Nora fight, escalating from reckless, tipsy passion into even more reckless and smoldering rage, except that instead of going to the bedroom and fucking or spooning or both, we ended it on the couch in the living room, sitting two feet apart in front of the bay window, watching the night change slowly into dawn.

That was when Nora first said it. It was startling but at the same time it felt predictable, like when you've been trying hard to remember a word or a song lyric and then all of a sudden it comes into your head when you're thinking of something else.

"Is that what you want?" I said.

"Yes. No. I don't know. But what else can we do?"

We sat in the living room quietly, feeling together the new and ugly and necessary resolution, while the room lit up with sunlight that brought the small pastel building blocks and the plastic play stove and the Fisher-Price dolls into sharp, bleak relief. Then Nora went to pick up Sandy and take her to school, and I showered and came straight back to the ward dressed in the same scrubs I had left in nine hours before. No one noticed. The day passed in a bleary, weird fog of sessions and hand-holding and questions in front of the seahorse tank, and then Ellie went to supervise the girls in the shower and I found myself alone in the kitchenette, cooking and blinking away tears of weariness and misery and exhaustion. The trays were out on the counter and I had already placed the side items into the small white compartments—the blanched patch of iceberg salad with its squiggles of purple cabbage, the single sweet clementine—and was turning to get the salt down from the spice rack for the rice when I saw the pill bottles and remembered.

The memory was small and compressed into one moment of one shift in an endless stream of shifts, but as I stood at the rack it seemed to swell and become outsized, gigantic and clear and whole. It was a memory of Ellie from just after I'd started working in the ward. She was standing in the same place I was in now, cooking the same Tuesday-night rice and enchilada dish from the recipe in the white binder on the counter. She was moving briskly around the kitchen, her back turned to the little half-open swinging door, and it was clear to me from her unselfconscious movements and the way she was murmuring to herself that she thought she was alone. It was my turn to sit with the girls in the common area until dinner was ready, but Dorian had insisted on having a glass of ginger ale before dinner, and I had returned to the kitchen just in time to see Ellie take down a pill bottle from the rack, press open the top, and pop a pill in her mouth just as casually as you would swallow a Tic Tac or an aspirin in public. She turned back to the stove and kept stirring, and I waited a moment, hovering and uncertain, before I entered the kitchenette. After that I watched her carefully to see if she did it again, but then she took a leave of absence, and when she returned I never saw her go to the rack except for seasoning.

That day after the fight, standing before the same spice rack, I looked behind me, saw no one in the doorway, and took down the bottle that read DORIAN GLEN. 20 MG NEMBUTAL. TAKE ONE CAPSULE BY MOUTH. I studied the dosage for a moment, put two of the pills on my tongue, swallowed them with a long drink of water from the faucet, and placed the bottle back in the rack. I returned to the cooking.

By the time the rice and enchiladas were ready, the memory of the fight and the word *divorce* and the bleak sunlight afterward had begun to retreat. The events of the night before seemed like they had happened to a different person, or in an imaginary world like the ones Sandy used to describe to herself in lisping, incoherent whispers as she sat back on her ankles in her pinafore, moving Fisher-Price people around in their gaudy red and yellow house. I saw Nora and myself as figures shrunken down into bright plastic, all head and abdomen, standing inside Sandy's Fisher-Price living room with frozen mouths.

Around me, by contrast, the kitchenette grew baroque and sensory, the lines of the counter and the cabinets bowing ever so slightly inward, the temperature warming with the heat of the oven, the air thick with the smells of cumin and garlic and chili powder. I took the dinner trays, one in each hand, and went strolling through the ward to the common area, where Dorian and Addie sat watching TV in a glowing sphere of fluorescence.

"Set it down there," Dorian commanded, without moving her eyes from the screen.

"I believe the word you are missing is *please*," I said.

"She didn't mean to be rude," Addie said. She reached for both of the trays and set them down on the table, but when I went to hand her the silverware she waved it onto the table next to the trays. “I don’t want a spoon,” she said. “I don’t want to eat. I want to hold your hand.”

She looked up at me from her place on the sofa, damp blonde tendrils clumped in glossy, wavy sections around her face. Her brown eyes were large and questioning, her skin still rosy from the shower. A few drops of water slipped down her neck. Her bruises were so faded as to be nearly imperceptible. She looked like a healthy, attractive young woman who had just lifted herself out of a suburban pool, not like a patient with broken, reset bones and jolted organs and bad dreams who lived in a locked ward. But had she said that? Or was it the pills that made it seem as if she had said that?

“I have work to do,” I said.

“Please?” she said again, and this time she was definitely saying it, or saying something that my brain was translating into it, her lips moving around the unusual words. “It will only take a minute. It’s part of the sessions. Like building a habit.”

I looked around the ward, but Ellie and Dr. Lark were nowhere in sight. Dorian was staring straight ahead at the screen like an indifferent babysitter, with her jaw set and her hand moving mechanically from her tray to her mouth. So I sat next to Addie on the sofa and took her hand, hesitantly, like a brother or a middle school boyfriend, pressing my palm to hers instead of interlacing her fingers in mine. Her skin was cool and damp and the pear-scented body wash the girls used in the shower clung to it. I concentrated. There was something familiar and inevitable about the distance between our thighs and the faint heat of her body so close to mine.

Then I realized what it was. It was like sitting on the couch with Nora in that faraway night behind me, limber and spent with fighting, only this time instead of the impassable gulf between us there was this sensation of hands touching, of skin merging into skin. I closed my eyes as all of my body slipped into Addie's trembling hand.

After the protestors have drifted away for the evening and the girls are lying in bed, Dorian has a relapse. Her cries pierce the softness of the nighttime ward with its muted lights and the water murmuring in the tank like a quiet fountain. It is a terrible, shrill cry, one that gathers into itself all the screams she has not screamed since the treatment began. She beats her fists into the pillow. I gather her into a hold from behind and stay with her until she calms down, Addie watching from the other bed with an expression of something like empathy, Dorian's tears slipping down my wrists and tickling my veins. Everything is sheer and far away through the Nembutal, even the strength of my body, which feels light and inconsequential as I wrap myself around Dorian, one feathery, disappearing figure flanking another. We are as paper dolls, folding into ourselves and flat.

As she quiets down she shifts over to her side and her temple, misty with sweat, presses back against my chin. Her red, flushed ear is at my lips. I whisper into it as one might whisper secrets into a seashell.

"Why tonight, Dorian?" I ask. "Is it the excitement? Missing the sessions? The protestors outside? What brought it on?"

She says nothing. She only presses herself deeper into the hold, molding herself into the form of the clutch that subdues her. Something raw and inexpressible has seized her now, something that has no accompanying words, only gestures and cries.

"It'll be over soon," I find myself whispering. "They'll grow tired and leave and it'll be over soon and we'll all be by ourselves again and everything will be normal." Lying, making believe that I can predict the future. A fraudulent gypsy, a parent wildly improvising for its wailing, beleaguered child.

I draw her close into the hold, a slaying embrace, subduing her with a violent, discomfiting affection.

In the morning Dr. Lark tells us we have to resume the sessions.

It is shift change and Ellie and I are getting ready to leave. The relief nurses, Ida and Jerry, have just come in. The protestors have gathered again outside with their signs and chants, fortified with new recruits, strengthened and united by the media flurry. Their cries and songs and prayers come floating through Dr. Lark's window as he looms over us in his lab coat, freshly showered and shaved, his voice booming over the din outside.

"It's important to maintain a sense of order and discipline with the cure," he says. "It's what Dorian and Addie need. They've made a lot of progress. They need to make more progress, Addie especially, if they're going to become caregivers. We're almost to the stage where we can begin to think about rebirthing therapy. That's the last stage of the cure. It's absolutely vital that you all stick to the session schedule and try as best you can to get the girls to that crucial point."

We all nod. He lets his gaze linger on each of us, but on me for a little bit longer. I turn to follow the other nurses out of his office, but he puts his hand on my shoulder and stops me.

"Simon," he says. His voice is the grave, leaden voice of a policeman who has just pulled you over. "Simon, we need to talk."

"Sure," I say, and I stand waiting and feeling sick, my shoulder tensing under his hand, but he shakes his head.

"Not now," he says. "Tonight. After the girls are asleep. Not to worry."

He gives my shoulder another squeeze that feels more like a chokehold than a reassuring pat and when I turn to leave it is with my pulses skittering up my bloodstream and my throat tightening. On my way out of the ward I pass Ellie standing by the reception desk, waiting for a policeman to come walk her to her car.

"You told him," I hiss.

"I had to," she snaps. "The test was positive."

Out in the lot the protestors look rested and showered and freshly energized, dressed in sweatshirts and ski jackets against the morning mountain chill, their *Love Life* and *Abortion Kills* signs bright and newly made out of gleaming patches of cardboard and colored posterboard.

The local police stroll warily around the borders of their phalanx and the perimeters of the ward, sometimes stopping to chat with the lead organizer, the one with the glasses and the passionate voice and the megaphone. Everyone seems to filter through her, I notice: the reporters never stray far from her; the new protestors greet and check in with her first before they do anything. Even the local businesses who have sent donations direct their shipments to her: bottles of water from the Kwik Mart, coffee from Mountain Brews, sugary cartons of donuts from One-Stop Donut. She is now talking to a barista from the Mountain Brews, who is standing a few feet from the edge of the lot where the news vans are parked, and I notice she is wearing her maroon sweatshirt over a knee-length flowered dress instead of jeans this morning, and her hair is pulled back in a ponytail. It has a flattering effect; the exposed slope of her neck softens the fervor of her eyes and the dress reveals the curves of her calf muscles, thick but beguiling. I notice the way the white crew socks and blue high-top tennis shoes she wears truncate her legs. There is something wardlike and appropriate about this, I reflect: the extension and denial of gratification, the hybrid feelings of pleasure and dismay. This is the woman,

I thought, who has devoted all her life and talent and skill to rescuing the voiceless and the unborn. She is the one Dorian and Addie have taken to calling, with a hint of awe, *the warden.*

I have to pass her on the way to my car. When she sees me, she stops in the middle of her conversation and locks eyes with me. The steely self-possession of her gaze, singling me out from the crowd, makes it seem as if the chanting has subsided and we are the only people on the lot. She calls out to me. Her voice has a practiced metallic ring, a clearness honed from years of chanting and yelling at congressmen and abortion doctors.

"Hi," she says. "Can I speak to you for a second?"

"I'm actually just on my way home," I say. "Maybe another time."

Then she leaves the barista standing with his cartons of coffee and brown bags of creamer and wooden stirrers and comes and plants herself directly in my path.

"I know who you are," she says. "You're the father." Her eyes slice into mine: hazel, unrelenting.

"Please leave me alone," I say. "I need to get home."

"I know who you are," she says again. I push past her, but she follows me to my car, speaking urgently yet with a practiced calm that never allows her voice to rise, to violate the private cadence of her talking and looking at me. "I know who you are and I think you should know who I am. All is not lost. There are options and resources. I can help you. Think of your baby. Think about the blessing you have received from the Lord. God wants you to have your child."

I am at the door of my car and halfway inside, but she still stands nearby at a respectful but unyielding distance.

"Take my contact information," she says, slipping the little card into my hand, and then, "I can help you," again, as I am starting the engine, and finally, "I will pray for you," spoken with such a clear, firm sweetness that it follows me down the winding mountain roads into town, an echo in the chilly air that greets me as I step out of the car again or drifts above me as I lie in bed with my heart racing, my eyelids trembling, my limbs shaking under the thin sheet.

All day I lie in the sunlight, falling in and out of a half-sleep while the wind stirs gently through the open window and brings in the sound of students streaming to class, their lilting chatter and their shouted greetings, and the clang of wind chimes from neighboring porches. Sometime around noon I slip into a fitful dream where the sounds from the windows fade and I am back in the hospital room pacing while my wife gives birth to Sandy. When I come closer to the bed it seems as if it is Addie giving birth to my first child, and then it's Nora again when she turns her head and moans in agony, a writhing Addie-Nora, the identity of the woman slipping back and forth like the images on a hologram card bending in the light.

In the dream I cannot come closer to the bed. I can see from my position at the far end of the hospital room that there is something wrong with the baby's movements, something about the way it is slipping, screaming, away from the world. It has turned itself around, is clutching desperately at the insides of the crying woman on the bed, and two masked doctors at the end of the bed are pulling it by the ankles, trying to drag it out. One of them turns to me just as the second ankle disappears back into the womb and the baby is lost inside and the Addie-Nora woman begins to howl with fresh, piercing cries of wretched suffering. I see that the doctor is Mel, still in her flowered dress under the white doctor's coat, still with the streaming hair and the gentle, firm voice. "The Lord has given you a gift," she whispers.

When I wake it is five o'clock in the evening. The air coming through the window is cool and brings with it the sound of cars pulling into driveways, doors opening and closing, dogs and children being called in from the yard, shuffling patio chairs and dishes being set out on glass-topped yard furniture, and balcony and porch doors sliding open and shut. It is the gloaming, the time Sandy always loves most on her weekend visits. The horizon is twilight blue and the trees are growing dark and severe; the students are all at dinner down on campus or at the sandwich shops and pizza places along the square, and the families sit outside on their picnic chairs. The houses are no longer ill-kept in this light, with flaking shutters and unmowed yards and curbs piled with garbage bags; the twilight melts these details until each yard becomes a flowing ocean of grass and the air surrenders to the winking lights of the fireflies. Sandy loves to stalk these tiny, pulsing beacons of yellow until she has assembled a handful of them to bring back to me where I sit on the steps, clambering onto my knee with light floating from between her palms.

I hold this image behind my eyelids until the room grows dark and I have to shower and dress for work. It has been twelve hours since the last Nembutal and I can feel my muscles beginning to twitch and pine. My image in the mirror is fuzzy and distorted when I stand at the bathroom counter and run the electric trimmer over my head.

When I arrive at the ward it is shortly after six and the mountains are covered with shadow. The lot is nearly empty now, the protestors mostly gone for the day or in the process of leaving, packing up coolers and sweaters and signs. Inside, Ellie is talking to Dr. Lark in his office and the seahorse tank is shining and bubbling brightly. Addie and Dorian are sitting on the sofa watching a show about something called a coy-wolf—a "coyote-wolf hybrid," the announcer is explaining as Dorian looks up from the tray on her lap. It is the first time since Ellie gave me the news that I have seen the girls without Ellie or Dr. Lark nearby. I want to talk to Addie alone, but the two of them are deep in a shared eating ritual I have never seen before, in which Dorian peels single threads of string cheese from the little log on her tray and Addie accepts them passively in her mouth. Addie's hands are resting on her stomach all the while, and her eyes never leave the television, where the male biologist's voiceover is explaining the migration patterns of the coywolf over an animated map that shows dozens of black cartoon creatures with pointed ears and dagger-short tails, crossing the rivers and mountains of North America toward the Canadian wilderness.

"Dorian, I'd like to talk to Addie for a few moments alone," I say.

Dorian meticulously peels another strand of cheese from the log and coils it into Addie's open mouth before she answers. "Not now," she says. "Maybe later. Addie needs her nutrition. We know everything for sure now. The test had a plus."

"That's what I want to talk to you about. Addie," I say, and her eyes shift over to mine, but Dorian cuts in, smoothly, and coils another thread of cheese into her sister's mouth before she can answer.

"Seeing as how the child needs nourishment I thought you'd be happy I'm taking care of it," Dorian says, and just then Dr. Lark's office door opens and he and Ellie come out. I take the empty trays from the table and turn back toward the kitchenette. "But I'm so glad you stopped by," she yells, "because I've been meaning to say *congratulations*."

"The coywolf made its way north to the Algonquin Park by following the railroads," the biologist on the television says, his voice earnest and brisk. The black cartoon animals are racing now across the animated continent. "It has passed through city after city unharmed, but it is a creature of the wilderness."

***

At midnight, when the girls are asleep, Dr. Lark calls me back into his office and shuts the door. He has his white coat off and underneath he is wearing khakis and a white T-shirt and a plain black belt. The effect is that of a man relaxing on a Sunday afternoon at home or watching sports with other men, not a man about to chastise and lecture and shitcan another man in an office. I am prepared for a reprimand and a termination and I expect that he will go to the other side of his desk to deliver it, but instead, to my surprise, he pulls a bottle of scotch and two clear plastic cups from the bottom drawer of his desk and takes a seat in the chair next to me. He pours us each a drink.

"Bottoms up," he says, taking a sip and wincing just a little at the strong taste. He looks over at my untasted shot and raises his eyebrows at me.

"Oh," he adds, "I almost forgot." He reaches into his pocket and withdraws an orange pill bottle and shakes two pills into his hand and passes one to me. The other he pops into his mouth and washes down with another sip of the scotch.

I stare at him, motionless, the untouched pill and drink in my hands. Dr. Lark puts his drink down.

"Relax, Simon," he says. "I only want to understand what happened. You're both of the age of consent. You've been working for me for a long time. Both of the girls know you and trust you. I know you and trust you. We're all human. We all make mistakes. My main interest is in trying to understand what transpired so that I can work toward proceeding with the treatment and the cure. If you're honest with me, then I can understand better how to manage this situation."

He smiles and gestures at the pill in my hand.

"So go on," he says. "Desperate times call for desperate measures, right?"

I swallow the pill and the drink, not taking my eyes off him. He fills my glass again, all the while talking about the malady and the cure. Soon his voice begins to thicken and my heart slows down. My muscle fibers stop twitching and my vision clears. Above him, the hands of the clock on the wall seem to advance in great intervals, like the darting needle of a giant compass.

This is what I tell him:

That it started because of Nora.

Or rather, it started because of not having Nora, or discovering at some point after I moved out that I hardly knew Nora, that the woman I had been with was a different woman when she had a child. The woman I had been with was easygoing, spontaneous; the woman she became after we had Sandy was possessive and stern, subject to long bouts of crying, alienated from sex. When we decided to separate she began to look for anything and everything that would keep me away from our daughter: the long shifts, the dingy apartment I moved into. Once she found an empty pill bottle inside my car door and questioned me, but she had nothing else to go on. Begrudgingly, we began the dance of custody, the shuttling of Sandy from doorstep to doorstep, the coordination of after-school pickups, parent-teacher meetings, and long weekends where our daughter volleyed back and forth between us with her pink backpack and her crumpled homework assignments.

Things were raw then. Everything around me had that hallucinatory echo that things have in moments of great shock or pain. That weird sensation that the magnetic field of the earth has shifted, its currents reversing their flow, the direction of daily life undergoing a sudden, total change. I went through the old routines. Sometimes I forgot what we had decided and found myself standing at the supermarket, contemplating a box of pasta and wondering what she would like for dinner, or opened my eyes in the morning expecting to see the smooth curve of her shoulder next to me. Then I would remember her absence—an illogical absence, a sudden, terrifying absence—and it seemed as if the poles of the earth reversed again, sending my life abruptly in another direction.

It is hard to say at what point in a breakup process healthy desire reasserts itself—not the desperate, burying kind that leads to indiscriminate sexual encounters but the untroubled appreciation of other people for who they are. I think I felt it at first as a twinge, a split second of admiration, of possibility. At first, little things: I noticed how Addie's shoulders were rounded and small in her scrubs and how the downy hairs lay gleaming along the back of her neck. I noticed the hollow at her throat and the shape of the collarbone that framed it. When I was out buying groceries or running past the square I sometimes thought about her in the ward, the way she looked sideways or down, an endearing fidget or an involuntary smile. These things gathered in me and I felt, underneath my loneliness, the faint brimming of desire.

It was in those moments that Addie came to me, holding her copy of the book open like an attentive student approaching a teacher after class. I remember she pulled it out once when we were all walking back from the garden and Dorian and Ellie were trailing a little ways behind us.

"Can you read this to me?" she said, pointing at a passage with jagged blue underlining. I read aloud:

> *Yea, in the very moment of possessing,*
> *Surges the heat of lovers to and fro—*

"Where did you get this, Addie?" I said.

"From the library." She pointed to some lines lower down on the page. I read again:

> *And pain the creature's body, close their teeth*
> *Often against her lips, and smite with kiss*
> *Mouth into mouth,—because this same delight*
> *Is not unmixed; and underneath are stings—*

"This was in the library?" I said.

She ignored me. "I want to know what it means," she said. "The stings that hide underneath."

"This is hard to explain, Addie. It's a very mature poem. Maybe it would be better to ask Dr. Lark what he thinks about you reading it."

"I don't want to ask Dr. Lark. I want to ask you. That's why I brought it."

I stared down at the page again. "To be honest, Addie, I'm not really very good at this stuff. It seems like author is saying that the lovers get kind of crazy. That they want to show love and affection for each other, but they hurt each other too. Even though they're trying to show love."

"Is that what it's like?" she said.

"Is that what what is like?"

"Showing love."

I reflected. "Sometimes. Sometimes we hurt people when we try to love them. But not always. I think when two people are in the right place, when things are healthy between them, this kind of hurt doesn't happen."

"Am I in the right place?"

I looked at her. We were walking on the pathway back to the ward and the sun was shining on her hair and the garden work had given her a healthy glow, one I never had seen on her skin when she was inside the ward all day. She was looking up at me like the same student might look up reverentially at the author of the book. I noticed that she came just up to my shoulder, and at the same time I noticed that her hip was grazing my thigh and I felt against my leg how round and soft it was.

"I'm not sure if I'm the right person to answer that

question, Addie," I said.

"I'll never be in the right place," she said, "because of my disorder."

She had stopped on the path and turned her chin straight up to me. Her eyes met mine and in that moment my heart went out to her, to this young woman who had never seen a world beyond the ward, who knew nothing of the life described in the books she read. In that moment for me she stopped being a patient and started to be a real woman with yearnings and urges like any other real woman, with the same yearnings Nora used to have before Sandy and before the new apartment and before the school. An unsullied, pure desire. That was Addie's desire.

"It would help me to know when and how often you met her in the garden," Dr. Lark says.

"How often?"

"Yes. For the cure. It would be helpful for me to know what stages she was at. What sessions we had begun."

"It was a month ago. Maybe eight or nine times."

"Just to clarify," he says, "you *are* still married."

"Technically, yes. But separated."

"Did Addie know this?"

"Yes."

"When did you tell her?"

"Early," I said.

"What did she say?"

"It didn't matter."

“That’s what she said?”

I thought back through the haze of the pill and the scotch to the garden plot with its tiny green tomatoes and its hidden carrots with fronds arching out of the ground, and to Addie with her long, pale thighs pressed against mine.

“Not quite,” I say.

It didn’t matter to her because she barely understood what marriage was. For the girls, that was something that happened *on the outside*, as if the world was divided between people who lived in the ward and people who didn’t and there was never any chance that those worlds would join. She spoke of the world outside as a television interviewer might ask a hundred-year-old man on his birthday what had changed most about America since he was young: disbelieving of the past, flippant, almost condescending. In the garden when we were alone together she sometimes seemed to gloat about her separation from the world; other times she was rancorous and dejected by turns.

“Why are you a nurse?” she asked me once. We were kneeling together, pulling weeds in the garden bed on an overcast day. She was leaning against my shoulder and her hair was pooling over me, and beyond her the clouds were slipping in dense clumps across the horizon.

“Why am I a nurse? So I can help people. So I can take care of people who are sick.”

“Why didn’t you become a big famous doctor? And come up with big famous cures? Like Dr. Lark?”

"I got married when I was very young and started a family. I had to get work right away. I didn't have time to go through medical school and a residency and everything."

She was silent for a moment, wondering at this. "You have a family?"

"I did. I had a wife and a child. I was married."

"Are you still married?"

"Separated."

"So you don't have a family anymore."

"I still see my daughter. But only every other weekend."

"So why don't you go back to school then? If you only see her every other weekend."

"Things change. We're still working out the custody arrangements. In time I might be able to see her more often."

"I don't think that's what it is," Addie announced. She moved down to the next seedling and squatted in front of it. "I think it's because you're an underachiever. You don't like school."

"That's not true. I just don't have a lot of money for school."

"But now look what you have to do if you stay here forever. Instead of coming up with your own things to do you have to do whatever Dr. Lark says."

"There's an element of that in every profession, Addie. Even Dr. Lark has had to take orders from the doctor he trained under and from the doctors who review his research articles. Don't you think you'll have to take orders someday? When you have a profession?"

"What kind of profession would I have? What would I even do?"

Her tone was teasing, demanding; I thought she was bantering with me, but when I saw her eyes wide and artless gazing back I realized it was a sincere question. Quelled, I thought to myself. Then I said, "Haven't you ever thought of a profession? Something you'd like to do? Think about the things you enjoy. You like learning about animals, don't you? Would you want to be a vet, or a vet's assistant? Or work in a kennel?"

"How am I supposed to do that?" She threw down her handful of weeds. "When you don't trust me in a kitchenette by myself? When I have to learn over and over again to hug and shake hands the way other people do? You think someone, some head doctor at an animal hospital, is going to let me work around dozens of other people and sharp tools and equipment? You really think that's ever going to happen?"

I was silent, still forming a response, when she spoke again.

"This is what I'm good for," she said. "Making sure that people like you have a profession. Making sure Dr. Lark has things to write in his research articles. I'm incurable. This is who I am."

"You shouldn't let them goad you," Dr. Lark says.

"What do you mean?"

"The way they bait you." He takes a swig of his drink and keeps talking in an automatic, practiced way, as if he were answering a question at a conference. "The way *she* baits people, especially. You and me and everyone else. It's not like with other patients, with the nonsevere cases. Dorian and Addie are manipulative. They have rage inside that has to come out. Until that happens, everyone else is disposable. Everyone else is a sacrifice to their rage."

But, I think, Dr. Lark can be manipulative too—the sessions, the strange lines of questioning, the way he plays them against one another and has Addie asking Dorian questions. There have been times when I've thought Addie would be better off without Dorian, that there is too much togetherness here. That the girls need separate identities and space, like any woman would need separation and space, even from her most cherished sister.

It is four o'clock in the morning. Time is passing in great, slow gulps, and the memories of the garden are fading in and out.

I am having a great realization.

I know what my mistake was, what it seemed to me I was preventing or doing for her or helping her with. Not the malady, but the recovery. Not the desire and the rage, but the sessions and the hand-holding and the restriction of the world outside and the too much togetherness. I wanted to save her from the cure.

You can guess how the rest of it happened. It happened in stages, by degrees. I watched myself descend as if I were watching someone else, an ill-fated protagonist on a television drama. I watched my body grow closer to hers as if it was someone else's body in place of mine. Someone else's hand reaching out. Someone else's illegal caress sliding down a forbidden thigh; someone else's skin receiving the impress of her untaught hands. We acclimated to each other's touch the way streams of water from twin faucets, hot and cold, merge to create a steady, comfortable warmth. Each day we went just a little further in the garden, the ground at our feet tangled with rotting blossoms.

"Did she ever mention anything about wanting a family? About wanting to conceive?" Dr. Lark says. "Did she ever mention pursuing anyone else besides you?"

"Never," I say.

"Think," he urges.

"I was the only one she was ever with."

"You're sure, then."

"I'm sure."

I know I was the first one because of the blood. It slipped down her thigh, just a little bit of it, and smeared across her skin like a dash of paint. She rolled away from me in the garden. It was a hot day and her body was moist in the sun.

I lay stunned in the light, stunned at the fragility of that first encounter, at the sensation of delicacy and caution that surrounded it. The weeks of buildup. Teaching her to know desire and to rouse it secretly, to train it, to practice it as one practices meditation or instruments, a slow disciplining and undisciplining, a slow bringing of skill to the rhythm of the fingers. Silently in the dark in her bed she practiced for me. In the garden, at last, she opened, her knees and thighs falling apart, hair tumbling in the sun, eyes turned up to me with curiosity and something like dread. (Why did I dread it too, always feel this dread at the onset of the lull between one pill and the next, always feel this dread at the crawl of women's eyes?) I pressed myself into her against the membrane and lunged beyond it into her unpracticed body. All this time she looked up at me with a tomboyish ardor, with a body long made immune to pain.

Afterward I think I was more frightened than she was. She used a corner of the towel beneath us to blot away the little stain of blood. I reached out instinctively to help, but she laughed and waved my hand away the same way she had waved away the condom and said she was immaculate. She actually *laughed* then, laughed disbelievingly like someone trying to make the best out of some bad news, there in that sinister garden, with the distressed murmurs and loud excited shouts of the nonsevere cases drifting up to us from beyond the hedges. She pressed her slender, naked body against mine and murmured something nonsensical in my ear. Something about the different types of fear.

"The fear that thrills," Dr. Lark says.

"Yes." I remember.

When I finish talking it is 6:30 in the morning and the window is glowing with the first traces of sunlight. The sound of car engines and slamming doors drifts in from the lot outside, where the protestors and the reporters are setting up for the morning and the nurses are coming in for the day shift. The ward, too, is coming alive: the pipes screech awake for Dorian's and Addie's morning showers, the breakfast dishes clatter in the kitchenette, the television jabbers, and there's the thin, dusky smell of cheap coffee brewing.

Dr. Lark has not stirred in a long time, and for a moment I think he's drifted off or has forgotten me, but then he shakes himself, sets his empty glass down, and takes his phone out of his pocket. He hits a button and tilts it toward me so I can see the screen. I see its winking red light freeze and the REC at the top right-hand corner of the screen go still, the frequency wave freeze above the little timer that reads 5:15:07.

"Thank you, Simon," he says, in the same not-unkind voice but now with a different kind of look to go along with it. It is the look of Dorian before an attack, the fierceness pooling in her eyes, the aggression of her muscles mounting. "I hope you don't mind that I took the liberty of recording this. For my own records, you know. Although I could just as easily email it to other people."

My heart begins to race. "No," I say.

"Nora," he says. "That's your wife's name, right? What's your kid's name again? Sandy? What time does Sandy get to school? I'm guessing Nora drops her off and then goes straight to work. I could email her this now and she'd see it by noon at the latest."

"No," I say again. My body curdles at the shock of nasty surprise and I grab for the phone, involuntarily, but a pill fog soaks my limbs and eyes. He easily moves it out of my reach.

"Don't embarrass yourself," he says. "Won't do any good. It's already in the cloud."

"Please," I say again, and I am ashamed to hear the note of begging, cloying desperation enter my voice. "Please don't tell her. I'll do anything."

"This is what you'll do," he says, calm and brisk and authoritative like the biologist describing the coywolf. He stands against the desk and looks down at me. I begin to stand up too, but he waves me down again and the power of his hand is like a real push, wrenching me back into the chair. "You will walk out of this ward and you will not speak to Dorian or Addie or Ellie or anyone on your way out. You will go straight to your car and you will get inside it and go home and sleep this off. When you get up you will compose your resignation letter and you will send it to me here at the ward by way of courier service. I will release you from the two weeks' minimum notice policy. You will call down at Knoxville General to see if you can get on the rotation at the ER eventually, maybe in a few months, when something opens up. I'll make a couple of phone calls there. I'll write you a reference. In return, you will never set foot here again, never call here, never write here, never attempt to contact Addie or anyone. You will not seek employment elsewhere without talking to me first. You will not take a paternity test even if someone asks you to. You will not agree to anything without my consent. Do you understand?"

I nod. Beyond us, outside of the window, the chants are starting up again and many voices drift tinny and hollow into the silence between us, as if the protestors are echoing Dr. Lark, as if they are not protesting him or the pregnancy or the abortion but rather me and what I have done, like an angry, singing jury.

"If I ever hear that you have tried to contact Addie, or that you have come to the ward, or that you have tried to interfere with any of the processes or procedures I will begin here—if you ever interfere in any way with the cure, if you speak a word of our conversation today to anyone—I will send this file to Nora for use in her divorce and custody proceedings. Is that clear?"

I nod again.

He opens the door and stands behind me as I pass into the ward, where I feel his gaze lighting up my back. I stop for just a second to appreciate the light in the common area, the lurid fluorescence making the arriving nurses seem at once deeply human and also frozen and unreal, like wax figures in a museum. Everything is strangely suspended, the ward paused and waiting for its cycle of motion and activity to begin, just as the butterflies in the garden plot used to pause when they had climbed to the tops of the flowers, in that split second before they lifted their wings. From the sounds and noises in the bathroom I gather that the girls are in the shower still; Ellie is looking questions at me from the kitchenette, but then she sees Dr. Lark watching us and understands that she cannot ask. I push out into the reception area, out into the lot where the protestors and the news vans have gathered and where the cries and chants sound more energetic, more full of promise, in the dawn.

As I stand before them the magnetic tides of the earth seem to reverse themselves again, and I find myself staring down a yawning vista of time, of empty, monotonous hours spent in haunts of the idle and unemployed: the town square with its desultory bluegrass pickers; the public library with its dim flickering lights and racks of bestsellers and old men who play chess on the picnic tables out back; the wooded trails that lead down to the reservoir where midafternoon dog walkers amble; the cantina with the dollar beer nights where the patio lights buzz and flicker, drawing brown-and-white moths that beat senselessly against the bulbs.

I watch that arc of time arch its back languidly like a cat across the coming months, across her trimesters, which are also my trimesters, and I turn away from it just as sharply, without thinking, and walk straight up to the leader. She is in the front where all the battered women gather. She is not wearing her glasses and the effect is startling, her eyes a wide warm brown. They are already directed at me as I come toward her and stop just inches from her dense, wholesome body.

"I've changed my mind," I say. "I'm in."

She puts the megaphone down and moves closer, her eyes never leaving mine.

"I don't know your name," I add. "I'm Simon."

She extends her hand. Her grip is bracing and firm.

"Welcome to the cause, Simon," she says. "I'm Mel."

Chapter 5

Dorian, Addie

Dorian

Simon vanishes around the time that the reporters and most of the protestors disappear. We were used to seeing him in the morning, coming in and out of the kitchenette with the breakfast trays; now it is Ellie who carries them, each with their single-serve portions of cereal and unripe bananas and little cartons of milk. She slams it all down on the table.

One morning, about two months after Simon's departure, we are watching *The Exotic Snub-Nosed Monkeys of Shangri-La*, and the pink faces of the monkeys with their wise eyes and hairy jowls loom on the screen. "These Yunnan snub-noses live in the forests of Shangri-La, the forests at the highest altitudes," the voiceover gushes; the camera pans out to reveal trees shrouded in mist. We stare. Everything is off: the rhythms of the shift change, the transition of the ward from nighttime quiet into daytime bustle and noise. It is a delicate mechanism, the ward, an entire ecosystem like the monkeys have in their mountain forest. It requires a precise and unvarying balance of life forms.

Addie feels it too. "Where is Simon?" she says every morning, to no one in particular, as she stands on her tiptoes at the tank and sprinkles plankton for the seahorses to eat. Always hungry, forever eating, most of the seahorses have congregated around the drifting plankton; a few have hooked their tails around the sea grass and anchored themselves to the stalks, their snouts swinging back and forth while their lower bodies stay rooted. They look like charms on a charm bracelet, still and statuesque except for the gentle sway.

Through that kaleidoscope of color, beyond the lush violet and deep yellow corals and the orange polyps that bloom like flowers, I can see Addie's other hand resting on her stomach. The tank lights throw their colors over that hand, bathing it in purple shadows, so it looks as if her hand is an extension of the tank or something that has crept forth from it. Her fingers mimic the bend of the seahorse tails, their slender, inadequate firmness. There are flecks of light from the tank in her eyes and highlighting the lines of her set, still jaw.

"I asked, where is Simon?" she says again, louder—this time to Ellie, who only answers with an angry look I do not understand and goes back into the kitchenette.

Addie does not understand it either, I can see, and she is about to try again when Dr. Lark comes up behind her at the tank.

"I told you. Simon left to take personal time," he says. "It's important now that we just stay committed to the sessions and the cure."

The faint lines around his eyes and mouth have developed into long creases, and the crescent-shaped shadows under his eyes have deepened to a tropical purple. He has not shaved today, and his jaw is spiked with hard, silver thatch.

"We can't let changes to our routine upset the rhythm of the sessions," he says. "We have to continue with the sessions in their proper order, as usual."

The play of light on Addie's face conceals the play of something else, a flicker of anxiety or uncertainty that sends ripples to the surface. "But why did he leave?" she says, for the umpteenth time. "Was it because of the reporters and the protestors?"

"Right now the most important thing to focus on is your recovery," he says. "Simon left because he had a family emergency he needed to handle. The reporters and protestors left because they got what they wanted. Everything is back to normal. And right now, you girls need to get ready for your appointment."

"What appointment?"

He has turned to leave but he stops, ever so briefly, to look back: first at Addie, then at me, then back at Addie. There is another flicker of something. Annoyance? Exasperation? Professional interest. The doctor eclipsing the man.

"The ultrasound," he says.

But that is not all she wants to ask, I know, as he returns to his office to prepare his remarks for the reporters. She is not asking because she wants to know how the cure will mingle with the new rituals of the pregnancy. She is asking because she does not know how to confront these new rituals themselves, these rites of fertility and motherhood. These rites that are happening to her body but are mine now as much as hers.

I wait until he has disappeared around the corner. "You didn't plan for what would happen next, did you?" I say. Her face is motionless behind the moving violet shadows of the tank; she looks down when I step in closer. "You didn't think that far ahead. Is that it?"

She shudders at my proximity, presses that protective hand more firmly against her belly.

"You thought ahead for all of the details in the garden, but you didn't think ahead about what to do when it actually happened. Did you?"

She wants to go back to the sleeping quarters and sit with her dumb palms flat on her womb and weep, I can tell, but I grab her wrist before she can turn away from me.

"Not to retreat now," I say. "Never to retreat."

So we stay in front of the tank in the weird bath of shadows, in a tense, fidgeting proximity. There are still a few lingering protestors outside, ones who stayed after the others left, and their voices sound like the dejected cries of a retreating army.

ADDIE

While Dorian is finishing her cereal I take the dog-eared copy of Lucretius and sit across from her in the common area, careful to hide the cover from Ellie as she storms back and forth from the common area to the kitchenette, bearing away the dirty breakfast dishes.

Just yesterday Ellie gave me a book called *So You're Expecting a Baby*, with illustrations of the week-by-week development of the fetus and little information boxes about nutrition. Someone has underlined or put asterisks next to much of the text and on the inside someone else has written, in glaring red pen, *Property of Stand for Life Library Do Not Remove Without Permission*. It has an index too, this book, and a list of helpful resources to consult.

Yet it is still the Lucretius that seems to best explain the mysteries of gestation, and how the couplings in the office and the garden gave way to new, young life. I turn to Book IV, "The Senses," and read:

And when perchance, in mingling seed with his,
The female hath o'erpowered the force of male
And by a sudden fling hath seized it fast,
Then are the offspring, more from mothers' seed,
More like their mothers; as, from fathers' seed,
They're like to fathers.

In Lucretius seeds are exchanged during intercourse and

the female sex is made when the woman is a strong and dominant lover. If the male is the one who guides and overpowers, then his seed conquers and the child will be male. If both the man and the woman dominate at the same time—if, "by Venus' goads," they experience pleasure together, their features will mingle and the child will bear the seeds of both the father and the mother. The best way to conceive is in the manner of "wild beasts," he says, with the lowered breasts and the raised loins. Yet who had really overpowered, Dr. Lark or me? Had I overpowered or had Simon?

The ward after breakfast is strangely empty without him. Dorian sips steadily from her milk carton, the white liquid scooting up the straw in slower and slower bursts until it is just froth and bubbles and an obnoxious sucking sound. Her eyes never leave the television.

"Strangely beautiful, endangered and evasive, these snub-nosed monkeys have remained hidden to the camera in their high alpine homes in the Chinese Himalayas," the announcer says breathlessly. "Until now. For two years, this award-winning filmmaker followed the journey of two monkeys. Brothers. Join us to watch their journey into maturity as we follow the lives of the exotic snub-nosed monkeys of Shangri-La."

The music swells over the small pink infant faces of the brothers just as Ellie marches back with a rag to wipe off the empty table. I ask her again: "Ellie, do you know what happened to Simon?"

"I don't know anything," she snaps.

"But did you see him leave?"

"He left this morning. I don't know why." She leans in closer to snatch a crumpled napkin off the table. "Give me time," she says.

Right now she wants us to hurry up and change into our street clothes and go out to the van—the white van that we always ride in to our annual checkups or our tense yearly Thanksgiving dinner with Stella, with its stiff, detached drivers who wear khakis and green collared shirts with the *Patient Transport* logo on the front and try to make conversation. The universal transporters of the houseless and the raving. I picture them going in ceaseless circles from institution to institution. Ward, hospital. Hospital, ward. Highway.

Dorian, at first, refuses to get ready—out of rebellious habit more than real defiance, I know, since she has always had a secret, giddy love for these little excursions. She loves the warm roads bathed in sunshine and the boxy strip malls with parking lots full of glittering cars, the commanding spires of the megachurch and the tourists hiking in their ski jackets, all behumped with fanny packs and camera bags like distorted neon camels. As for me, I am indifferent. The life outside the ward is not an available life. Its mountains, its sunshine, its movements of people and traffic are like the dumb projections of a television screen, actors and sets that switch off as abruptly as the television does once we pull back into the gray gravel parking lot of the ward.

"There will still be a few protestors," Ellie tells us when we have changed into our own bland khakis and white T-shirts. "The van will park just in front of the door. A security guard will walk with you until you get inside."

"I thought the protestors would have gone away by now," I say. "Aren't there other things for them to do?"

Ellie gives me a blank look.

"Not in Tennessee," she says.

We are standing in the waiting room near the front doors, waiting for the security guards to meet us, when the receptionist at the front desk calls Ellie over.

"Ell," he says, handing her a slip of paper. "For you. A Dr. Coe. Said she couldn't get a hold of you on your cell so she tried here."

"Is that about Simon?" Dorian asks, as Ellie unfolds the pink slip of paper with its bold WHILE YOU WERE OUT heading and holds it away from Dorian's eager eyes, skimming it quickly.

"No," Ellie says. "Come on." She leads us out to the automatic double doors that wing in and out like the flippers on a pinball machine. The rows of relatives waiting in blue armchairs to visit their nonsevere cases look up with mild curiosity at the uniformed security guards who come forward to link arms with us. They look at my stomach especially—first at my stomach, then at my eyes, then away. As if the stomach were the main thing and the eyes were an afterthought. Ellie is still looking down at the folded piece of paper, so Dorian tries again.

"What is that, really?" she says. "It's not about Simon?"

"No, Dorian. Get in the van."

"Is it about the protestors?"

"No."

"Is it about the cure?"

"*No.*"

Ellie shoves the note into her purse. She is like a flustered mother on the Discovery Channel *Families and Pets!* shows, herding her children and their dogs and guinea pigs and rabbits to their various appointments and activities.

"Get in the van, girls," Ellie says. "We'll talk about it later."

Dorian

Then we are coursing down the mountain to the hospital, Ellie and Addie and I, past the reservoir that shimmers and glints like the great sheets of aluminum foil Ellie spreads out in the kitchen, past the runaway truck ramps with their great slats of dirt, down into the outskirts of the town, where grocery stores and hardware stores and home decoration stores sit squat and boxy and firm, like paperweights holding down the rippling landscape around the mountains. Addie sits next to me in the back with the seat belt stretched over her belly, shifting uncomfortably because she has to keep a full bladder for the ultrasound. Ellie sits in the front seat next to the driver, staring out the window or looking down at her phone, lost in distraction.

The driver is polite like all the van drivers: he feels like he should try to talk to his disturbed, vacant passengers. He has a drawl, like everyone we have ever encountered outside the ward, and when he talks he glances at us in the rearview mirror, so that I can see his green eyes and the peppery gray hair sticking out on either side of his hat.

"You girls are from Tennessee?"

"We're from a house not far," Addie says.

"Grew up round here, then."

"Yes."

"So you've been down to see the World's Fair park and the Sunsphere since they opened it up?"

He means the tall golden ball that's on our right as we speed by, its weird steel flashing in the sunshine, its hexagon-shaped support structure braced on a green lawn crowded with students playing Frisbee.

"Never," I say.

"What? Never been to the Sunsphere?" The driver feigns surprise. "I used to go all the time when it opened for the 1982 World's Fair. Back then it had a restaurant up top and you could get a rum drink called a Sunburst. That was more'n thirty years ago but lots of folks around here remember that."

"You know a lot of people in Knoxville?" Addie asks.

"Sure," he says. "I know everyone around here."

"Do you know a guy named Simon?" Addie says. "I don't remember his last name, but he has a tattoo."

"That's enough, Addie," Ellie snaps. "Can it."

"I'm just asking," Addie says.

"I know what you're doing. Stop."

The driver purses his lips and looks straight ahead with a practiced neutrality. We ride the rest of the way in silence, listening to the local traffic report, Addie wincing and yanking the seat belt away from her stomach.

We pull up at the hospital complex. It is broad and massive, with swooping driveways and parking lots and parking garages curling around it and traffic pouring toward it and away. Ambulances line up at the emergency drop-offs with their sirens quiet, waiting. The main entrance is flanked by raised garden beds and concrete planters. Its glass doors open and shut rapidly as people go in and out. Ellie and I each take one of Addie's arms and conduct her toward a bank of shining elevators that take us to Women's Health, Second Floor. This floor has a small lobby with planters of fake flowers and a toy box for the children and glossy pamphlets about annual exams and mammograms and birth control and domestic abuse. In this place, I notice, people do not gape at Addie or at me walking beside her and holding her hand, as they do in the waiting room of the ward.

The examination room is tiny and clean and alarming, with its counters covered in jars of cotton swabs and dispensers of hand sanitizer and posters about uterine cancer on the walls. Ellie and I help Addie into a white hospital gown with a pink pattern and support her as she climbs onto the crunched-up bed.

"Are you ready to see your baby?" the technician says brightly. She is a young blonde woman, maybe five years older than Addie and me, and she wears a white lab coat with a stethoscope draped around her neck like a snake.

Addie nods and allows her to spread the cool gel across her swollen stomach, but as I stand next to her and hold her hand I can feel that she is bracing at its coldness, at the stranger's touch and its brisk, medical efficiency. She is bulging under the gown, her belly button stretched tight and wide across the skin on her stomach like an open, glaring eye.

"Let's see," says the technician, glancing at a file. "You're in your second trimester."

"That's what they tell me," says Addie.

The tech forces a laugh and looks at me. "Are you two sisters?"

"Parents," I tell her.

"I see." Her facial expression dissolves into a rehearsed, blithe smile.

Ellie has been scrolling around on her phone but now she looks up. "They're up at the care ward together," she offers.

"I see," the tech says, her cheerless smile never wavering. "And this is your first pregnancy, Addie?"

"Yes."

"Any extreme body aches or swelling?"

"The skin on my face," Addie says. She touches her cheeks. "It's patchy."

"Some skin discoloration is entirely normal," the tech says. "We call it the 'mask of pregnancy.' Let me explain what we're going to see today." She wheels the cart with the screen and the tangled wires closer to the bed. "I'm going to confirm that your baby is developing normally, and then I'll show you an image of your baby. Now, let me explain what that image will look like. It will be black and white. The bones of your baby will appear as white. The tissue around your baby's bones will look gray, though, and the amniotic fluid that cushions your baby will seem black on the screen. This is how all of the babies look. It's just a function of the technology, and it helps us see what we need to see more clearly. While I'm running the ultrasound, feel free to lie back and relax, and feel free to ask me questions at any point."

"Okay," Addie says.

She cranes her neck a little, trying to see the monitor, but the screen is turned too far away from the bed, so she looks at me and raises her eyebrows. I inch down to the foot of the bed and sneak a look. The image on the screen is blurry at first and then clears, like the static on the old television we used to have in the ward. The nurse slides the little bell-shaped wand over the gel on Addie's belly and a picture materializes, a fuzzy black-and-white image that looks like a rock formation, a large stone piled on a smaller stone. Or is it more stones than that? I try to focus on the white, glowing bones, but as she shifts the wand the image focuses into not two stones but four, a symmetrical outcropping of bodies. I cannot make out where the bones begin or which way they have formed.

"Now what's that?" the nurse says, in a friendly tone that fails to hide a note of alarm. She picks up Addie's file to double-check, but Ellie has already come around behind her and is peering into the image.

"What?" Addie says, frightened. "What is it? What?"

"Twins," Ellie says.

Addie

Back in the ward Ellie and Dr. Lark are fighting over the results—fighting quietly, in that subdued angry tone, the way I would imagine that people fight in public on the outside, where you have to try and be quiet and not yell and say *please* and *thank you* and smile when people drop you off somewhere or when they accept your payment and give you change. I listen for news of Simon but it is hard to make out what they are saying; they speak in hurried murmurs, sometimes interrupting each other.

"The second one shifted," Ellie says. "It's rare but it happens. That's why they didn't catch it before."

"Rocks shift," Dr. Lark says. "A pile of gravel shifts. Tectonic plates shift. But a small human being? They don't catch a small human being before it shifts?"

"It was a mistake," Ellie says. "What do you want me to do? Sue the hospital? Take her to another hospital? That's the closest and the best one."

"Let me think," Dr. Lark says. "What did you do with those files? Those case studies I told you to pull?"

"They're on your desk," Ellie says. "All the rebirthing ones."

"Don't tell me there's more of them that I'll find if I *shift* those ones over."

"Of course not."

"Did you hear that?" Dorian says, turning toward me. We are in the common area and the television flashes and gleams. I have rested both my hands on my belly, one for each of them. "One sister has shifted over and made room for the other."

"I wonder which one came first," I say.

We sit peacefully together, my hands resting over their heads, all of our beating hearts in a quartet of proximity. Dorian's side presses against me. There is no urge to lash, to pinch, to be anything but bundles of flesh full of beating hearts. Nestled by my thigh is the dog-eared copy of Lucretius, with the conception passages carefully underlined and the pages worn and crinkled from being turned down and unfolded and turned down again. I pick it up and read the lines again:

> *And when perchance, in mingling seed with his,*
> *The female hath o'erpowered the force of male...*
> *Then are the offspring, more from mothers' seed,*
> *More like their mothers; as, from fathers' seed,*
> *They're like to fathers.*

With Simon in the garden I had prevailed; I had been the

one above. And in Dr. Lark's office he was the one who prevailed; he was the one who was above and who drove down into me on the floor beside his desk, the stubble on his chin scraping across my neck. It was sudden, the way he did it: always he said no, always he told me he was a professional, and then one evening he was talking to me about the cure, going on and on about the cure, and how he knew now that it could work *this* time because of the way I was behaving toward him. He looked tired and his eyes were wild, like the nonsevere cases who walk the hedgerows pulling their hair out strand by strand. Something came over him and he seized me.

He did not linger, afterwards, as Simon often had, reaching his fingers down to trace and caress me and try to get me to feel what he had felt, asking me to tell him where the sensation was. Instead he removed himself from me quickly, using his hand to tug himself out, and the space where he had been became a void again, a hollow wall of membranes made tender and alive by the brisk way he had entered and thrusted. He buckled his pants—he had not even taken them all the way down—and told me to get out of his office. There was a different look on his face now, something like shock or fear.

"But I want to stay here with you," I said.

He had forgotten to set his glasses back on his face, and when he wiped his hand across his eyes I could see that it was trembling. "Get dressed, Addie. And don't tell anyone about this. They wouldn't understand—they wouldn't believe you.

It's better if we keep it between us. This is very important for the cure. Do you understand?"

I went to the sleeping quarters and laid with my pelvis tilted upward and imagined the seed ripening inside into the kind of cells that had become me and Dorian.

The male seed had dominated, Lucretius would say. So the child would resemble the father. But which child? If there were two, and I had dominated with Simon but Dr. Lark had dominated with me, did that mean the seed of each child belonged to a different father? Would there be a girl twin made of Simon and a boy twin made of Dr. Lark? And how to know for sure which one was which?

Is that what is in the rebirthing files? Do they have the answer to the question of the sex? What did he put into my own file, what did he write, that night that he dominated? Back through the corridor I can see Dr. Lark in his office, reading—mouthing the words of the documents to himself like an enchanter slowly repeating the words of a new spell.

Dorian

The night of the ultrasound appointment, Dr. Lark comes out of his office and tells us about a new, culminating habit. A habit to crown all the others.

"It will be a habit of re-enactment," he says, standing in front of the tank with his clipboard. His wire-rimmed eyeglasses are oval-shaped and magnify his eyes so that the bloodshot pupils stand out in stark relief. They are thin and crimson, those little paths in the white part of his eyes, like the slow trickle of a line of aphids down the surface of a leaf. "A habit of rehearsing the memory of your birth, like revisiting a site where a trauma has happened. There is a rage inside, and a wildness. Some say such a rage is genetic; others say it happened when you were younger, when you did your crime. You return to the birth canal; you talk it out and you try to determine the source of that wildness. Some call this *catharsis*."

"Will we be born at the same time?" Addie says.

"Yes. I will be there to talk both of you through it."

"What will we be born out of?"

"You will construct a canal. It will be a long-term project. It may take some time."

"Will we be born through the same canal?"

"You'll each have your own. But you'll be born out of them at the same time."

"Will we be able to see each other?"

"Can children in the womb see? Of course not. You won't see anything. You'll only be able to feel. Others will help you through. They'll talk you through, with their voices."

"Will I have the babies first?"

"No." Dr. Lark's voice sounded brusque and a little condescending, like the judges on *People's Law Prime Time* when they issued verdicts. "You will have the rebirthing in order to have the babies. So that you can exorcise the rage and the wildness. It is the last stage in the cure. The most important thing now is that you focus on the sessions. You have to work at it, build up to it."

So we return to the sessions and hold hands across the table and stand in front of the tank where the fry are starting to take on distinct features, like the stone formations in Addie's belly. Some of them are plump and linger in the sea grass with one eye on either side of their heads gazing through the water; some of them are yellow and cluster together in little clans; some of them are an iridescent plum color and drift and rotate slowly past the colorful algae bursting from the rocks. I feel as if the beating of the hearts that is in Addie is thrumming and upsetting the water, sending waves crashing against the glass where my fingers rest and where her fingers rest, transmitting pulses to me.

During these sessions Dr. Lark asks questions, but he is absent and distant by fits, sometimes bending forward eagerly at one of our answers, sometimes leaning back all of a sudden, slumped and forlorn. When he does this I see that his khakis are baggy around the waist, his belt cinched and yet still loose in the loops, as if his girth is not substantial enough to exert tension on it, as if his body has settled into weightless orbit.

"Tell us what Dorian said and then tell us what you see, Addie," he says. His collared shirt opens at the throat onto a patch of tangled black chest hair. "Go ahead."

Addie looks at him blankly. She has a hand resting on either side of her belly now, one for each tender, unseen head.

“Go ahead, Addie,” he says, a little more impatiently than normal. “Goddamn it. Say something. Say what Dorian said first, then say something of your own.”

She looks at me in confusion. Ellie, too, looks stricken. She sets down the rag she has been using to wipe off the table and comes over.

“No one has said anything yet, doctor,” she explains. “The session just started.”

He looks at her in irritation, then at me, then at Addie, before he leans back in the seat.

“Then you say something, Dorian,” he mutters. “For God’s sake, just say something.”

They are becoming more frequent, these episodes of blankness and mistake and distraction. Ellie says it is because of the cure; Addie says it is because of the twins. What does it matter? The sessions are the same every day, day in and day out; we all know the sessions; we could talk through them in our sleep. They are as circular and predictable as the rhythms of the bees around their hive in the ash tree out by the slumped and abandoned garden, and yet there is something palpably different now, some reversal, some strangeness. It is only when he tells me to speak, for God’s sake just speak, and then Addie and I look at him together in silence, that I realize what it is. The sessions and the canals and the rebirthing are not a routine to keep up normalcy for us. They are to keep up normalcy for him.

The next day Dr. Lark tells us that we are to remain close every day from now on. There is only one place my sister can go without me, and that is her canal. Addie will construct this canal by herself. It will be her space to go to when she chooses, and I am forbidden to go near it. "You need to learn that some things are sacred," Dr. Lark says. She is supposed to build this canal like a bird, taking bits and pieces of things that she found from the old house where we were abandoned. Ellie takes her back to the house to scavenge. I can't imagine why anyone would want to go back there; I hated being in the dim living room with its boxy television that time I went back for the pendulum. But my sister comes back with a wheelbarrow of glinting objects. She sets up a workstation and works at night, like a robber.

The canal takes four nights to build.

The first night she prepares the foundation, crumpling and bending chicken wire.

The second night she prepares the blankets, draping them all along the curved foundation she has made.

The third night she fills the canal with matting from the house: old clothes we'd worn, blankets, tablecloths.

On the fourth night my sister begins decorating the birth canal. She balls up bits of red and silver wrapping paper and pokes them into the crevices of the chicken wire, where they glint and shine. She places our mother's jewelry all around the top of the canal, lining its upper surface with necklaces and dangling earrings. The top of the structure flashes. My sister crumples and hangs. I watch from between my bound fists as she stuffs the old birthday bags, the curling fingers of ribbon, and the mazes of bows with their endless layers and intersections into the crevices. By dawn she is finished. She climbs into the canal and sits so that the shape of her head and shoulders is visible under the curve of the blankets. I watch from under my bound hands and she cries.

Watching her cry is worse than feeling the heat of her sweat beside me. It is as if all those liquids are both inside and outside of her simultaneously, the wetness of her face and the shadowy wetness of the seahorse tank. The whole lab feels suffused with tears. Nobody can approach her when she sits in the canal and cries like that. She stays there until it is nearly time for breakfast. I want to tear the structure apart. I want to bring my bound fists together on the top of her skull. Ellie and two of the restraint-trained nurses from the other side take me in their laps and hold me there.

"We'll take you back to the house, too," they say. "You can build your own."

But they will have to force me.

I can't think of a single thing I would want to take.

Chapter 6

Ellie

"Tell me more about this procedure," the doctor says. "Rebirthing, I think you said it was?"

She is sitting at her desk in front of her diplomas and looking straight at me through wire-rimmed glasses. Her gray bob is parted perfectly down the center and falls neatly down either side like a curtain drawn back to show the deep inner rooms of her face. Inside those rooms, beyond her glasses, behind the attentive pupils and the focused gaze, there is a neat and efficient arrangement of sense, an orderly furniture of rationality that shines forth. She has her hands folded on the desk. Her shoulder blades are pulled back straight and something about her posture makes me pull my shoulder blades back, too, and speak a little more forcefully.

"Rebirthing," I say again. "He wants the girls to pass through a 'womb' to simulate their birth. He thinks this will help to cure them. To get rid of their rage."

"He wants to talk them through," she says, and as she tilts her head the curtain of hair falls forward. "As if he were the mother, or the parental figure. To try and get them to talk about what they experienced there. To access that first moment of parental recognition."

"Yes. He's writing something, I think. Something to read during the rebirthing session."

"Yes. I thought so. It's a script. This is common practice at rebirthing sessions. The therapist and his attendants read from a script of questions, where they ask the child how he or she feels inside of the womb, how it feels to be so close to the mother, and whether he or she wants to be born."

"So this is normal?" I say. "This procedure?"

"Not exactly," she sighs. "Attachment disorder is not very well understood in general, and there have been a lot of misdiagnoses and a lot of faddish cures. Rebirthing is one of them. Psychologists are divided about its effectiveness. Some have seen very good results, and others have said that it only makes the child angrier and more resistant. In any case, it could be very dangerous for a pregnant woman. How far along is she?"

"Seven months."

"So, eight months pregnant by the time he'll hold the session," she says. "Yes, that sounds risky."

"Yes."

"You must be very concerned about the girls."

"Yes."

"And what about him?" she says. "Do you trust him?"

The curtain falls back again for a moment and her hazel eyes peer keenly, but this is not an accusatory or a probing question; it sounds like the kind of question Mel would ask me. I am surprised to find that I feel at ease with her and in this environment with its motivational posters and diplomas and stacks of medical journals. I am comfortable working in hospitals and around sick people, but I have always hated being a patient, ever since my mother died—hated sitting in little rooms waiting for specialists to come out and meet me, hated consulting a doctor about my own or another's health. But this doctor is different: more straightforward, with kinder eyes.

"I used to," I tell her. "But the more I learned about him, the more I began to distrust him, and now I'm not so sure he has the girls' best interest in mind at all." I hesitate, unsure if this is the right time to raise the paternity question or the question of Simon's dismissal. "When I try to ask him about the pregnancy he's not as concerned as he should be. It's all about the rebirthing procedure, nothing else."

"I see," she says. "How long has he been working with these patients?"

"Years. Most of their lives."

"Okay," she says. "Let me think about the best way to handle this. It's a little complicated if there's no evidence of malpractice on his part. Maybe the best thing you can do now is keep an eye on him and let me know if you see anything. Take notes. Write everything down." She picks up one of the white cards on her desk. "In the meantime, please feel free to call me if you think of anything else. I'll give you my cell number as well."

I glance at the handwritten numbers on the back of the card and tuck it carefully into my purse. "I don't know how to thank you," I tell her, reaching out to accept her handshake. "I really appreciate this, Dr. Coe."

"Call me Rachel," she says.

"Patients died this way," he said once, and then I noticed it—that blank way he looked at us, his palms upturned on his knees in a gesture of helpless acknowledgment. It was then that the feeling came: that brooding feeling of unease, the same one I'd had when I realized I'd missed my period or when I looked at my mother and knew the cancer was getting worse. The girls were sitting on the couch. The nature shows were playing; it was dinnertime, and Simon and I were bringing the trays while Dr. Lark was just lounging there in street clothes, staring at the TV like someone's father just home from the office. Dorian gazed at him, her face a geography of bruises, with oceanic patches of blue among puffy, rising landscapes of deep purple.

"Did you try the other kind of cure?" she asked. "The first kind?"

He said nothing at first, then: "Yes. I have tried that cure. I've tried every kind." I held my breath. Dorian stared. "It has to fail before we know how to make it work," he said. I went back to the kitchenette with that dark feeling of crisis, those remembered shocks of pregnancy and death.

I had the same feeling when he started to talk about the rebirthing, and so the afternoon after he made his announcement about the procedure I went to the UT med school library and looked it up on PubMed. It was six in the evening, and the library was just closing. My phone was chirping like an electronic cricket with texts from my ex-boyfriend at the hospital. I shut it off and paid three dollars to print an article, which I went to read in one of the locals-only dive bars just off of the strip where students took their visiting parents for dinner. It was dark inside. The jukebox was mercifully broken, and I sat at the bar drinking a High Life and reading the article by the light of a neon Coors sign.

The article was about an adopted girl named Glory Lewis who'd had attachment disorder. It reprinted a few lines from the transcript of her rebirthing case, which had been recorded and presented at a trial. I read:

> **GLORY:** It hurts! I can't breathe!
>
> **DR. MENSI:** I can't loosen it until you decide you want to come out. You have to be born to get to the air. Are you ready to be born?
>
> **GLORY:** I don't know. I don't know! How do I get born? Where do I come out?
>
> **DR. MENSI:** You come out when you are ready to see your mother. Do you want to see your mother?

She's right here with me, waiting for you to be born. Ms. Lewis, can you feel the movements of your baby?

MS. LEWIS: (reading from a card) Yes, I can, doctor. I'm so happy to have this baby. I can't wait to see what she looks like and to hold her and love her.

DR. MENSI: Do you hear that, Glory? Your mother wants to hold you and love you. She doesn't want you to kick and to fight anymore and to be angry. Do you want your mommy to hold you? Do you want to be born and to get better and stronger and to let her take care of you?

GLORY: (weeping) Yes, yes, I want to be born! Please let me out. How do I get out?

DR. MENSI: You have to fight hard to get out. It's a hard world. You have to really want to be born.

GLORY: (still weeping, inaudible)

DR. MENSI: Do you hear that, Ms. Lewis? Glory doesn't want to be born. She's giving up. Is that right, Glory? Are you saying you give up?

GLORY: (silence)

"Glory's death by suffocation is thought to have occurred

during this silence in the recording of the rebirthing session," the article read. "The national press the story received led to a widespread investigation of rebirthing therapy, and Glory's doctors and adopted mother were charged with three counts of child abuse in 1998. Still, proponents of rebirthing therapy insist that, under safe and carefully monitored conditions, the technique of being 'born again' has had highly beneficial results for patients suffering with the disorder."

I choked on my High Life and the men at the bar looked over at me, startled. *People have died this way*, he'd said. *I've tried every kind of cure.*

Of course, I called Stella first. I got her number from the receptionist at the ward and called her while sitting on the hood of my car outside the megachurch, waiting for Mel to get home. On the first try there was no answer, so I left a message and let her know it was me calling from an outside line about Addie and Dorian. Then I waited five minutes and called back again; she answered on the first ring.

"Yes, Ellie," she said, her voice angry and alert and intense, like a mother who's been expecting a call from a truant officer about a wayward adolescent son. I pictured her standing in the kitchen of her suburban Minimal Traditional house in Farragut while her husband, the personal injury lawyer, prowled back and forth across the tiles, his suit jacket off and his sleeves rolled up and a scotch in his hand, barely repressing his courtroom bluster long enough to listen to her side of the conversation. She would be wearing the high-rise designer jeans, flowing white blouses, and chunky statement jewelry she always wore when she came to see Addie and Dorian on their birthdays. Her hair, dyed black, would resemble Dorian's, but in every other way her features would be fainter and less prominent than those of her nieces, as if she had stamped out her every resemblance to them with spray tans and salon hairstyles and deep bronze eyeshadow.

"It's about the girls," I said. "I have some concerns about their treatment and I was hoping you would be willing to speak with me privately about it."

She was silent for a moment.

"Does James know you're calling?"

"No, he doesn't," I admitted. "I didn't tell Dr. Lark I was calling you because I didn't want him to react badly and alarm the girls. I'm sure it's nothing. I'm just concerned. I thought you would want to know."

There was another long silence. I heard the clink of a Zippo and a heavy inhale. "Go ahead."

"It's about a new form of therapy," I began cautiously. "'Rebirthing.'"

In the calmest, most understated way I could, I told her about the construction of the canals, the changes in Dr. Lark's behavior, and Simon's sudden termination. I mentioned that the girls had a hard time processing big changes in their routine and reminded her of the need for Addie to maintain her health throughout the pregnancy, and for Dorian to stay calm and not have a relapse. When Stella was still silent except for the quiet, focused inhalations of smoke, I told her about the article I had read, and finally about the fate of the little girl named Glory.

There was another long pause when I finished. "Is that all?"

"Is that all?" I said. "Well, no. I was hoping you could help. I was hoping maybe you could drive down and talk to Dr. Lark. Maybe talk to the girls. See if they want to be placed with someone else."

"You want me to drive down and talk to the girls. You want me to try to get them placed somewhere else," she said in a low, steely tone.

"I was hoping you might consider it. Yes."

"You've got a lot of nerve." Now she was raising her voice and the slow inhalations and exhalations gave way to a breathless, panting rage. "You've got a lot of nerve calling me up like this. Those girls put you up to it. They put everybody up to it. I ought to tell James about this. You ought to know better."

"Wait," I said. "Wait. Please, just listen."

"No, you listen," she said, cutting me off. "It's bad enough I got to put up with all this harassment ever since that goddamn girl got herself into trouble. Reporters calling my house all the time again. Just like fifteen years ago after they found the girls with his goddamn body. I have to get an unlisted number, I have to get security bars put in my windows to keep cameramen from breaking into my home, I have to take my daughter out of school so the other kids don't torment her for the sins of her family. Those girls are not victims. Those girls are cold-blooded killers. They're fucking crazy, just like their mama was. And now you call me and you want me to come talk to them? You must be out of your mind."

"No," I said, helpless. "It's not like that. It's not the girls. It's *him*. Dr. Lark. James."

"James has been the one guiding light in those girls' lives. It's only because of James that they haven't killed each other and they can sit and eat a Thanksgiving dinner without having to be put in straightjackets. Don't you dare talk to me about James. And don't you dare call here again."

"Please—" I begged, but it was useless. She'd already hung up.

With Stella out of the picture there was no one left but Mel, and Mel had no medical authority or expertise. So I looked up "attachment therapy Eastern Tennessee" and came up with an alphabetical list of seven experts to call. In my messages I said only that I had a child with the disorder and that I was seeking a consultation. I left my cell number and the ward number since cell service is spotty in the neighboring hills. Three of the therapists called me back. Coe, Rachel, M.S.W., Ph.D. was the only woman, so I called her first.

It is easy to hide my concerns from Dr. Lark, but it is more difficult to hide them from Addie and Dorian. They follow me around the ward now when he is not on duty, Dorian escorting her engorged sibling along like a midwife. "Have you heard any more news?" Dorian says, standing in the doorway of the kitchenette. Addie is just behind her, shiny with sweat, her belly sticking out above her waistband.

"I'm working on it," I tell them. "Just give me some more time."

"How much more time do you think?"

"I don't know, Dorian. I'm trying. It may take a little while. You have to trust me."

"The twins are kicking," Addie says. She looks forlornly down at her stomach.

"Yes, you'll feel them move more from now on," I tell her. "Remember what the doctor and the ultrasound technician said? They'll kick more in this trimester and change positions more often. Lots of changes are happening to them. They're getting more fat on their bodies and they can turn themselves, and they can even hear now."

"I still don't understand how it's twins," Addie says.

"Of course you do, Addie. The doctor explained it to you."

"But how do I know which seed came from which? What sort of features each one will have?"

"Your children are not seeds," I say. "What did I tell you about reading that book?"

"I'm not reading that book. I'm just asking."

"You *are* reading that goddamn book. I told you, I'm going to take it away. Where's the pregnancy guide I gave you? That explains everything about the kicking and the twins."

"That book doesn't make any sense. I don't have the same things the women in that book have."

"What are you talking about? You have goddamn

children growing inside of your body. So do the women in the book."

"They make themselves things to eat for their cravings and go to breathing classes and have baby showers with their friends. I don't make myself things to eat and I can't go to breathing classes and I don't have friends to give me baby showers in their houses."

I am not sure if this last remark is sincere, but when I look at her, the expression on her face is mournful, and the patches of skin on her face, darkened by pregnancy, seem to flush with a bright new color.

"Is that what you want?" I ask her. "A shower? We can hold something for you. I'm sure Dorian would be glad to plan it. Wouldn't you, Dorian?"

"I don't want to have a shower," Addie breaks in. "I'm just saying. The book you gave me doesn't explain about the seeds."

"And I'm saying that if I see you with that book about the seeds again I'm going to take it away and throw it in the garbage. Go get ready for dinner."

"But—"

"I said *go*."

It is not until the girls are in bed and I am walking around checking off the nighttime round duties on the staff clipboard that it hits me. I walk back into the sleeping quarters and tiptoe around to Addie's single bed, where she lies asleep on her side, her blonde hair streaming over the pillow and another pillow placed between her knees. Careful not to disturb Dorian, who lies snoring with her mouth open on the opposite bed, I lean over Addie and touch her shoulder gently.

"Addie. Addie." Her skin is humid with sleep. "Addie, wake up."

"What?" Her voice is thick and fatigued; her eyes are still closed, and the weight of her body seems to sink even more deeply into the mattress.

"Addie, listen to me. What did you mean earlier when you said 'which seed came from which'? What were you talking about?"

"Which seed?" she mumbles.

"Addie, this is important. Think. What were you trying to ask me in the kitchenette when you said you didn't understand about the seeds? About where each seed came from?"

"I meant," she says dozily, like a small sick child who has just been awakened to have its temperature taken, "which one came from which. Whether one came from him and one came from the other one."

"What other one? One came from Simon and one came from what other one?"

"The other one," she repeats. "Dr. Lark."

"She told me there was *another* one," I tell them. "Not just Simon. So she thinks one of the twins belongs to Simon and the other one belongs to Dr. Lark. He fucked her. Once. In his office. No clue where I was. No clue where the fuck you were. They fucked *in his office*, around the same time you started banging her in the garden. She doesn't remember exactly when, and she doesn't have any proof—and now she thinks one of the twins is yours and is going to look like you, and the other one is his and is going to look like him."

They are sitting on the bench outside the megachurch sharing the bottle, Mel in her nighttime jogging pants and sweatshirt and Simon in a faded black Ministry T-shirt and jeans, his wallet chain draped over his thigh like a torn shackle. They are both looking at me. Mel's expression is calm, with her long practice in such times of crisis; Simon's entranced in the fog of Nembutal that makes each piece of news take longer to reach him, like a foreign correspondent speaking on satellite delay.

"This is who you, a grown man and a father, have an affair with," I tell him. "A teenaged girl who doesn't know anything about her own body. All she knows about sex is from nature shows and that ancient Roman crap she reads. For fuck's sake."

I don't usually moralize like this. I'm surprised to find these sentiments emerging from my mouth and not Mel's. But she intervenes smoothly, cutting me off just as I'm about to launch into another assault on Simon.

"We need to stay focused on the present, on the now," she says, quiet but firm. "We need to decide what to do with this new piece of information. There's no proof, you said.

Or that's what she says, anyway. She's a mentally ill young woman and he's a powerful man with a lot of people on his side. We're going to need evidence. Did she tell you what happened afterward? Did she tell you if they ever talked about it again?"

"All she said was that he was upset afterwards and kept muttering about the cure. They never talked about it."

"We have no proof that it happened, but I think we have to believe the girl. The man can't be trusted with her. He's a criminal. He's blackmailing Simon to cover up his own sins. He doesn't have Addie's best interests in mind, to say the least," Mel says. "We need to get her away from him as soon as we can."

She pauses to give Simon an opportunity to speak, but he is still staring at me, squinting, as if anticipating something I have not yet said. I want to slap him. The image of Dorian thrashing comes back to me, the way she lashes out and hits. Is this what that impulse feels like?

"As for Simon," Mel continues, "he can't take back his sins, but he can try to make things right. He's already separated from his wife. He can provide a home where the babies will be safe. But all of that's in the future. The important thing is that we get Addie away from Dr. Lark as soon as we can. We also need to find a secure place for her to stay with her children. A rental, maybe. An apartment."

"Them," I say. "You mean get them an apartment."

Mel looks at me blankly.

"You mean get *them* an apartment," I repeat, impatiently.

"Addie and Dorian. They can't be separated."

"Of course we don't want to separate them," Mel says. "But it may not be God's will that they always stay together. Our first priority is to rescue Addie and the unborn children. We may not be able to rescue them both right away; she's the one in more immediate danger, so we have to think of her first."

I'm about to protest but Simon breaks in.

"The notepad," he says, almost inaudibly.

"What?" Mel says. "What notepad?"

"She said he went over afterward and wrote in the notepad," Simon says, looking back and forth from Mel to me. "He only writes in that notepad when he has an idea about the sessions or the cure. He had sex with Addie and then he wrote in the notepad. We have to find out what he wrote. *You* have to find out what he wrote," he continues, raising his eyebrows at me. "Because that might be it."

"That might be what?"

"Our proof."

It disgusts me now to be near him: his disheveled clothes, his stubble, his sour breath. When he does his rounds in the lab or conducts the sessions, he mumbles to himself. Sometimes he wanders back to his office and sits there "reading" for hours, his feet propped up on the desk, but when I walk down the corridor to retrieve things from the supply closets I can tell he's just staring without really seeing anything. His shoulders, once broad and muscular from weekends of golf and squash, have sunk, and his face is like a lunar eclipse, the bottom half covered in dusky shadow and the top half lit by the glitter of his peaked, feverish eyes. Whenever someone catches him in a blank stare, he looks up and seems startled for a moment that we have noticed him, that we are even there.

"I haven't been sleeping well," he always says. "Nightmares."

Things no longer get done in a timely and efficient way—the sessions get postponed or start late; doctor's appointments get forgotten or are only remembered at the last minute—but this also means he's become less guarded about his notes, absentmindedly leaving notebooks on the table in the common area or strewn among files atop his desk instead of locked in the manila filing cabinets that line the wall. One night, when he wanders off to the common area to join Dorian and Addie in front of the television, I go back to his office under the pretext of looking for a copy of a prescription and take two notepads from underneath a hill of medical journals on his desk. On the outside he has scribbled the rough dates of their composition: April, May, and June of this year, around the time we began the sessions for the cure. I hurry through the pages of close blue scrawl: observations about the sessions, references to relevant chapters in journals or books.

> *May 8—Holding Therapy in c-area. Hands for ten minutes. Both girls spoke, avoided eye contact (see Russell 1987 on remedial hold. ther. with adolescent women?)*

Bruises on D's left arm
Addie—more deferential to questioning.
Dinner as usual

Pages and pages of this follow: mealtimes, questions to ask the girls, snatches of conversation, vegetables we planted in the garden, notes about what the girls preferred for dinner and what nature shows they enjoyed the most, bits of medical vocabulary so specialized and abbreviated as to be practically illegible. There is nothing helpful, nothing incriminating. I am about to give up when I come across an entry from late May, around the time of the garden blooming and the tryst with Simon—the time, I assume, of the encounter with Dr. Lark. It is a single page, with no date and only one sentence written across the middle of the page:

Addie—Capacity for touch.
Breakthrough.

Was that the seduction? Was that all he wrote? I flip further through the notebook and find another oddly sparse notation, as succinct and bewildering as a shorthand memo in another language:

AD—genetics versus environment?
2nd gen?
Early intervention

Multiple case studies—genetic patterning.
Lifelong observation—multigenerational.
(Unprecedented!)

AD, I know, is the disorder—but genetic patterning? Early intervention? Then it hits me and I sit down heavily in his office chair, the cryptic handwriting shrieking up at me from the page.

The breakthrough.

"It's not just the girls he's interested in," I tell Rachel, breathlessly, in her office.

It is midafternoon and the sunlight is slanting through the blinds; it lights up her face and hair so that she looks blonder and less gray. The plain silver chain around her neck, hanging just above her crisp blue button-down, twinkles like a piece of tinsel. I have come straight from work to meet her at the end of her workday. I am still in my hospital scrubs and a little frantic, while she has the same relaxed and efficient stance, shoulders pulled back, but there is something quizzical now, something distracted, in her expression.

"He's interested in *their* girls. The twins. He wants them to grow up in the ward so he can study their behavior. He wants to do a multigenerational, lifelong study. He wants to keep Addie and Dorian in the ward and he wants to raise the twins in the ward. And he wants to do it all in order to make some kind of life's work, a magnum opus."

"I think I understand," she says. "He wants to sort out the

distinctions between nature and nurture. To decide to what extent the patients' rage is genetic and to what extent a product of the family and social environment."

"I think so. He thinks it would be an unprecedented study. No one else will ever have worked so closely with four related patients in this way before."

"He wants to keep four patients with this disorder in the ward?" she says.

"I don't know. I don't know if he knows anymore. He's obsessed. And that's not all," I say. "I spoke to Addie about her pregnancy last week and she said the children could be his, Dr. Lark's, that the two of them had an encounter together. Back in April or May, she thinks. One time. She doesn't know when."

Dr. Coe raises her eyebrows at this.

"And you read this in his private files?" she asks, quietly.

"In one of his notebooks."

"May I see it?"

I extend the little book to her and she flips through it absently, stopping here and there to bring the blue scrawl closer to her eyes. She spends a lot of time on the page that I have marked with a Post-It note, the one about the multiple case studies, and seems to extrapolate from the brief, terse notations a larger, invisible web of information. I glance around the room, fidgeting, reading the titles on her bookshelves: *Parenting with Attachment Disorder. Adoption and Attachment. For the Love of a Child.* In the corner of her office there is a small consultation area with a round table and a toy box, and I imagine Dr. Coe sitting at this table talking to Addie and Dorian, describing the different treatment options for their children, while the twin toddlers toss and bang the loose toys on the floor. Addie and Dorian look back at her and nod in unison, earnestly, their hands clasped together.

Ten minutes pass this way. Then Dr. Coe sets the notebook down on the desk and pats it thoughtfully.

"Ellie, I want to thank you for bringing this to my attention," she says. "It is puzzling. There's nothing obviously incriminating here, but it does seem like the case needs some immediate outside intervention, proof of malpractice or not. You say Addie told you she had a sexual encounter with this doctor. Did the encounter happen in the ward?"

"Yes, she said it happened in his office."

"Did anyone see her go into the office?"

"I don't think so. I didn't see her, and I was the one who was working that night. But it wouldn't have seemed unusual. The girls often went into his office individually for private consultations."

"Did she keep the clothes she was wearing?"

"No. I mean, she has them still, but she put them in the hamper afterward and they got sent out to the laundry with everything else."

"So it would be her word against his," she says. "That's difficult. Patients with attachment disorder often misrepresent or misstate the facts. I'm not saying that's what happened here," she says, raising her hand at my little noises of objection. "I'm just trying to show you how it would be very difficult to compel him to take a paternity test. Lawyers will easily be able to find doctors who will testify that attachment-disordered patients lie. And since another man has already been identified as the father, it will be even harder."

"What about the media? Can't the reporters get involved again?"

"You might be able to get public attention on your side again. But the attempt to force an abortion was already a big scandal, and it will be hard to replicate a media frenzy like that. Most people will have moved onto other things, and there's no proof. If Dr. Lark is the father, it seems like he went from wanting her to terminate to accepting that the pregnancy was going to happen to realizing that he could use the children as part of his ongoing research. If he's that deeply embroiled in this scheme, he'll have known better than to incriminate himself further in any way. Even this notebook. It's going to be hard to make anyone, a watchdog company or a lawyer or anyone, believe that these lines mean what you think they mean. He has a lot of supporters in the medical profession. Probably the best thing we can do is keep our eyes on him and wait to see if he makes a mistake."

"Just wait?" I say, desperate. "That's it?"

"That's not it, but it's what we can do right now. You have access to his files and his office. If you or I or anyone makes him suspicious, he might restrict that. So it would be best to proceed as normal while we think about next steps. When did you say the rebirthing is scheduled?"

"November 7."

"November 7," she repeats. "That gives us three weeks. I'll think about who I might get in touch with. And you stay alert and let me know what's going on when you can."

She stands up and extends her hand. I shake it and reach for the notebook with my other hand but she lays hers gently over mine.

"If you don't mind, I'd like to hang on to this," she says. "Let me know if he asks about it in the meantime."

On the way out I pass through a lobby where a little girl of five or six is wearing a helmet, shrieking and pelting one of the chairs in the waiting area with mittened hands while her mother leans over and talks to her softly, trying to get her to stop. There is something so sad about this helpless process, about the contrast between the forlorn mother-and-daughter pair and the blithe, mass-produced posters on the wall that show smiling families above slogans like *Persistence, Not Resistance* and *Helping Families Heal.* For a moment I wonder why people continue to form families at all.

Outside, against Rachel's advice, I sit in my car and call the number for the state medical examiners' board. After waiting on hold for half an hour and being transferred three times, I finally speak to a woman who listens quietly, tapping on her computer keyboard, as I give a statement about the whole situation: the doctor's strange behavior, Addie's condition. When I am finished she asks several pointed questions about Addie's psychiatric history.

"You know, patients suffering from reactive attachment disorder frequently make false accusations of sexual misconduct," she says. "It's well documented."

"She's not lying!"

"I'm just saying, these patients are known to be highly manipulative. Is there any evidence to support her statement?"

"She's *pregnant*."

"So you said. But Dr. Lark is not the only adult male who has had access to this patient, correct? And at least one other man has admitted to engaging in sexual activity with her?"

"Yes, but—"

I hear the keyboard click again. Then she thanks me for contacting the state medical board and assures me that they will forward my complaint to the Tennessee Department of Health. My name will be kept confidential, she says.

"To the health board?" I say. "What happens then?"

"They'll give your complaint a priority code based on the severity of the allegation. Then, they'll send your complaint to the regional office in charge of investigating that facility. They may get in touch with you to request additional information. You'll get a letter when the regional office decides whether or not adequate evidence exists for the Department to take disciplinary action. Either way, the facility will be investigated."

"How long will it take?"

“I can’t say at this time,” she says. “If you have any more information you’d like to provide, just call.” She rattles off a number, but I hang up without writing it down and sit in my car, staring at the blank screen of my phone.

I am too antsy to go home to my apartment, so I go instead toward the University of Tennessee med school complex. I park and enter the medical library, where tables of students are studying in intense postures of concentration: some scribbling on legal pads; some sipping from white cardboard coffee cups; many wearing regulation hospital scrubs. I am still in my nurse’s uniform, too, so nobody glances at me for longer than a second or asks for my ID when I pass through the metal detectors and go to the computer at the reference desk. My first search for *Lark* turns up a wealth of articles and books about delirium, respiratory diseases, and schizophrenia, but *Lark + attachment* turns up the right title, *When Caring Can’t Fix It: A Guide for Parents of Children with Reactive Attachment Disorder (RAD)*, by James Lark, M.S.W., Ph.D.

The thin paperback lies on its side on a shelf in the stacks, way back by the emergency stairwell where a few students are pacing back and forth and speaking in low voices on their cell phones.

I scan the table of contents:

> I. Introduction: What is attachment disorder?
> II. The story of “Theodore”

III. Outpatient treatment: Holding therapy, catharsis
IV. Rebirthing: The future of recovery?

I am just about to flip to the rebirthing chapter when something in the acknowledgments section catches my eye: "This book would not have been possible without the guidance of Dr. Rachel Coe. She is responsible for all of the merits of this book; its deficiencies are my own. I also owe a great debt to the staff at the care center, where the majority of this research was conducted under her supervision, and to the patients there, who taught me everything I know."

I set the book back on the shelf and walk past the silent students and out of the library. I drive to my apartment, where I sit on my sofa drinking a beer and staring out at the street with my stomach lurching into my throat.

Of course they know each other. Of course she was his mentor. I recall her measured demeanor, her even tone, her calm perusal of the notebook. *He wants to decide to what extent the patients' rage is genetic.* I realize now that the quizzical expression I saw when she said that must have masked zeal, captivation, interest. The breakthrough. It would be hers too, the breakthrough by her esteemed mentee: an achievement of medical scholarship that would burnish his reputation and her own. But then why did she want to keep the notebook? To warn him of my treachery and show him the evidence? Or to scoop him herself, perhaps—to try and take credit for the idea?

Outside the twilight throws a dark sheen over the road

and the grass, and the twinkle of the fireflies is lurid and severe. The beer tastes sour and makes the pit of my stomach full and sick with hops and carbonation.

Why didn't I know about his mentor? He hardly ever talks about his training, I reflect, that's why: he only ever says that he trained in many wards, that he tried all sorts of cures. *I've worked in many other places. Many people have died this way.*

Why did I trust her? Because she was a woman, I realize; because she was a woman I thought she would be an ally. I did not stop long enough to think that women, too, can be powerful and malicious.

My cell rings. I look at the number and answer it as evenly as I can, cringing a little at the sound of his voice, at its slyness and insincerity, at the once-familiar background noises of the waiting room near the security desk where he sits the evening shifts at Knoxville General.

"Ellie," he murmurs.

"Thanks for calling me back," I say, with what I hope is a note of cheerful brightness even though this feels like a bald-faced lie. I stand in the darkening living room and look out into the dismal front yard.

"No problem. What's up?"

"I have a favor to ask," I tell him. "I want to know if you still have control of the security clearance."

He is silent for a moment. I can hear the voices of the security officers on the other end asking visitors to place their bags on the belt, calling them *Sir* and *Ma'am*, telling them to step on through.

"If I do, what do you want with it?"

"I want to know if you could help me keep a visitor from getting into the hospital. And I want to know if you could help me get a patient out. Maybe before discharge."

"That depends."

"Depends on what?"

"What does she look like?"

"Forget it," I snap. "I shouldn't have called."

"Wait, Ellie, wait," he says, still laughing at his own joke. "Of course I can do all that. But why? And when?"

"I'm not sure yet. I'll call you back."

I hang up without saying goodbye, open a fresh beer, and walk out onto the balcony and switch off the light, so that all I can see is the darkening sky and the low line of trees against it and the fireflies like falling embers all through the air. In the back there are even more, and they seem to be winking together in a great, suspended, iridescent maze. The tightness in my throat and stomach is hardening into something like resolve, and I am startled to find myself picturing the two of them here, Dorian and Addie, sitting out in the shared backyard watching their toddlers wobble and fall in the cushiony grass, chilling bottles of formula in my refrigerator, reaching into my linen closet for fresh towels.

No, I think, looking out into the dusk, no, I am not crazy. I am not Mel with her thankless charity work and her endless lobbying and her sacrificed life, and I am not Dr. Lark with his heroic delusions. But I am surprised at what I am suddenly willing to do to ensure that the girls get to a safe place, that they emerge from the ward into a network of resources and caregivers, to the safety of a backyard like this one, to the independence of a life like this. I will not be a mother, but I will be the champion of these mothers, these doomed bearers of the perpetually unwell.

CHAPTER 7
Simon

She says that grace will come to this little apartment over the town square. The realtor has gone downstairs to check on another available unit. Mel and I are standing at the window in the living room looking down at the street below. It is late afternoon, and the lunch customers have all paid their bills at the street's artisanal pizza restaurants and Southern-cooking cafés and Mexican-style cantinas. They are wandering back to their parked cars and their offices, college-aged waitresses emerging behind them to sweep the patios and clear away the half-empty, sweating glasses of sweet tea and diet soda. The awnings and the red bricks of the square gleam in the sun. Two bluegrass pickers sit on the edge of a giant flower planter. One has a banjo, the other has a guitar, and their fingers are strumming an agile farewell to the receding crowds.

"There's a playground right there"—Mel points to our right, beyond the square, where I can just make out the figures of children swaying back and forth on a swing set—"and there's a mini-market one block south that sells formula and diapers and milk and things like that. Plenty of storage space in the unit if you want to take your car out to the Costco and stock up."

She gestures at the counter that divides the kitchen from the living room, the freshly painted white wooden cabinets, and the pantry. The hardwood floors creak under her weight, and the sunshine coming in through the window lights up her hair and her profile.

"It's too much," I say.

"Not too much at all. Seven hundred. Has to be less than what you pay for your split-level."

"I meant it's too much what you've done for me. For Addie. For us."

"Nothing's too much trouble to help one of God's children," she says. "Grace doesn't have a price."

But it does have a price, I thought, looking at her tired eyes, at the beauty that was not like Ellie's sultriness but rather more handsome and maternal and long-suffering, a beauty now fading under a lifetime of stress and sleeplessness and putting others' needs before her own. Fighters pay a price for the good fight.

"You don't have to thank me," she says. "It's not about thanks. It's about the child. It doesn't matter that it's out of wedlock. You'll finish your divorce and you'll help Dorian and Addie and the babies get here and you'll marry her and you'll make it right."

I stare down at the bluegrass pickers. They've moved into "Orphan Joe" at a slower tempo, and the clutching, mournful way the banjoist moves his left hand up and down the neck of the instrument as he switches chords makes it seem as if he is looking for different ways to bring it closer, as one holds a woman's waist in a dance.

"You don't like it," Mel says. "Is that it?"

I look down at her again: at those faint lines around the mouth and at the corners of the eyes, at the faint trace of a worn-out bra underneath her white *I Stand 4 Life* shirt.

"No, it's perfect," I say. "Let's take it."

It is the third and last trimester. I have followed the swelling and the growth through Ellie, who comes to the megachurch on her nights off and shows me the pictures she has taken with her phone. In all of the pictures Addie is standing sideways to the camera to display her bump, sometimes pulling her top up all the way beneath her breasts to display her proud roundness, a roundness that still looks delicate and slim in a woman so young. She is no longer wearing the regulation scrubs in these pictures: sometimes she has a larger size of pink maternity pajamas with a fitted elastic band just over the waist that highlights the curvature of the belly; other times she wears the new maternity clothes Ellie has bought for her with money from the ward: loose, flowing cotton shirts with split sides and low-rise jersey pants. Dorian stands next to her grinning a malicious, imbecilic smile, her long black hair snaking down her back, her hand resolutely clutching her sister's.

When Ellie tells us the dates of the checkups and the ultrasounds I write them down on the wall calendar in the kitchen at the Stand for Life charity, which already bulges with the dates of other women's doctor visits and custody hearings and visits from probation officers. It holds, too, the monthly dates when the pro bono lawyer comes to the charity with her rolling suitcase of case files, her manila envelopes clutched against her flustered chest, her cell phone quaking and chirping with urgent interruptions. Mel goes to let her in and the women descend upon her in dishevelment and distress, their small children running forward too, and then stopping in the hallway and falling back shyly against their mothers.

But no one speaks to the lawyer before Mel does, and whenever the lawyer says anything the women look at Mel before they answer. I watch Mel fighting endlessly for these wasted and tired women, her own hair disheveled like theirs, her own needs unmet or only partially met; I watch her skipping meals, rising early for conference calls, staying up late to review WIC applications and sort out the vouchers. I've worked with others like her, doctors who split their time between ER shifts and the urgent care clinic down in Mechanicsville, nurses who take vacation time to go assist Partners in Healing volunteer surgeons in war-torn Rwanda and ruined Port-au-Prince. There is no reprieve in that sort of work, no downtime. The resources are always tight and the organizations understaffed; the people who work there are all doing the tasks of ten people.

She is both thrilled and lonely, I know, with only her battered and abandoned women to tend to, in that thankless charity center hooked onto the side of her father's titanic evangelical fortress. It is important work; it is God's work. But she must have desires, I reflect, looking at the shape of her body under the white T-shirt and the plaid flannel shirt and the faded boot-cut jeans that wrap around her body like a security gate. Standing at the window in the sunshine I remember that first sight of her outside of the ward, that moment when she seemed to me to come straight out of the books of the apocalypse, glowing with a holy strangeness like the woman clothed with the sun from Revelations. Now I remember the line every time her face changes when she is at a protest, every time it changes when she is screaming invectives at a politician or at a doctor emerging from the Planned Parenthood flanked by security guards, every time it changes when she goes forth to assail the pro bono attorney with questions about court dates and child support: *Who is she that looks forth as the morning, fair as the moon, clear as the sun, and terrible as an army with banners?*

Next to Ellie she looks different: intimate, conspiratorial. The family resemblance is like a performance that settles over them, the same lilt of voice and the same roll of the eye, the same sideways working of the jaw when they are angry and upset, the same restless tapping of the fingers on the knee. We three are sitting outside on the bench in front of the giant cross and the fountain, handing a bottle back and forth. It is nighttime and the sounds of the leaping water and the crickets in the manicured bushes drown out the periodic flares of engines on the interstate. The empty asphalt lot and the giant ramparts and steeple of the megachurch feel like a private, hidden garden.

"The next big thing is the rebirthing," Ellie says. It is a warm night and she is still in her scrub pants, but she has ditched the top and is wearing only a white camisole that shows stenciled traces of the curlicues on her lacy beige bra. Her cat-eye liner has melted and smudged in the heat and left blotches next to her temples. "The last session of the cure. He wants the girls to re-enact the experience of coming through the birth canal. He says it will be the final stage in the recovery process if he can get them to let all of their rage out."

"Re-enact their birth?" Mel says. She is wearing the same T-shirt that she wore to the apartment, and through the pleasant, spreading vapor of Nembutal I notice she is just as chesty, if not a tad chestier, than Ellie. Or maybe it's that they strain against the cloth of the T-shirt more, appearing rounder and fuller, while Ellie's are partially freed and exposed in the low neckline of the cami. "That sounds like New Age quackery. Is it for real?"

"It is real," I say, and the two women look over at me suddenly, with their eyebrows raised to the exact same height, like actresses following a cue. "It's always been his final goal for the cure. It's how he worked with other patients before he started the ward. He says lots of doctors have done it and many patients have been cured that way. You get the girls under blankets to simulate the womb and you talk them through their birth and they talk back and cry and kick and scream until the anger is exposed and he lets them out."

"Well, it's dangerous," Ellie says. "The girl is eight months pregnant. She can't be under a blanket getting hot and upset. And Dorian's doing so well. She hasn't had a relapse in months. Now he wants to try this and he says he has to do it before the baby comes. It's the last chance to cure them and to help them be mothers, he says."

"Jesus," Mel says. "Well, we've got the place, and it will be easy to get furniture and everything. It's just a matter of figuring out how to get them into it."

"Them?" I say. "Or just her?"

Ellie looks at me blankly.

"Both of them," she says. "Of course."

"Have you thought any more about how you're going to get her out?" asks Mel.

"I set up an appointment with the only other specialist in Knoxville who works almost exclusively with attachment disorders," Ellie says. "Her name is Rachel something. She's at the children's care place at Knoxville General and she's on the faculty of the med school at UT. But I talked to a nurse who works with her and she has a family too, a husband and a little girl. The little girl is only seven. I think because she's a mother it might help. Dr. Lark doesn't understand."

"What are you going to tell her?" Mel says.

"Everything." Ellie crushes her cigarette out beneath the heel of her white no-slip nursing shoes. "I'm going to tell her everything that's going on and I'm going to ask her to help us."

"I hope she will," Mel says. She takes a sip from the bottle, winces at the strength of the cheap Schnapps. "We need to get that poor girl away from that godless ward and that godless man."

In front of us one of the fountain jets pumps with a renewed vigor and sends up a clear, arching spine of water, as if to echo Mel's tone of solemn, majestic fury. We drink and sit and stare at the cross. A feeling of quiet solidarity spreads between us. We are a little string of misfit avengers, a heroic trio getting drunk on our beacon of righteousness.

After I got sent away from the ward I found myself staring down painfully empty stretches of time: sudden gaps in the evening; blank, unending weekends punctuated only by the occasional, sweet, but too-brief company of Sandy's visitations. All the old rituals of dinner and nature shows and gossiping in the kitchenette fell away and left only a void. I floundered. Sometimes I took ER shifts at Knoxville General and attended restraint training workshops to keep up my certification. I took long, pointless walks around the downtown Knoxville square, where the bluegrass pickers sat absently strumming their banjos and singing to no one, walks that took me all the way out to the reservoir past the parked cars of weekend-drive tourists snapping pictures. The reservoir water shimmered and broke into sunlit patterns so bright they left searing patches behind my eyelids when I closed my eyes. Even when I returned from these excursions there was still time: always time, neverending time, the painful, searing, cruelly abundant time of the suddenly alone.

I began to follow the rhythms of the ward at home. This was almost unconscious at first. It began as a way of wrestling down and taming that yawning gap of time; it became a sustaining routine, a form of monotonous, necessary sustenance. I ate breakfast and lunch and dinner at the same time the girls did. At ten, I pictured the hand-holding sessions, alone at a table staring at my knuckles. In the afternoons, I thought about the girls standing in front of the seahorse tank and wondered about the messy, overgrown vegetables in the garden. And during their breaks and their mealtimes I flipped the television on to watch the same nature shows: those lanky marsupials going slow in the rainforest, the smooth glide of snakes up the scaly bark of trees gleaming wet with rainfall.

When I began these routines at home I began to experience a strange, intimate connection to the remembered sessions in the ward. I began to feel as if I was living in sync with Addie, the mother of my child whom I could not see, as if I was sharing her space and her life again. Time passed between us in unspoken harmony. At night after dinner I sat stupidly in front of the shows about gorillas and wolves and pythons with a slow feeling of stillness dropping into my brain and my bones, sliding through my joints and moving my shoulders away from my ears and shifting my ankles so my feet splayed out on the coffee table.

At least one thing had not changed about this feeling, this life: every thirty days, on the last weekday of the month, the delivery service at the pharmacy brought me a folded white paper bag with the Nembutal prescription, Dr. Lark's name and my name printed on the bottle just above the Rx number and black lettering that read *Doctor's Authorization Required.*

Mel hung back at first, invited me to a few rallies and things, until she noticed my aimlessness and asked me to volunteer at the Stand for Life facility. "While we wait to see what we can do you can help me and the other women," she said. "You can work and get yourself right with God."

This is what it looks like to get yourself right with God at Mel's women's charity:

You cart donation boxes back and forth from local schools and churches to the back of Mel's white Volvo;

you put on a black usher's uniform and clasp the arms of elderly female churchgoers as they tap their canes along the rows of pews before the live sermons in the megachurch on Sundays;

you listen to Mel's father's preaching as it thunders through the loudspeakers out over the cascading arcs of water and the jets bubbling around the cross;

you glue wooden stakes onto the backs of signs that read *Moms for Life* and *Is Your Doctor a Baby Killer?* and *Abortion = Homicide*;

you prepare a little car seat with a bottle and a blanket and a baby doll smeared with red food coloring to simulate blood and you stand fifty feet outside of Planned Parenthood on Saturdays holding the car seat out and screaming at the ashamed and bewildered teenaged girls who are walking with their angry parents and boyfriends and husbands and brothers to the facility;

you guard the doors of the unmarked I Stand 4 Life entrance from roaming, hostile fathers and brothers and boyfriends and husbands;

you call and arrange for Mel to speak at rallies and churches and right-to-life fundraising drives and listen as she reads aloud her short speeches and her impassioned, rousing sendoffs;

you open cans of SpaghettiOs and heat them in a giant saucepan and serve them to a shrieking, waiting roomful of unwashed and exuberant children;

you sit on the floor in a circle with Mel's women and hold hands while Mel strums a guitar and leads everyone in a rendition of "Lead Me, Lord";

you buy gaudy pastel boxes of maxi pads and tampons and unload them into the waiting hands of scowling postpartum women;

you slide the drain-opener snake into the shower drain and withdraw a long, snarled clump of hair, blonde and black and brown and red, all the pigments of the world gathered into a damp, dripping nest of follicles;

you hold the ball of yarn for Mel while she knits baby clothes and bitches about her sister;

you slip away momentarily when Mel goes to let Ellie in at night and dodge into the bathroom that never locks and lean against the door so that no one comes in while you unscrew the bottle of Nembutal and dose yourself next to a counter heaped with children's clothes and empty baby bottles and diaper boxes, feeling like a thief or a pervert, like a secret masturbator;

you go get the sticky, ancient bottle of peach Schnapps from the far corner of the cabinet, behind the Bisquick and the wholesale boxes of Fruit Roll-Ups and Capri Suns, and take it to Mel and Ellie sitting out on the bench by the giant cross;

you see Ellie safely out to her car and stand waiting your turn to leave while she lights a cigarette and juts her chin angrily and complains about Mel's fundamentalism;

you pick through box after box of donated clothes and go shopping for used furniture to take to the little apartment over the square, that little apartment where Mel says you will make things right by marrying Addie;

you explain, quietly, to Sandy on the first custody weekend after you start volunteering that these children are not as lucky as she is and that they are here because someone wanted to harm them, and that you and Mel want to protect them and make them better, and Sandy stands with her large eyes staring across the playroom at the alien kids who have no daddy and no personal toy box and no room of their own;

you tell Nora to pick you up at the megachurch where you and Sandy are outside in the fountain playing with four other children her age, where you and the children all have rolled up your trousers and you are picking them each up individually and setting them down again with a gentle splash in the water and they are screaming with glee, and you let your ex-wife park her car and stand leaning against it with her arms folded, taking it all in;

you protest when she looks you straight in the eyes and says she doesn't get it, that it is a sudden change and not a normal change, and something stinks about it. You protest this and laugh but stay on your guard, knowing she will keep hunting for what she cannot see and will not find, knowing this aimless search will make her worse, more temperamental.

Sometimes Mel witnesses these little exchanges, these quiet, angry conversations out by the car that take place when she is also outside with the children or sifting through the donation boxes in the trunk of her Volvo. During the last one, Nora asks what address to send the papers to, while Sandy clutches her legs, looking back and forth as if she is watching a tennis match. When Nora drives away with my daughter, Mel sets a box down and asks if everything is okay. "I'm fine," I tell her. Her brown eyes are large and questioning behind her glasses. “She’s a difficult woman, Sandy’s mother.”

When I say this I notice that I have taken to calling her *Sandy’s mother* rather than *my ex-wife* or *Nora*, speaking of her the way one speaks of a distant acquaintance.

“Why difficult?” Mel says.

“I don’t know. Everything is difficult with her. Her attitude. Her brain makes her difficult. Her ovaries make her difficult.”

“That’s no way to talk about the mother of your child.”

“No, it isn’t. I’m sorry.”

“Not sorry,” she says. “I just asked you a question. You didn’t answer it. That’s all. What makes her so difficult?”

“She doesn’t want me to have rights over Sandy. She’s vindictive about the custody.”

She is still standing by the trunk of her car, which is filled with heaping boxes of distended sweaters and well-worn, neatly folded onesies. “I see,” she says. “She’s upset. It’s about you, but she makes it about Sandy.”

“Yes,” I say, and there is something else, another truth to this point, but before I can trace that thought to the other thought where that other truth is, I find myself startled into silence by Mel’s eyes. They have not left mine for many seconds even though she is not speaking. All of a sudden it is Mel who knows another truth.

“You don’t think I can understand women and relationships,” she says. “You don’t think I can know what people think and why they behave the way they do. I’m crazy, I hate women, I'm an anti-feminist. Right? Crazy right-wing bitch."

"Of course I don't think that," I say. "Why would you say that? Why would you think I would think that?"

"Everybody thinks that," Mel says. She has not taken her eyes from mine. She is speaking rapidly and a little desperately, like she does to the young women in that short space between their car doors and the locked security gates of the Planned Parenthood. "They think I hate women. That I don't look out for a woman's choices. But who looks out for women who have no choices? Who knows what these women will think later? You think I don't believe in birth control? You think I want to scare women? I want to show them respect for their bodies, respect for life. Abortion makes their wombs disposable. It invades them. If we allow it, then what else can happen? Who else gets control over her body? Then we got data collection and regulation of family size and eugenics. Then we got the government ordering mandatory abortions. Then we got that tyrant over in the ward saying that girl has got to kill that baby. *That's* an encroachment on a woman's life. *That's* a violation of the right to choose."

I hesitate at this but she holds up her hand before I can interject.

"I know," she says. "I know it sounds crazy. But you have to think about the long-term implications of the problem. All the regulations and the medical oversight. You add a national health care system where the government is sponsoring those exams and you see what happens. We have to protect the women. Make sure they have services and support. Make sure they have someplace safe to be. Make sure they know they can get away from dangerous people if they need to. We have to do it through the churches and the local charities, not through Big Brother."

She turns back to her work in the trunk of the car and I stand looking stupidly at her sweatshirted back and thinking of the ultrasound photo Ellie showed us, the twins side by side in the little cocoon of Addie's body. Was that an encroachment? I pictured the transept moving over her young belly as I had once seen it slide over Nora's, the fuzzy black-and-white picture quaking into life, the infant forms emerging beneath the surface with sudden and terrible clarity. *Immaculate*, she would say, taking her sister's hand.

Two weeks later I overhear Mel talking to Sweets, and our strange conversation out by the trunk of her car suddenly falls into place. I am in the kitchen dicing onions and tomatoes for pasta sauce and Mel is in the room just opposite doing a cleaning inspection. This is the room where Sweets and her children and Donna and her children all sleep, in bunk beds, but Donna and the children are in the playroom and Sweets is sitting on her bare mattress in jean cutoffs and a tank top, her shaggy blonde hair loose and a Dum Dum stuck in the corner of her mouth. Mel is opening and closing the doors in the dresser, checking the contents, and they are talking about Donna.

"She didn't want to go," Sweets is saying, "but it bothered her last night. I heard her in the bathroom. Why she ain't want to go, I asked her."

"Some folks just don't like the doctor," Mel says.

"Sure, but if her stomach is giving her that much trouble why can't she just go get it checked out? I don't see what the problem is. She got insurance."

Sweets announces this with a loud sucking *pop* as she removes the Dum Dum from one cheek and inserts it into the other.

"That doesn't mean anything," Mel says. "Plenty of people feel poorly and they go to the doctor and the doctor says they're fine, and then six months later they find out they've got some kind of terminal disease."

"Don't shit me."

"I'm dead serious," Mel says. "It happened to my mom. She went for everything. Physicals. Blood donations. Annual women's exams. Checkups in between the physicals. That woman went to the doctor for every damn thing. If she had indigestion, she called him up. She thought she was being extra cautious. She didn't think that maybe he wasn't so good or that he might not see something. She trusted him. When they found her cancer, there was so much of it her whole entire ovaries were infected with it."

"Jesus," said Sweets.

"Nobody saw it coming," Mel says. "We all used to joke with her. We all said she would live longer than anybody else and that she was a hypochondriac, because if someone had just a little headache she said it was a tumor. He showed us the X-ray and her ovaries were just a big fog of cancer. He cried a little bit and he swore and he said he had never seen any cancer like that kind. A month later she was gone."

"Goddamn, Mel," Sweets says. "How long ago was that?"

"Fifteen years."

"That's good that you all had each other," Sweets says. "Your father and your little sister. You must have given each other strength in your hardship and trouble."

"My dad was a mess. I raised Ellie all by myself. Not that she ever thanked me. You should have seen the state of this place," Mel says abruptly, slamming the last dresser door shut. "I told you, Sweets, you can't wear cutoffs in here. No cutoffs, no spaghetti straps."

"All right," Sweets says.

I hear this as I pause to take a break from the pungency of the fat white bulb, my eyes filled with searing onion tears, and I understand: the campaigning, the Planned Parenthood visits, the rallies, the pro bono lawyer, the charity. Saving the others, I thought, for the one she couldn't save.

The timeline is urgent, Ellie says. We sit on the bench beneath the cross with the bottle of Schnapps and Ellie fills us in on the plan. She cannot sway Dr. Lark from the rebirthing; she cannot convince him the girls are well; she cannot convince him to release them for the final trimester and the labor. She has spoken to the lady doctor named Rachel and the doctor has agreed to contact Dr. Lark and see if she can assist at the rebirthing.

"Will she be able to get the girls released?" Addie says.

"She says if he agrees to let her assist, then she will look out for evidence of any trouble," Ellie says. "If she sees due cause she'll make a complaint and a recommendation to the certifying board, but she prefers to talk to Dr. Lark informally, as a colleague. She said if she saw anything wrong she would advocate for us, though."

"Well, that's something." Mel takes a long drink. "But I think if we could just get the girls *out* it would be such a blessing."

After Ellie leaves I follow Mel back around the building toward the side entrance and stop her before she goes inside. "You know it won't be easy to try and get them both out," I tell her. "There's a better case for Addie."

"They're sisters," Mel says. "They came up together."

"Yes, but Dorian has relapses and Addie doesn't," I say. The figure of Dorian weeping sideways in my arms, those moments of desperate rage, comes back to me. "It will be easier to get Addie out than the both of them."

"They're both God's children," Mel says.

"Yes, but think about the situation, with a sick woman who needs constant help and care living with a woman who has two small babies," I say. "Come on. You always say yourself what it was like growing up with Ellie. Her leaving the house and leaving you to take care of things here and the megachurch and your father and everything.

Don't you think the two of you had to split up at some point? Now she only comes to you when she needs something. Do you want to make the two of them into enablers and dependents?"

"Not enablers," Mel says, guardedly. "Helpers."

"We don't need the kind of help Dorian can offer around two newborn babies," I tell her. "It will be easier to get Addie out."

"I don't know," Mel says, her hand on the door. "Let me think."

It is easier to get Addie out because she follows instructions. She could be trusted with our furtive little secret of the garden; she could be trusted not to lash and bite and bruise. But Dorian is different: more volatile, more unpredictable, more sabotaging.

Of course they were always supposed to live in tandem, Dr. Lark used to say. "You have to work together to see together," he would intone, standing before Dorian and Addie in the light of the seahorse tank. And the two girls would look back obediently—or, if not quite obediently, then at least with some kind of private, unexpressed hope that the cure would work, that it would take them out of the ward and into the real world where people made love and fought and watched television and went to work and bought groceries. In all of those strange reveries and questionings in the light of the tank they saw a glimmer of that world where people were healthy, or where their disorders were at least secret and manageable.

But what if only one of them can be cured? I linger a moment outdoors after Mel has gone inside. What if the cure is all wrong because its basic ambition—to cure *two* women—is all wrong? There is the one woman: pliant, malleable; and there is the other: fierce, combative, passionate. Surely we treat and cure the passionate ones differently than we treat and cure the compliant ones? For Addie maternity might be a rehabilitation, a biological and genetic awakening of a desire to nurture and protect that was stamped out of her with those grisly, unspoken acts of a faraway childhood and the influence of a sad and disturbed mother. But Dorian? What if the cure cannot work the same way because her genetic wiring is different? What if it's Dorian, not Addie, who carries forth the damaged coding of the mother?

Then it would be a disaster to install them both in the little apartment over the square with its sunshine and its gleaming hardwood, to entrust them with the care of children who will grow up and act in the ways they learn there. Perhaps the daughters, too, would split into a good and a bad, a passionate and a calm sister: the first and the second twin, Dorian and Addie, Ellie and Mel. Like beads of oil dancing in a pan: that fiery separation and that inevitable and endless and blazing recombination of sisters.

***

Dr. Lark has upped the dosage. Where there used to be two capsules a day there are now three, arriving in the same humdrum, unannounced way as the other prescriptions, with no note or explanation. He has guessed at my increasing tolerance, I reflect, looking through the orange plastic at the threatening, beguiling capsules. That was how Marilyn Monroe went, from taking too many barbiturates. Clutching the telephone, they said, while she was splayed out on the bed. This was on a late-night episode of *Celebrity Scandals* that came on in the ward at eleven on a Friday (sometimes Ellie let them stay up on Fridays), as Dorian and Addie sat slack-jawed and bewildered by the unaccustomed garishness of *E!* The Entertainment Channel. That garishness, in turn, had been made suddenly available by the absence of Dr. Lark, by his waltzing out of his office earlier that night in his bachelor's dissolute blaze of khaki and polo shirt and Rolex and silver temples.

"What's a barbit? turate?" Dorian sounded out, as Ellie came into the common area.

"It's what you take that makes you calm," Ellie said.

"It's what she took too," Dorian said, and pointed at the shot of Marilyn on the screen, the one where she is laughing with the white dress blowing straight up over her thighs. "Did it make her calmer?"

"Too calm," Ellie said, and Dorian said, "I should think so," and Addie laughed a strange, braying laugh, and that was that. Dorian and Marilyn and me. Triangulated through a calm that kills. *Many patients have died this way*, Dr. Lark used to say of the cure. *Many doctors have died this way too.* But he will be more gradual, more cautious, in his assault.

In Mel's charity there are other Dorians and Addies, other configurations of the disorder. It is as if the women inside the ward have blended into the women outside the ward, as if all women are variations of the same sickness. Sweets, the one with Dorian's hard stare, comes up to me after Ellie has left and Mel has gone into her back room and I am in the kitchen making a list of needed supplies before I leave for the night. Sweets comes into the kitchen with her frayed cutoff threads trailing down her legs like streamers and her blonde hair loose and her chin jutting in that way recovering addicts always jut: that sideways movement of the jaw, the restless movements of the eyes up to yours and then down and away as they are talking. She leans against the long cutting board at the sandwich station and says, "You ever work in a place like this before?"

"Like what kind of a place?"

"Like this kind of a place. With lots of women."

"Yes. Before this place."

"They had women and children there?"

"Just women."

"So what do you know about us?" Sweets says. She presses herself back against the sandwich board as if she is trying to get more leverage to assault me with. Her jaw hitches back and forth around an imaginary lollipop.

"I don't know about every woman," I say. "I only know about some of them."

"Yeah, I think you're right," she says. "As a matter of fact, you know what? I don't even know if I agree with you on that. I'm not sure I agree with you on anything. I don't think you know shit about any woman in any place."

"Go to bed, Sweets."

She stops rolling her jaw and laughs a terrible laugh.

"I mean it, Sweets. Go to bed. Or I'll call Mel."

"All right, all right. Don't do that," she says, taking a few steps toward the door. "Don't you get Mel upset too. Leave her be. Why do you hang around her so much?"

"I help her out here, Sweets. She asked me to. That's all. Go to bed."

"I'm not impressed with the *helping out*," she snaps. "You had better not ever fuck with Mel."

"Go to bed, Sweets," says a voice somewhere behind us, and I turn to see Mel in the gray sweatpants and white T-shirt she always wears to bed, standing in the doorway with her hair brushed and smooth. Sweets saunters out of the kitchen.

Mel's tone is weary, unsurprised. "You have to be patient with them," she says. "They've seen terrible hardship."

Then there is Dorian before me, or a vision of Dorian, during the restraint, her teeth clenched and her eyes shut, tears streaming into her tangled hair as I clutch her to me, desperately reining in her limbs as they quake and jar against mine.

"I know it," I say.

***

"They're *friends*," Ellie says.

"What?" Mel says. "How?"

We are in front of the cross again, and it is late at night. Ellie is trying to light a cigarette but her hands are shaking too badly. Her voice and face are tight with the strain of keeping back angry tears.

"She was his *mentor*," Ellie says. "She's the one who practically *invented* rebirthing with him. She got in touch with him, and now he knows she's coming and that I went behind his back, and she must know that he knows I went to her. She can't help us."

"Jesus, Ellie," Mel says. "When did all this happen?"

"Today," Ellie says, and finally she is able to strike and light and take a drag, her hand still shaking. "He almost fired me. He was angry. I think if he wasn't so set on the rebirthing, he would have let me go. But he can't—there's no one else there who knows the girls well enough. I called the medical board too. They said they'd investigate but I'm pretty sure they just dismissed me as a kook. I tried everything."

"I'm so sorry, Ellie," Mel says.

"It's okay." Ellie pitches the cigarette into the fountain and for once Mel does not protest but sits still and waits. "It does mean we need to act fast, though," Ellie says. "We can't count on the doctor—Rachel. We need to get the girls out ourselves. Is the apartment ready?"

"The apartment is ready," Mel says, softly. "But, Ellie, we need to think about this a little more. We can't rush and make bad decisions. There are innocent people's lives on the line."

"Yes, and if we leave them there, Dr. Lark is going to rebirth them, and if they make it through that, he's going to come up with some reason why they still have to stay there, no matter what happens," Ellie says. "They might be cured, but they will never leave. You should see him now. You try to point out anything wrong, you try to say we should think or wait, and straight away he says you're against the cure, against the treatment, against the whole enterprise. We have to get them away from him on our own."

"All right," Mel says. "It's upsetting. I know. But we might have to change the plan a little. It might be better to get Addie out first. She's in the most danger."

"It doesn't matter what order we get them out in," Ellie says impatiently, "so long as they both get out."

"No, Ellie, that's not what I mean," Mel says. "I mean we might need to separate them. You've said yourself that Dorian is unpredictable, that she has relapses. Maybe we need to get Addie out first, get her safely into a new place and away from Dr. Lark. Then we think about Dorian."

"What? That's crazy," Ellie says.

"It's not crazy. Think about it."

"No. How can you say that? They have to get out together. If we manage to get Addie out he'll make sure Dorian stays there forever."

"But the safety of the children needs to be our top priority right now. It'll be easier to move Addie."

"No," Ellie says. "I'm not even going to think about that. Forget it."

"Ellie—" Mel begins.

"I said forget it," Ellie says. "I'm on the ground and I know how it is with them and how it is with him, and I'm not even going to consider what you're suggesting right now. So just forget it."

Together we stare at the fountain, feeling the weight of the silence while the arcs of water leap up and kiss the arms of the cross. Ellie and Mel. Mel and Ellie. Two statues with hard faces, their skin sealing into twin masks of stone.

At midnight Ellie leaves abruptly, with a frosty goodbye.

"Want to go for a drive?" Mel says.

"Now?"

"I don't think I can sleep."

"Okay," I say. I feel in my pocket for the capsules and place one under my tongue while she goes in to get her keys. We crawl through the parking lot in Mel's boxy white Volvo, its muffler battering all the way down the interstate, past the golden World's Fair Sunsphere and through the park to the little row of parking spaces at the back of the building over the square where Addie will live. Mel pops the trunk and calls me over. I leave off investigating the small hedge behind the apartment, the one filled with pulsing lightning bugs that remind me painfully of Sandy.

"I thought we might drop this off," she says.

I take the box of used baby clothes from her trunk and we climb up to the apartment the back way, up the steel gratings of the fire escape. Our footsteps ring hollow and full into the night. Inside, the apartment looks full and comforting, with a bright red area rug, a scratched wooden coffee table, a vase of cheerful silk daisies, and the yellow sofa we bought at the Salvation Army. We sit together and take it all in.

"You've done so much with the place," I tell her. "When did you find the time?"

"Sometimes I come here at night when all the women are asleep," Mel says. "Just to get away. When I start to think of all of the women and children in there, breathing and sleeping, and there are so many of them, and it feels like so much."

Her voice is tired. She is leaning back on the sofa with her hands resting on either side of her. I take one of them and squeeze it.

"You should let me help out more," I say.

"No. You've done plenty. And you have plenty of work to do still," Mel says.

In the lamplight her hair is soft, the individual strands of it framing her face, and the slender contours of her arm muscles stand out. She is solid and gentle.

"But you're right," she adds, almost to herself. "This apartment is for Addie. It's for you and Addie to make it right."

When she says this everything that is righteous and angry about her seems to collapse in the slump of her shoulders, in the press of her body against the T-shirt, and what is left is what I saw back at the protests, that serenity of confident dedication, but also that private longing and that loneliness. Instinctively I slip my hand up her arm to that slender muscle in her shoulder. Mel looks up and sees the same thing that I see, and there is a look in her eyes of horror at herself and at me. Her skin is warm against my hand and before us there is a sudden and unasked question, growing larger and larger in the stillness, looming and pulsing.

"Is it okay?" I ask.

"Yes," she says. "Yes."

She closes her eyes.

Chapter 8

Dr. Lark

One week before the rebirthing I begin to have my dream. In this dream the canals are the same but the rebirthing takes place in the old Bone House, with its glowing lungs and ribs and brains. The canals are in the kitchen. Rachel is there in her white lab coat, supervising, and my mother is sitting at the table coloring her X-rays and drinking from her glass of wine. I have talked through the entire list of questions. "Are you ready to be born?" I say to the murmuring, moving shapes in the canals. The girls inside nod yes, and then the blankets of the first canal are thrown off. It is Andy who emerges, black-eyed and bruised, his helmet pushed onto the back of his skull, his temples flushed with sweat, his eyes glittering. "Have I been quelled?" he asks, in the split second before I wake up.

It is always the same dream, and it encircles me like a fog as I drive to work, do the usual rounds in the ward, sit in my office and fill in reports. Addie waddles around the ward with thick ankles, the lighter and darker patches of skin on her face giving her the aura of a raccoon, and Dorian follows her, fetching her water, settling a pillow behind her lower back on the sofa. At least I've accomplished that much, I reflect, watching them, but then again anyone could have done the holding therapy. It's the rebirthing that will cure them, and it is the cure that they most fear. They dance around it, but it is coming. The ballet of the sick cells. Soon, once and for all, they will recombine and heal.

She cries, as women always do, when I confront her. But unlike most women she chokes it back. It flashes across her face for an instant when I go find her in the kitchenette. She freezes, her shoulders stiff, and then she puts down the wooden spoon and looks straight up into my face and calls me a criminal, a psychotic. The Dr. Kevorkian of therapy.

"I'm not going to apologize for getting in touch with her or anyone else," she says. "You're dangerous. Maybe when the therapy started it was a good thing and brought the girls closer together, but now I'm afraid of what you might do to them. You need professional help."

"You've been working with the girls too long," I tell her. "You're making up fantasies in your head."

"I am not. *You're* making up fantasies—delusions. You're getting rid of everyone here who could help them so you can do whatever you want. And she's going to come here and *help* you? It's sick."

"She'll be here because of you. Not because of me."

Then she calls me a crook, a blackmailer. "You don't know whose those babies are and you don't want to know whose they are. Simon confessed, so you let him take the fall. You got rid of him and now you're isolating Addie and Dorian so they can be completely under your control. Yours and no one else's."

"Watch yourself, Ellie," I warn her.

"I am watching myself. But I'm also watching you. And I'm watching out for them."

"Are you?" I close the space between us so that she is sandwiched between me and the stove, the boiling water steaming behind her. "You're watching out for them, so you call someone else to undercut me? To come along and in a single day reap the benefits of years of painstaking research? You're looking out for them, so you bring in someone who hasn't been living here, who doesn't even know them? I wish you'd just trusted me, Ellie."

Her eyes are filled with frantic hatred.

"You need to trust me," I tell her again. "You need to believe in this to make it work. Soon Addie will be a mother. Do you want her to fight and pinch when she's a mother? Do you want others to have to do the most basic things for her, the cooking and the washing and the cleaning? Is that what you want? For her to be disordered when she's raising her children? Or for her to have to give them up and let others raise them? Because that's what will happen. If she can't get well, the twins will be taken away and placed in a foster home. Or maybe, if they aren't well either, they will live exactly as Addie and Dorian do, and their children and their children's children will have the disorder. If that happens, does it matter who the father is?"

"I want them to get well," she chokes out. "But I want you to stop treating them. You're not well either. Get Dr. Coe, or someone else, anyone. They have no one now, except for me. I'm the only one who's looking out for their best interests."

"You can look out for their best interests until the rebirthing," I tell her. "Then you're fired."

She retaliates, begins to rattle off a string of insults, but I ignore her and walk out of the kitchenette, letting the door swing closed behind me. It is dinnertime. In the common area the girls are watching the third installment of *Orphans in the Wild* and eating from an economy-sized bag of tortilla chips, their eyes never leaving the screen.

"This little koala lost his mother to a traffic accident when a new highway was built through his habitat in the eucalyptus woodlands of Fraser Island in eastern Australia," announces a gentle female voice with an English accent. "Can animal rescue workers train this baby koala to fend for himself in an increasingly populated and deforested environment?" The music swells over an image of the slow-moving marsupial with its smiling jaw and furry ears as I pass through the corridor.

Back in my office the furniture is shoved back to make room for the canals, which wait like hungry animals. They seem to dilate, as a woman's body dilates in the hours before labor.

***

On the phone she is pushy and insistent, as all career women are. I picture her sitting in her house in the evening, still in her work clothes, with her shoes kicked off and a drink in front of her, unable to concentrate.

"What will the temperature in the room be like?" she says.

"Moderate," I tell her. "We'll keep the air on. It will be hotter for them in the canals."

"Sometimes the heat and discomfort is what prompts the breakthrough."

"We have to be careful."

"What about the transcript?"

"I'll read it. I'll take all the questions."

"It might help me to see it too. To give you a break."

"I think the consistency will be good for them. One person speaking."

There is a long pause.

"Okay," she says finally. "Whatever you say. Just know that I'll be there. Seven in the morning, yes?"

"I'll see you then."

After we hang up I stare at the script lying there on my coffee table, next to the empty bottle of Stoli. It has been marked over and revised a million times and I think it looks ridiculous, like the script a hungry young actor mulls over again and again before an audition. I have become an actor in a two-bit melodrama about a girl getting herself knocked up. Still, I reflect, the life within her speaks to that capacity for touch. If you had two patients with attachment disorder and you fixed it, and then they had their own children, what kind of research would that be? Daughters of sisters, sisters themselves, the strong descendants of the damaged and the disordered. Together they would live in the ward I have created.

That night I have the dream again. As before, I am in the Bone House, and the glowing jaws and teeth gawp at me from the windows. The canals are trembling and rocking with the force of the girls inside. But now my mother is gone and Rachel is hovering at the table where my mother should be.

"Are you ready to be born?" I ask the shivering figures—but this time when I whisk the blankets off, it is Addie who is there. Her legs are parted and she has just given birth, unassisted, to Andy.

"Sometimes you have to fail before you can make it work," she says.

When I wake up I am drenched in sweat and the autumn sun is boiling behind the blinds and spilling over my bed. I turn to the alarm clock. Five forty-five.

It is the morning of the cure.

Chapter 9

Dorian, Addie

Dorian

On the morning of the rebirthing we wake up early and get ready in front of the mirror in the bathroom, Addie moving gingerly around the toiletries with her bulky stomach.

"Hold still," Ellie says, and makes Addie succumb to a hair-brushing so vigorous that instead of smoothing her hair it tugs the strands out into a flyaway halo. This is Ellie now: always angry and distracted, always forgetting the briskness and velocity of her fingers. I do not want her to touch my eyes, so I apply the makeup myself, the way she showed me. First the purple liner, on the tender skin just above the eyelashes. My eyes glitter beneath twin arches of violet, greener and more startling than ever, bolder and darker than ever, like the animal eyes that glow in the desert night on *The Wild Animals of the Mojave.*

"Hey," Addie says, catching my eye in the mirror. "You're getting pretty good at that." Her own face is puffy and swollen, the mask of pregnancy like the strange bandit markings of a raccoon.

I finish my eyes and move on to my mouth, filling out my bottom lip with liner, darkening my frown into a red diva pout. "And what shall we wear to the rebirthing?" I say. "How do we attire ourselves for such a grand occasion?"

Ellie tosses me the familiar folded squares of ballooning linen, fresh from the laundry, with the elastic-waisted pants as bright and roomy as sails. They hit me in the side of my shoulder and fall to the floor.

"The same outfit," she says, "that you wear to everything."

Addie

Ellie marches us through the common area and down the corridor toward the faint noise of voices in Dr. Lark's office. She has her hand on the small of my back and her other hand on the small of Dorian's back, but there is a nervous pressure in her fingers, a jumpiness that gets into my bones and makes me feel jumpy too. I picture this sensation slipping into my womb and running along the spines of the twins and there is a responding pressure inside my belly, a faint quaking as the sensation thrums up their bodies and makes them twist and flail.

"Addie, what is it?" Ellie says, stopping us in the hallway. Her face turns to mine, flushed.

"Nothing" I tell her. "Just some little kicks."

In Dr. Lark's office, the room of the rebirthing, everything is hushed and quiet. The overhead lights have been shut off and the room is lit only by the small Tiffany lamp on Dr. Lark's desk, which bathes the mahogany in a warm halo and leaves everything else in the room awash in fuzzy shadows. He has hung a blanket over the mini-blinds to block out the morning light. The bookshelves stand shrouded in blankets too, like silent monks at prayer, their robes trailing into scarlet pools along the floor. Even the clock face is covered, as clocks are covered, I have heard, in the houses of death, the mourners sitting under a symbol of time frozen and stalled, the hands pointing stiffly toward the hour of expiration. All the plaques and diplomas and awards and certifications have been taken away and the desk is pushed against the wall, leaving a gaping space in the center of the room, on the rug. In the middle of this space are the two canals, both shaped like igloos, both draped in folds of blanket, both pierced with the strange artifacts from the house: a shimmering earring here, a scarf folded and knotted there. In between these small, haphazard shelters Dr. Lark sits with a woman I have never seen before.

"Girls, this is Dr. Coe," he says, and the woman comes from a sitting position up onto her knees so that she can reach out and shake hands, first with Dorian, then with me. She is older than Dr. Lark, maybe fifteen or twenty years older, and her hair falls in smooth silver arcs on either side of her face. Her brown eyes have a very direct look, a look that makes it seem as if she knows what you are thinking. Next to her Dr. Lark looks boyish and rumpled in his mustard-stained lab coat and unironed khakis and peppery hair that is at least three inches longer than normal, sprouting around his forehead and ears like the untrimmed hedges by the abandoned garden plot. I gravitate toward the woman, but it is Dr. Lark who holds up the edges of the blanket, his eyes manic and glittering.

"Get in," he says.

Dorian

And then Dr. Lark is arranging the blankets over both of us, so that I am enfolded in the darkness of the canal, the walls of mine pressing up against the walls of Addie's, the space under the blankets warm and damp. It is stuffy in the room and it is even stuffier under the blankets. Dr. Lark is pressing down on the edges of the blanket and he is telling Ellie to press down, to hold her hands on either side of my canal so that I am pinned under and cannot get out. Under the muffle of the fabric, through the beating heat of the blankets, I can still sense the presence of Addie and the twins.

"This is tremendous," I say, raising my voice above the thickness of the blankets that I am coming to regard as sacks: rough, scratchy things that prickle at me like the carpets of pine needles that surround the garden plot. "How long do we sit here before we get reborn?"

"As long as it takes," says Dr. Lark.

Addie

We sit in silence for ten minutes, maybe more, with nothing but the gentle rustle and press of the shuffling, shifting bodies on the other side of us, and the sound of Dorian's impatient, angry panting and her restless movements inside her canal. The heat of my breath, condensing, makes the temperature inside my canal rise. In my stomach the kicks come harder now, more furiously and rapidly, and in my belly there is a flutter of hearts. We are inside of it and they are inside of it, inside of me, fidgeting and twitching as Dorian and I fidget and twitch, all of us blind, all of us surrounded by a damp, amniotic darkness.

There are more minutes of shifting, the sound of a pencil scratching across a clipboard, the faintest birdcalls pushing through the shut window and the shrouding, light-smothering fabrics.

Then Dr. Lark says, "Dorian, tell me what you remember. Tell me about an early memory with you and Addie in it. Tell me about the house in Nashville and about the first time you remember learning how to hit."

Dorian stirs in her canal and the sides of my own absorb some of her jostling. She does not answer. She will not break, I know, or at least she will not break right away; or it could be that she doesn't have an answer and doesn't care enough to lie. If I don't remember, she doesn't remember either. Dr. Lark tries the question again, expectantly, as if asking a sick patient to confirm symptoms he has already privately observed. There is another smothering silence. I feel moisture collecting at my temples, under my armpits, around the folds of my stomach, and in that crease of skin that forms just under the waistband.

Then, in the sharpest moment of that heat, on the crest of Dorian's breathing, there is a subtle shifting outside of the blankets, a temporary release of pressure that seems to indicate some kind of hushed, unspoken conferral.

Now the question comes again, but in a different voice: the woman's voice, low and throaty, a roughened and mature voice of calm self-possession that somehow buries within itself another, more volatile layer: an unpredictable quality that sends shivers thrumming up my abdomen and into my throat.

"Tell me what you remember, Dorian," this voice says, lingering over the name with a dignified, intimate authority. "Tell me and tell the rest of us about an early memory of you and Addie. Tell me about the first time you remember learning how to hit."

Beside me Dorian stirs in her canal, less impatiently this time and with more purpose, and I can tell that she feels the thing that is in the voice too, that underlying current of something that seems like raw emotion and also the antithesis of raw emotion: like the recognition and quelling of some unshakable rage. It hangs in the still, humid air inside the blankets as a hawk glides above the forest in slow circles, dropping imperceptibly, by inches, to its prey.

To my surprise, Dorian begins to speak.

DORIAN

"It was not the first time I learned how to hit. It was the first time I knew that hitting had an effect," I say to the voice that has crept under the blankets like a spider.

"What kind of effect, Dorian?" This is Dr. Lark's voice, floating and official.

"A sleep effect," I say.

We wait.

It was around the time of the first pendulum story or shortly after it, I am sure, the first time I understood the sleep effect. We were six and we were in the old house and they were sitting in the kitchen having one of their "discussions." We were in the living room watching television. The lamp by the couch gave off a small glow and the gauzy curtains over the windows parted to let in a pool of light on the linoleum where I sat with Addie. The window sash was tugged up to let in the breeze, and on the sill a small black oscillating fan turned its face back and forth to us. Each time it rotated toward us it blew strands of Addie's hair across my cheek and sometimes into my mouth.

We were watching *Gorillas in the Wild* on the Nature Channel. The gorillas sat on a hill, black and furry and muscular. The announcer explained that the gorillas were resting through the day's heat and grooming each other. They were grouped in twos and threes on different parts of the slope, picking insects from each other's backs.

The kitchen door was closed but we could still hear the

discussion rising and falling. At intervals I heard the voices pause to drink and the clink of bottles set back onto the table, first gently, then with more force. They were talking in low tones and then their voices took on an urgent quality, dropping suddenly and fiercely, trembling with the effort to stay hushed and then rising suddenly.

My attention was divided between *Gorillas in the Wild* and the sound of their voices. On the screen the great gorilla, the silverback, lumbered on all fours toward the peak of the hill, the muscles in his back heaving, his giant domed head looming over the heads of the others. In the kitchen the voices grew louder and louder and we waited to hear if she would hit, if she would fight him like the females who sometimes got mad and hit at their mates, who waved their hands away and crawled majestically up the hill.

Just as the silverback was reaching the crest, Addie crawled on her hands and knees over to the kitchen door, scooted up against it, and cupped her ear to the wood. Her face gathered into a look of concentration.

"What?" I said. "What? What?"

She put a finger to her lips to shush me and beckoned me over with her free hand. I crawled over the floor as she had done, on my hands and knees, and took my place beside her at the door.

We listened.

***

Addie

"What were they fighting about?" Dr. Lark says. It is hard to think in the slow, static heat with my limbs and abdomen cramping from the way we sit and sit and sit. I think back to the voices speaking frantically in the kitchen, the rise and fall, the one voice—her voice—climbing the register while his hardened and grew firm at a lower pitch.

"I don't know," I say. "They always fought."

But then I remember a pleading note entering his voice, and then it was her voice that grew more and more firm, at the same time that it grew shrill with a desperate resolve. A bottle dropped hard against the floor and shattered. Neither Dorian nor I flinched. We sat facing each other, sitting back on our ankles, our knees touching, our ears pressed up against the wood, straining to hear over the swell of horns that accompanied the silverback's slow, majestic crawl up the slope.

"No," I say. "It was because she was sick, he said."

"He was upset because she was ill?" Dr. Lark says.

"No," I say. "Not ill like that. He said she was sick in another way. He wanted her to get help. To leave. He wanted to take her to get help and he wanted Stella to come stay with us."

Who was going to help her? The first time he said it, it seemed like that word, *help*, was the word that it was: getting help with dinner, getting help with carrying in groceries from the car. But then the way he pronounced it, kept saying it, gave it some awful, tragic quality. Now his voice was louder than hers, so loud in its pain that I could hear it as clearly through the door as if he were shouting directly into our ears.

I am silent, remembering this. The twins kick and twist.

"What happened then?" Dr. Lark says. "What did they say?"

"I don't know."

"You don't know because you didn't hear? Or because they didn't say anything else?" the woman's voice cuts in, smoothly.

"I don't know because they got up," I say. "I don't know because we had to run away from the door."

Run, I just said, but didn't we crawl? In the kitchen the chair legs scraped back against the floor and the sound of her crying grew louder. We shot across the carpet on all fours, Dorian and I, back to our spot in front of the television. When the door burst open and she came through it, still weeping, and ran into the bedroom, we were seated again in that little halo of light in front of the screen, our hair stirring in the wind from the fan.

The silverback gorilla had reached the top of the hill and straightened himself slowly into a standing position. He stood with his great chest bared, his awful muscles flaring, commanding the slope. The music surged.

***

Dorian

Trying to remember without holding her hand, trying to look together and to see together, feels different to me inside these canals. I cannot feel her skin or the grip of her palm; I can only sense her stirring inside her canal, feel the way her shifts and fidgets ripple the walls of my own. But her voice still comes to me, muffled yet clear, and the associations it brings awaken all the sounds and smells and temperatures and colors of that memory between us. In the spaces of the canals, back and forth under our respective blankets, the story forms. It is as if a small animal, a little herding dog, were trotting back and forth between us, slipping first into her canal and then crawling under the blankets into mine, its tail wagging, moving our memories closer and closer.

"What happened after she went into the bedroom?"

This is the woman's voice again: steady, even.

"She cried," I say.

She must have cried for half an hour in that bedroom. The crying was not muffled, not like the way Addie sometimes cried when she did not want our mother to notice. It was loud and for us to all to hear, to be included in. It battled with the sound of the television and the whir of the fan and the heavy sound of bootfalls in the kitchen as our father went to get another beer. The refrigerator door sucked open and there was a *clink* and then the door sighed closed again, the bootfalls returning to the table, the creak of the wooden chair receiving the weight of his body. It was dinnertime, but there were no cooking smells in the kitchen, no sounds of running water or clanging pans. Addie and I sat together, tense and still, waiting.

On the television the gorillas began to lumber up the hill on their long arms and legs toward the silverback. Some of them were alone; others bore their wide-eyed, wrinkle-faced young on their backs.

Soon his weight yawned away from the chair and the bottle came down and the bootfalls crossed the kitchen and he appeared in the doorway of the living room and stood there for a while, watching us. I do not remember him well. He had a tall, wiry frame and wrists that were sinewy with muscle, and his bare arms often had fading, metallic streaks of grease from his work at the garage. But it is hard to know his face anymore, anything about the features. I remember not a face as much as a look that I would describe now as a resigned sadness but that at the time struck me as something else, something that made me look away.

"What would you have said it made you feel then, that look?" comes the woman's voice, the voice with the metallic ring. "What would you call it if you were there again, right now?"

"Defeat," I say. "Weakness."

"Why defeat and weakness?"

"He always lost."

"He always lost what?"

"He was the weaker of the two."

The woman's voice is silent, waiting.

"She always won," I explain. "He always did what she wanted. He could never make her do anything that he said."

"I see," she says. "So what did he do after he lost this fight?"

"He went to lie down on the couch."

"Did he seem upset? Was he crying?"

"No. He was tired."

"So what did he do then?"

"He came to the sofa."

"By himself?"

"With his bottle."

"What did you do then?"

"We watched the gorillas."

"So he went to lie down because he was tired," comes Dr. Lark's voice. It is a little strangled, as if he is trying not to sound too eager. "Then what happened?"

"He fell asleep," I say.

"And?" Dr. Lark says.

He fell asleep. The crying in the bedroom died down, then quieted entirely, and there was only the sound of the television. *Gorillas in the Wild* was over and a new show was coming on, *The World of the Chimpanzee*. The opening credits rolled over a line of chimps loping on long arms across a grassy expanse, their weird bald faces shining in the sun. The fan moved its face from side to side, and the faraway buzz of a lawnmower came through the open window.

Behind us there was the sound of our father's breathing,

the breathing of a deep sleep, coming at long intervals from the sofa.

On the television, the setting changed from the wild chimpanzees on the grassy clearing to captive chimps in a zoo, sitting in a cluster under a tree.

"Violence is a normal part of life for chimpanzees," explained the voiceover. "New studies show that chimpanzees are the only species we know of that is more violent than humans. While some researchers have concluded that violence among chimpanzees may have been caused by human interference with their food sources and habitats, a new study at the Yerkes National Primate Research Center in Atlanta suggests that episodes of chimpanzee violence stem not from human contact but from the number of males and the population density of a given chimp community."

As he spoke the camera rose above a crowd of zoo visitors, some in hats, some taking pictures. They were all pointing and gesturing excitedly toward two of the chimpanzees, who were fighting. One of them, the larger one, was ambling calmly away from a tree toward a large crop of rocks, while the smaller one shrieked at his retreating back, beating the ground with long, furious arms. As we watched, the smaller one scooped up some mud into a ball and began to pelt the larger one. Still he walked away with his majestic back turned, this elder chimp: elegant, imperturbable. Enraged, the smaller chimp seized a large stick from the ground and chased the rival, striking at his back, screeching. The crowd of visitors hollered and pointed and took pictures. The chatter of the chimpanzees filled the living room and overpowered the long, dragging breath of our father on the couch.

Addie stirred beside me.

"I'm bored," she said. "Let's play a game."

Addie

How is it she remembers it all so well? The shrill violence of the smaller chimpanzee, the neck of the fan twisting slowly as if it were shaking its head at us? But that's Dorian, living from moment to moment of passion, vividly remembering and then submerging her anger, recalling it in those hallucinatory bursts.

My memory is different. It is more spare and only comes in short beats after Dorian's, as if she were wandering through my recollections and opening doors, throwing open windows, switching on lights. Those parts she wants to animate become brighter, starker, more colorful; the parts she does not say remain closed and dusty and blank.

Inside it is growing more and more damp and it is hard to concentrate with the sweating and the thick air and the shifting of the heartbeats in my belly. I can feel them trying to beat together, those twin hearts, and just missing the rhythm every time: as if their heartbeats are syncopated, the rhythm slanted and asymmetrical.

"What game?" Dorian had said.

"Truth or Dare."

"Okay. Truth or Dare?"

"No, I picked so I go first. Truth or Dare?"

"Dare."

"But you always pick Dare. You never say Truth."

"Fine. Truth, then."

"Tell me the truth," I said. "Who always wins? Her or him?"

"She does," Dorian said promptly.

"Why?" I said. "She's always crying."

"She always wins because he can't make her do anything she doesn't want to do. Plus, she's stronger," Dorian added.

"Who do you love more?" I said.

"Her."

"How come?"

"That's enough," Dorian said. "I already answered two truths. Now it's my turn. Truth or Dare?"

"Dare."

"Okay," Dorian said. "I double-dare you to hit him with the bottle like the chimp hit the other chimp with the stick."

We both turned to look back at the brown bottle standing upright on the coffee table, the one he had set down before he went to sleep. He had pulled the label off and ripped it into tiny pieces that blew like confetti across the table each time the fan purred its breath over us.

"We'll get in trouble," I said.

"No we won't," Dorian said. "She's asleep."

We listened together for the sound of her muffled crying and heard nothing. On the television the scene had cut away from the zoo to a group of chimps sitting in a nut grove with their furry legs splayed, bringing down rocks and stones on top of the single nuts they had plucked. Their movements were blunt and forceful and their heads were bent in concentration.

"This nut grove is prime real estate for roaming gangs of chimpanzees," the voiceover intoned. "These chimps may look playful and relaxed, but at any moment they are ready to fight back in case of a raid." As if on cue, one of the chimps stood up to his full height, grabbed hold of a tree branch, and shook it violently, startling the other chimps and sending nuts raining to the ground.

"Fine," I said. "I'll hit him with the bottle if you hit him with that stick."

I pointed at the brass fireplace poker hanging up next to the little brass shovel and the black brush our mother used to sweep the ashes back away from the rug.

"He'll wake up," Dorian said.

"No, he won't," said a voice behind us.

Dorian

She seemed taller all of a sudden when she stood up straight and looked down at us with her long skirt trailing over her bare feet and her arms crisscrossed with scratches from where she had clawed herself in the bedroom, worn out and yet majestic all the same, like the gorilla when he unfolded himself on top of the hill. She was standing in the doorway of the hall that led from the bedrooms out into the living room, tall, shadowy, and—I think now—criminal, her eyes red-ringed from the crying, but not sad now, not fierce. With a different sort of expression that seemed like curiosity. Her voice measured, calm.

"He won't wake up at all," she said. "He'll just keep sleeping."

"Really?" Addie said.

"Really," she said, and it was the same voice she used when she told Addie to take the spider away from her shoulder, a low and steady voice. "Try not to get scared about what I'm about to tell you. Do you think I would tell you something that would make him angry? Do you think I would tell you something that would put you in danger?"

"No," said Addie.

"What about you, Dorian?" she said. "Do you think I would tell you to do something that would bring you harm?"

"No," I said.

"Then listen closely to what I'm about to say. Look at him. Do you see what happened? He went to sleep. He wants to be more asleep than he is. That's why he came out to sleep here, where you are. He wants to sleep more deeply now, and for longer."

We looked at him lying perfectly still on the couch, his mouth slightly open, his chest rising and sinking under his dark-blue mechanic's uniform. He was younger than our mother, and the skin on his cheeks was smoother, and his eyes were not red from crying like hers always were.

"He's like the hedgehogs we watched on the television," our mother explained. "The ones who get into their little scratchy nests in the winter and go into a deep sleep, so their heart rate goes down and they can stay warm. You have to make him hibernate. You have to make him sleep with the poker. Do you think you can do that, Dorian? Do you think you can do that without getting afraid?"

Her eyes were puffy but fierce, and her eyebrows were raised, waiting. Addie was looking at me too, her eyes wide, awed and a little jealous. She looked at me and they both looked at me together and they were waiting for me to decide.

The chimps were dozing in a thick forest grove. It was nighttime in the wild, and the camera was showing a series of close-ups of the wildlife and foliage that surrounded the furry, slumbering bodies: a damp, dewy spider web so magnified that you could see each individual strand, the bright green leaves of a bush trembling under the weight of the droplets that surged onto it from an adjacent waterfall, a tree frog with its sky-facing eyes and webbed gelatinous hands and feet clutching a tree branch. "These chimps may be sleeping," the announcer said, "but the jungle never sleeps."

I went to get the poker.

Addie

When our mother spoke that way, quietly and calmly, I felt afraid, more afraid of her than I felt when she was yelling at our father in the kitchen and crying in the bedroom. Her voice seemed as remote and bodiless as it had when she told me to remove the spider and take it outside. But when I looked back at our father sleeping, at his slack, unsuspecting face, I felt an energy stir in me and a wildness that seemed to come from the television, from the images of the chimpanzees, until I looked at Dorian standing and watching him too and I realized that the feeling came from her.

"Listen very closely to my instructions," our mother said. "Can you still do that, Dorian? Can you listen without becoming afraid?"

"Yes," Dorian said.

Dorian's dark hair was bound in a ponytail and she was wearing gray sweatpants and the pink long-sleeved shirt our mother always dressed her in, the one with the pattern of green dinosaurs all over it. She stood next to the couch with the poker dangling from her hand and looked at him. The poker was the same length as the distance from her waist down to the ground and it was made of golden brass, smudged here and there with ashes from the fireplace. He still slept soundly. Each of his inhalations seemed as long as his exhalations, all of his breathing long and delayed and symmetrical. His body sank into the couch, so heavy with slumber that it seemed each breath merged him more deeply with the sofa cushions. Was there a sounder sleep than this?

"Listen to me," our mother said from the doorway. "The

first stroke is the most important one. It needs to be right. You'll need to grip the poker better than that, Dorian. Maybe take it by the middle, instead of at the end. You'll get more control over it that way."

Dorian wielded the brass poker in her hands like a tiny baton twirler, got a firm grip on the middle. Still he slept.

"Raise it back and wait," our mother said.

Dorian reached the poker overhead, her arms fully outstretched. She paused, her small arms trembling.

"Breathe, Dorian," our mother said. "Take a sharp breath in. Inhale. Exhale. Now bring it down. One stroke. As hard as you can."

Dorian let her breath out in one whoosh and brought down the poker. It flashed for one instant in the light and then it connected and slammed his head back deeper into the pillow. It was like the way our heads slammed back on the roller-coaster seats at the amusement park they always took us to whenever one of us had a birthday. When the coaster started to go fast, really fast, the force of the air made our whole bodies go flat against the cushions. That was the way his head was pressed into the sofa now. Like all the pressure and wind of the world was against him.

Then he opened his eyes.

The pupils were foggy and glazed, and there was a trickle of blood coursing down over one of the eyelids. It dampened his eyelashes and made them look even blacker.

Dorian froze.

"Dorian, raise it again and strike," came the voice. "Now.

Forget about the eyes."

Dorian reached the poker high and brought it down again, harder, in a series of sharp staccato strikes—frightened, I think, by the weird glassy stare and that little scarlet rivulet. She shrieked as the attacking chimp had shrieked, and the force of the blows drove his head more deeply into the cushions. I could no longer see his eyes open in between the blunt, rapid strokes. But I saw his arms clumsily grope for Dorian, his hand finally making a lumpy claw around her shoulder. Dorian screamed and I screamed and I ran forward to stop his arm, to pry it off of her. She tried desperately to twist away while I grabbed at his fingers and tried to uncurl them. But his hands were too strong from gripping tools and fixing engines all day. I seized the beer bottle in a panic at the sight of Dorian dancing and twisting, screaming as if her shoulder was on fire, and I smashed it down over his claw. The bottle exploded against the veins in the back of his hand and he yanked his hand away, and underneath it Dorian's shoulder welled with sudden trickles of blood, splinters of brown glass sprinkling over her dinosaur shirt.

"Listen to me," our mother said, calmly, her voice somehow cutting through Dorian's screeches and the sound of the blows. "You're almost finished. Hold your hands over his mouth."

I put both my hands over his mouth and pressed down, hard. The force of my hands made the blood come faster from the wounds in his cheeks. His eyes were closed and his arms flailed, but they were weaker now and fell back to his chest easily when Dorian struck them. She took aim again and hit his skull, hard. I could feel the whoosh of the air separating around the poker as it came down. I closed my eyes and pressed down on the mouth as firmly as I could, the warm moisture of the breath dampening my palms in short coughs and then not coming at all, the same way the air goes out of a balloon when it sails away from you in a circle and then comes to rest at your feet, crumpled and flat.

"That's enough," our mother said, never raising her voice by even a decibel. "Dorian, go and put the poker back where it belongs, next to the fireplace. You girls have a seat and rest and watch your program."

Our mother faded from the doorway and went back into the bedroom. Dorian went, obediently, to hang up the poker. I took my hands away from the flat slack mouth and the red-smeared features, the saggy, ragged face of the man in his deepest sleep, and went to sit back on the carpet in front of the television. Dorian took her place next to me. There were dots of glass and slashes of blood all over her dinosaur shirt. It looked as if she had been painting or doing an arts and crafts project. The fan hummed peacefully at us. For a moment the sound of our panting blotted out the sound of the television and we both sat breathing heavily and letting the currents blow the damp strands of hair off our foreheads.

On the nature show the chimpanzees had left the nut grove and moved into a clearing where they were foraging for more food. The camera showed a shot of the entire clearing with the roaming chimps before it cut closer to one chimp who was thrusting a stick into the hole in the middle of a log and tapping it around in a clumsy circle. "This chimp is using a specially fashioned tool to penetrate this swarm of army ants," the announcer explained. As we watched, the ants surged angrily onto the stick, and then the chimp brought the stick to his mouth and gobbled the ants down.

From the bedroom came the sounds of the closet door and the dresser drawers opening and shutting.

Our father slept.

We watched the chimp eat his fill of ants and move with the others downstream. They were moving in a roundabout way back to the nut grove when our mother appeared again in the doorway with her purse and her suitcase.

"Girls," she said.

It was the same voice but it sounded different now: disembodied, panicked, tracing our spines with cold fingers of alarm.

"Listen very carefully to me now," she said. "I need to go around the corner for some things and I need for you to stay right where you are. I want you to start counting. Can you do that for me?"

"Yes," we said in unison.

"Count to two hundred," she said. "By the time you get done counting I'll be back."

"One," Dorian began.

***

Dorian

We counted obediently until the front door had sucked open and shut behind her and then we stopped and looked behind us at the pulpy thing on the couch. Addie wanted to know if I was scared.

"I'm not scared," I said. "What would I be scared of?"

"Of him when he wakes up," she said.

"He's not going to wake up."

"When she comes back in," Addie said, "he's going to hear the door and he's going to wake up."

"He won't wake up."

"I'm going to ask her to be quiet when she comes back," Addie said, "so she doesn't bother him."

We both looked up at the grandfather clock with its stern oval face, its two spidery fingers reaching apart to twelve and six, the pendulum swaying and tocking.

There was an endless series of minutes.

On the television the chimpanzee show had ended and a new show about lion cubs was coming on.

"We already saw this one," Addie said.

"They just play the same ones again and again," I said. "We should change it."

"We have to get permission," she said.

"Lions will prey on lions they don't recognize as part of the pride," the announcer told us. "This lioness hides her cubs from the rest of the pride to protect them while they're young."

We stared at the blind, squirming cubs, their brown fur and tiny ears all jumbling together as they clustered around the teat.

"You were scared," Addie jeered, when the clock had chimed nine and we had been sitting for hours transfixed before the television, first watching the lion cubs nurse and tumble and then watching two more programs, one about crayfish and another about the ecosystem of the Amazon River basin. We had consumed an entire box of Pop-Tarts, the silver wrappers crinkled and littered all around us, and Addie's mouth was red with cherry filling. The blood on my hands and on my shirt had dried and hardened into crispy, dark scabs. "I saw you when he opened his eyes."

"You were scared too," I said.

Had I been scared? There was the blank expression in his eyes when they fell open, the same way the eyes of a doll I used to have fell open when you tilted her backward and forward, the plastic eyelids clicking awake and shut. This doll used to cry, too, if you pressed her stomach one way, or giggle if you pressed her stomach another way. The gurgling, automatic sounds came out of her vinyl-and-plastic body without any variation, so that the sadness of the crying and the hilarity of the giggles and the clicking of the eyelids were all part of the same dull, heartless mechanism. That was how the falling open of his eyes and the little grunting noises he made when the blows hit sounded to me. So why was I afraid? It was the reaching out of the arms, I think now: that futile effort of the doll to come awake, to fend for itself.

Addie disappeared into our bedroom and came back out with a bundle of pastel blankets, one already wrapped around her shoulders, the other one trailing from her hands. She kept stepping on it and almost fell twice before she plunked down next to me on the carpet. Beside us, the grandfather clock gave the short chime of nine fifteen.

"Let's get the pillows and sleep out here," Addie said, "in case she comes back."

Neither of us wanted to sleep on the couch next to him, so we shoved aside the empty Pop-Tart wrappers and slept on the carpet in front of the television, where the cool air of the fan sang over us and the warm colors pulsed from the screen. I laid next to her under the blanket. My arms were sore from lifting the poker and I felt very hungry and alone.

The next morning we awoke to the sound of knocking at the door.

Addie stirred next to me. "Maybe it's her," she said.

"Why would she knock?"

I crept out of the blankets to the window next to the door and pulled aside the curtain just the slightest bit to see out. In front of our door, standing in his light-blue uniform, was the mailman who used to sometimes linger on our porch and talk to our mother when there was a package to sign for. He would hand her the stylus and the device with the brown screen and she would sign it and take the package and then he would remain there in the doorway, asking her about work and about our dad and about her children. About us. On the week of Christmas she always bought a card for him and gave it to him to open and read on the porch and he would take out the folded bills and thank her and she would smile and wave away his thanks. *It's nothing*, she would say, in her high, happy voice, the voice that so suddenly and easily warbled into tears. *Absolutely nothing.*

I let the curtain fall and walked back to where Addie sat on the carpet rubbing her eyes, her blond hair tangled around her shoulders.

"It's the mailman," I announced. "He has a package."

"Should we let him in?"

"What for? She's not here to sign."

Addie shrugged. She took the remote, aimed it at the television, and turned the volume all the way up, as high as it would go.

"In some cultures these beautiful black birds are considered bad luck or pests," the announcer's voice boomed. "But new research suggests that these unique creatures are smarter than almost any animal in the animal kingdom, even rivaling the apes. Join us today on *Birds of the World* to hear the unique story of the American crow."

The light and the noise splashed over us and a new day was beginning. Behind us, he slept.

There was another endless series of minutes.

"When is she coming back?" Addie said.

"I don't know," I said. "Maybe she got lost."

It was noon and the sun outside was blazing through the curtains into the room, lighting up the litter of Pop-Tart wrappers and empty Cheetos bags. We were sitting on the blankets watching crocodiles slink through the river, their eyes and scaly foreheads looming up from the water. Our fingers were a bright, artificial orange, and there was orange around Addie's mouth and streaks of orange on the stomach of her shirt where she had wiped her fingers. She picked up a Capri Sun, turned it upside down, and expertly pierced the bottom with the pointy end of the straw. The plastic straw wrapper clung to the back of her hand and she shook it away impatiently.

"What if he wakes up before she gets back?" she said. "What are we supposed to tell him?"

"Tell him she went out," I said.

"What if he gets mad?"

"He won't get mad," I said.

"What if she never comes back?" she said. "What if he never stops hibernating? Will we go live with another family?"

"I don't know," I said.

Afternoon fell and then nighttime. Still he slept. The shows came on and the animals roamed and slept and ate and then the shows were over and new shows began. We watched shows about the cheetah, about the hummingbird, about the Eastern coyote. All day, the animals stalked and flew and hunted. They groomed themselves and they groomed each other and they napped and they fought and they nursed their young. On and on he hibernated. Back and forth went the fan with its whirring, windy face. Beside me, that night, Addie stirred and thumped restlessly, twisted her face and fists in the blankets, began to cry. She cried on and off all night, her tears wetting the pillow we shared, and I laid awake longing to cover her mouth with my hands and make her stop. In the morning she sniffled herself awake and I saw the dried, gluey streaks on her sleeve where she had been wiping her nose.

Outside it was overcast and the grey light in the room collapsed over us. I laid and listened for the sound of his breathing under the sound of Addie's little sobs and heard nothing. My stomach was very empty.

On the television the show about the chimpanzees was repeating. Again I watched them shrieking and wielding their sticks, clobbering nuts open with the rocks, forking the buzzing ants out of their hiding place. Still Addie sniffled.

Without warning, I began to cover Addie with blows, raining my fists down on her shoulders, along her stomach, on the side of her neck. She rolled away from me under the blankets and screamed, covering her head and her tangled hair with her arms, tugging the blankets over her body. I hit even harder, waiting to see the angry red marks my fists would leave on her skin, gripping her hair, listening for her screams to become more vivid and desperate.

Why was Addie the only person I knew who was not like that doll with its rattling eyelids? Not like the plastic, artificial sound of our mother crying or of our father grunting softly on the sofa in that hollow, foggy moment before he raised his arms? She was something else, something that was made of me too. Our flesh was not the same as the flesh of others. Our eyes had a different expression. I must have recognized her expression because it was the same one that I knew was in my eyes, that blank, focused stare in the moment when she lifted her gaze to me, right before she pressed her hands over his mouth.

Addie's shrieks grew louder and she reached out to claw at me, to pinch me. Underneath her screams I heard the pounding of the mailman at the door. This time he did not stay and wait but instead turned the knob and let the door sway open on its hinges, and suddenly a blast of air and light was in the room. We froze, tangled in blankets, our arms wrapped around each other. He stood in the doorway in his uniform with his bag slung over his shoulder and watched us.

"Hello, girls," he said in his friendly way. He was tall and his face was tan, like our father's. He was holding the same package I had seen in his arms yesterday morning. "I'm sorry to barge in," he said, "but I heard screaming and I wanted to make sure everything was okay."

"Everything is fine," Addie said.

He looked long and hard at her as adults do when they think you're telling a fib and they're waiting for you to break down and confess.

"Is your mom home?" he said. "She's got a package here."

"No one is here to sign," Addie said.

"What about your dad?" he said.

"He's hibernating," Addie said, and pointed at the couch.

The mailman stepped over the threshold, looked in, and then, suddenly, stepped back and swore. For a second he held his hand over his mouth.

We sat tangled in our blankets on the floor and watched him as he retched in the doorway.

Then he leaned down, still coughing, and beckoned to me and Addie. We unwound ourselves from the covers and padded over to him in our bare feet with our dirty hair around our shoulders and our clothes smeared with Cheetos dust and dried blood.

"Listen to me, very carefully," he said. "Is there anyone else in this house?"

"Our mother was here," Addie said, "but she went out."

"Okay," he said. "Okay. Okay."

But the way he said okay was not the way people usually said it when everything was fine or when they agreed with you about something. He kept looking nervously over the tops of our heads.

"Is there anyone else in this house?" he said. "Has anyone come into this house since your mother left?"

"No," we said.

"Listen, girls," he said. "I need you to come with me, out to my truck, right now. Would you like to ride in the mail truck? Would you like to do that?"

"We have to get permission," Addie said.

"No," the mailman said, and that stalling tone fell away and he became more certain. "You don't need to get any permission. I want you to come and follow me out to the mail truck. Right now."

"But what if we get into trouble?" Addie said.

"Listen to me. No one is going to get into trouble. Come out of the house and follow me."

"But she might come back and look for us," Addie said.

He grabbed our shoulders and steered us out onto the porch.

"Come with me," he repeated.

So we linked hands and followed him, blearily, out onto the lawn. The day was still overcast, but there was a stabbing gleam of cloud-covered sunshine in one part of the sky and all of the houses looked as if they were made of plastic. The driveway was empty; our mother's car was gone and newspapers were tossed carelessly onto the pavement in a little heap. I don't know how long we'd been inside, but the walk out to the mail truck seemed endless. The grass tickled the arches of my bare feet. The street in front of our house and the mail truck parked there and the newspapers and everything were all too vivid, too glassy and strange, after the close space of the living room and the colors of the screen.

With this, I fall silent. There is nothing else to say, I think, except that the inside of the truck smelled like cardboard and ink and there were no seats and we rode the whole way to the police station wedged in between white cartons filled with mail, endless envelopes with handwritten addresses.

They are quiet while I am quiet, remembering this.

"Do you remember anything else, Dorian?" says the female voice. "About what happened at the police station or after the police station?"

I shrug under the blanket, in my canal next to Addie's canal, and for a split second it is the same blanket that we huddled under on that living room floor, the same one we fought and clambered and held each other under while he slept and the fan whirred back and forth over us and the grandfather clock banged out the time, swaying its pendulum like an accusing finger.

"That's it," I say. "We came here."

"And where is here?"

"The ward."

"Dorian and Addie," Dr. Lark's voice says. It is an excited, jumpy voice, a frantic voice, like the voice of the mailman when he said *okay, okay*. "Are you ready to be reborn?"

I nod, and I know, somehow, that through the blankets Addie is nodding too.

"Yes," she murmurs.

In a split second they whisk the blankets off and the light breaks all around us, the fresh air coming like a series of cold slaps on our perspiring skin, as harsh and sudden as the air in that moment when the mailman swung open the door.

The tall, draped bookshelves lean in like reapers and the blankets around us are dark, messy puddles. Addie's hair is matted around her face. Her breath comes in long, heaving gasps, and her body is quaking in a way I have never seen it quake before.

Three faces are peering at us: Dr. Lark's, Ellie's, and the woman doctor's, the one with the voice. I want to look at her, but it is Dr. Lark's face that stands out in the starkest relief to me, an eager face dilated in glee, a face as sweaty as our faces, still wearing the fading emotions of the past hours the way the worshippers still smile their fervent smiles on the television after the Sunday sermons, when the choir is singing its farewell.

"Welcome to your rebirth," he says. "Welcome to the cure."

Addie

When the blankets come off, the air stings my skin and I close my eyes against the shrillness of the light. In my stomach the twin stones turn and they are like small animals scrabbling and heaving, scraping their claws against the insides of my belly, clamoring to be released. Before me, three faces swim. His is the one that speaks. I try to focus on what he is saying but the sounds are hollow, pulsing from his lips in a sequence that at first I do not understand. One of them, one of the twisting, heaving creatures, is his. Does he sense the way it scrabbles and kicks?

"You had courage," he is saying. "You had the courage to be born. You were brave. It takes a lot of bravery and determination to change. The wildness that was in you is over now. What happened is in the past. Now you will go forward and be your own family, find your own way, without that rage and that hostility."

Dorian takes my hand while he is speaking and she senses it too, the kicking and the twirling. The blows are coming so swiftly now that I can barely look at the faces, and suddenly I feel a slender arm lifting me up off the blankets and smell the scent of floral lotion and hibiscus conditioners. Ellie.

"They've had enough," she is saying. "I'm going to take them back to the sleeping quarters now and have them lie down."

"Fine," Dr. Lark says, but he is talking excitedly to the woman doctor now, the one with the haunting voice, and she is talking back just as excitedly, and they barely notice us as we pass out of the dim, shrouded office and back down the corridor and across the common areas into the bedroom. Ellie is propelling me on one side and Dorian on the other. Once we are out of earshot, Ellie is on her phone, hissing to someone and looking over her shoulder.

"It's coming now," she says. "Now. Now. No, it's early. I don't know why. The stress and the excitement. You need to get here. Now."

Now the kicks and the cramps are coming with renewed force. I dig my nails as hard as I can into Dorian's hands to keep from crying out, but the effort makes me double over in the doorway to our sleeping quarters. They help me over to the bed.

“What’s happening?” I say, sobbing, clutching at Ellie. “Is it because I was born? Is it because I was born?”

“No, goddammit,” Ellie says. “The twins are coming.”

Chapter 10
Ellie

They meet us by the side entrance in the white Volvo. Mel is driving. Simon is in the passenger seat. He hops out and runs around and opens the door, and Dorian and I help Addie into the backseat, still writhing and moaning. We crawl in on either side of her. When Mel hits the accelerator, our tires spin a little in the gravel and I look back fearfully out of the rear window at the ward, but all the dark windows look the same. The only light is coming from the main reception area and from Dr. Lark's office, where he and Dr. Coe must still be sitting over their brandy glasses. In the car we are packed in close, and Addie's contractions cause her to double up against me. Each time she moves she disturbs the stack of picket signs at our feet, and the slogans tilt up at Dorian and me.

"Abortion equals death," Dorian reads out loud. "Human rights start at birth. Planned Parenthood kills babies."

"Stop it, Dorian," I snap. "Mel, what the fuck."

"Excuse me," Mel snaps back, her angry brown eyes meeting mine for a split second in the rearview mirror. "We were at a rally. We came as soon as we could. We weren't just waiting around for a sudden crisis."

I have not seen Mel for weeks, not since the argument about splitting up the girls, and I have forgotten her sudden and awful spite. We travel in silence down the dark roads that surround the ward, past the sleeping farms with their fields of ruffled soybean plants, sipping the crisp nighttime air that flows in through the cracked windows. Dorian holds Addie's hand and looks out at the land. On her lap is the small duffel bag I made her put together with their things: their medicines and several changes of clean clothes. Addie leans back and groans, clutching her dog-eared copy of Lucretius with her free hand. In the front passenger seat Simon looks thinner than usual in his giant *I Stand 4 Life* sweatshirt. His skin is pale and there is a sheen of sweat on his brow. As for me, my body is still coursing with adrenaline and I am desperately thinking of the next steps, the new, improvised exit plan.

As she drives, Mel keeps her eyes on the road, but every few minutes or so I notice she glances at Addie in the rearview mirror with a strange, almost hostile expression. Her brows tighten and constrict and it is like the anger of a parent scolding a sulking child. *But she is having them*, I want to cry out at her, *what can you blame her for?* We turn onto the interstate and get in the lane heading toward Knoxville General, and only then does Mel speak. Her eyes lose that expression and soften to their usual mildness, their usual patience in moments of feminine catastrophe.

"So when did the contractions start?" she says.

"Probably sometime during the rebirthing." Beside me Addie continues to groan, each new spasm causing her body to quake against mine. "No one noticed because she was under the blankets and they were too distracted by the procedure. I got her away and into the bedroom and walking and breathing, and I got Dorian to watch her and to pack the bag, and I called you right away."

"And him? Does he know?"

"No, but if he goes to look in the sleeping quarters he'll figure it out."

"Then he'll come to the hospital."

"I think so. I might be able to keep him out. I don't know yet."

Now we are pulling into the hospital complex with its glowing all-night bustle of activity, heading toward the emergency drop-off where the sliding doors usher in and out a steady stream of doctors, nurses, and medics with stretchers; patients on foot and in wheelchairs and with walkers; patients with wheeling IV bags and on crutches and holding *Get Well* balloons; friends and families chatting excitedly with the news of pregnancy and birth or healing and recovery; friends and families dejected and slumped with the news of sickness and death.

"Are you ready, Addie?" Dorian whispers to her weeping sister in the backseat. "It's time."

***

I see the girls through check-in. Addie is installed in a hospital bed in a long wing of the ER where rows of beds are separated from each other by curtains. She is still squeezing her goddamned copy of Lucretius like a stress ball, and Dorian is standing there wiping her brow and timing her contractions like a proud father. I ride the giant elevator down to the main waiting room and walk back out past the metal detector and over to the security desk where he sits in his gray uniform with its black trim, his badge dangling over his upper right pocket. He is clean-shaven and his black hair is shorn in a buzz cut close around his skull. His shoulder muscles seem even bigger, straining against the cloth of his uniform. He is watching the series of monitors below the counter of the service desk, but his mouth and eyes work into a slow grin when he sees me.

"Ellie," he says. "In the flesh."

"Tim."

I have not seen him since I went back to work at the ward, and this moment of recognition brings a fresh but diminished wave of adrenaline after the sudden crisis of the evening, like a small tropical storm that emerges from the fading whirl of a hurricane.

"I have a favor to ask."

"Here she goes again," he says to no one in particular—the other officer on duty is seeing patients through the metal detector—"always asking for the favors. Jesus, Ellie, can't you just catch up with a guy?"

"It's about what we discussed on the phone," I tell him. "I have a friend who's in trouble and she's here for treatment, and I need to make sure that a certain person doesn't come in to see her or find her, and that no one else knows she's here." I take Dr. Lark's business card out of my purse and slide it across the desk. "Can you help?"

He takes the card without removing his eyes from mine.

"A friend in trouble, huh? Who's this guy? Her boyfriend?"

"Sort of."

"What'd he do?"

"He's not a good guy. I don't want him here."

Again, without taking his eyes off me, he slides the card into his pocket. I can see him working his jaw the way he always used to when he was thinking about something or noticing something, and suddenly I remember him doing that when we were lying in bed together. He used to avert his eyes from mine and pull my hips more tightly against his, and I could feel the motion of his jaw against the crown of my head.

"Seriously, Ellie," he says at last. "You show up here out of the blue and you've got all these demands. I don't know what to think. I'll tell you what. I'll keep your guy out if you go have a drink with me. I get off at midnight. We can just go around the corner to Railbenders for half an hour and then I'll get you back here so you can check on your friend."

"Please, Tim, can't you take this a little more seriously? It's important."

"I *am* being serious."

His obstinate eyes lock onto mine.

"Midnight is too soon," I tell him, impatiently. "I can't be far."

"Railbenders ain't far."

"Okay," I agree. "Okay. Fine."

"Okay," he says, and suddenly the jaw is still and he is all business once more, picking up a pencil and a clipboard. "Tell me what this asshole looks like. What's his name again?"

The nurses move Addie to a private room in the eastern wing of the hospital and I find her there with Dorian, still clutching her damp, tattered book. Dorian is sitting in the chair by her bed in a tomboy's stance, knees falling away to the side. She is holding her sister's hand. The nurse on duty is taking Addie's vitals and I can see Addie wince a little at the stranger's movements, at the unaccustomed warmth and briskness of her touch.

It is strange to see them interacting with the wider world, strange to see them in a place as vulnerable and human and universal as a hospital—and yet, I reflect, they have spent their lives in a type of hospital, under measurement and supervision. But for once the procedures are not just about them. Dorian seems to sense this too and looks with a kind of awe at the routine wrapping and unwrapping of the blood-pressure cuff around Addie's upper arm, at the tube that falls down her side like a snake, at the slow drip of the IV into her sister's body.

"Your vital signs are good, Addie," the nurse says.

"My stomach," she groans.

"I'm going to invite the anesthesiologist in to administer your epidural. Do you feel ready for that, Addie?"

Addie nods weakly.

"Then I need you to sit up for me and open your gown at the back."

The nurse helps her into a sitting position with her head bent toward her chest, exposing the smooth skin at the base of her spine. Addie looks like a small child who has been yelled at and put in timeout.

The anesthesiologist is a man in his late twenties or so, with a full head of thick brown hair; healthy, glowing skin; and squat, muscular thighs that strain against his hospital scrubs. He wears a regulation-blue plastic head cap and has a small white mask over his mouth. The girls draw back when they see him, startled by his alien bulkiness and vitality. Dorian tenses in her chair, and for a split second I think there is going to be a struggle.

The anesthesiologist laughs a warm, reassuring laugh.

"Try not to worry," he says. "This will help with the discomfort."

In a series of smooth, practiced gestures he swabs the injection site with the local anesthetic, slides the guide needle in, and fixes the catheter in place by taping it along the center of Addie's shivering back.

"You'll start to feel this in about ten minutes," he says. "It's very important that you stay in bed now and that you don't try to walk. The nurse will be back periodically to check your blood pressure and your babies' heartbeats."

Addie groans an acknowledgment. The nurse helps her settle back among the pillows and smooths her tangled hair away from her forehead, but it is not until both she and the anesthesiologist have left that Addie relaxes fully back and closes her eyes.

"Do you want me to read to you again?" Dorian says.

Addie nods.

Dorian takes the book from Addie's hand, unfolds a dog-eared page, and begins:

> *But, now again to weave the tale begun,*
> *All nature, then, as self-sustained, consists*
> *Of twain of things: of bodies and of void*
> *In which they're set, and where they're moved around.*

With their wide eyes and sweaty, tufted hair, they look like feral cats brought inside, tense from all the different noises and smells, alert and prepared for the attack.

I leave the girls for the moment and go in search of Mel and Simon. They're not in the waiting room and they're not in the snack area by the vending machines. I double back through the hallways I still remember from my training. The eastern hallway by the delivery elevators is mostly made up of supply closets, and it's darker and quieter than the bustling ER corridor where the girls are. I linger for a moment, relishing its calmness and its empty hallways and its doors half-shut against dozing patients.

Down at the far end of the hallway is a supply room with the door half-open. A pool of fluorescent light pours out onto the clean, polished white floor tiles. I pass this door, expecting to hear the familiar soft murmur of shift nurses or pharmacy personnel loading prescriptions onto a little wheeled cart for distribution, and I am startled to hear a low, throaty, teary voice that sounds like Mel's. I pause in the little patch of light and push the door further open.

Mel is standing there, pleading and crying, and Simon is standing on a footstool in front of the long rows of orange plastic dispensary drawers. One of the drawers is open and he is grasping a handful of pills. All around him, on the counter, on the floor, are more white pills, scattered like the beads of a broken necklace.

"Mel!" I demand, aghast. "What are you doing in here?"

She looks panicked. She bursts into tears.

Simon makes a slurring, incoherent noise and turns to me with that hangdog look, a mournful mien as low and ashamed as a dachshund's. He tries to step down off the footstool, lurches, and catches himself against the counter. The pills that were in his hand scatter onto the floor with a noise like rain on a tin rooftop. He falls to his knees, in a daze, and begins to collect them. I can see traces of vomit on his T-shirt and the muscles of his right arm twitch and strain as he tries to prop himself up.

Mel makes a move toward him but I grab her arm and

hold her back.

"Who let you in here?"

"Oh, Ellie, it wasn't his fault." Mel speaks quickly, hysterically, over her choking sobs. "He knew someone here with a key. It wasn't his fault. He started taking it, you know, in the—in the ward. And Dr. Lark kept him on it, and he kept sending it to him, and he wanted so badly to quit, but it kept coming. And he tried and tried and there was a whole week where he did it, he was in one of the beds at the charity, and Sweets watched over him. He was sweating and throwing up and he had the shakes the whole time, but he did so well and we were so proud of him. But he was miserable, and then when the pills came again Dr. Lark had messed up the prescription. I think he got so distracted at the ward that he started prescribing the wrong things. He sent—I think it was Tramadol. It wasn't the right thing. And so we just thought maybe something, just to get him through this delivery and to get him out of his pain so that we can get him some help when this is all over. Oh, Ellie," she cries again, "don't blame him. He needs it. It's not his fault."

Simon lets out another incoherent moan, from the floor, and Mel makes another move toward him, but I pull her toward me, hard. I turn her so that we are facing each other, her arms gripping mine in desperation, her body crushed against mine, her moist, red-ringed eyes in my face.

"Mel. Mel. Listen to me. Take a few deep breaths. There. Breathe. You need to stay away from him. He's sick, Mel. He's not in his right mind. He needs help right away. We need to get you and him out of here, away from this room, and we need to go downstairs and tell someone that he's here and that he needs help. Mel. Listen. Please. You need to breathe. If you can just breathe everything will be okay, I promise."

She is gulping air, she is trying to breathe, but the thing that is making her face contort into fresh sobs seems to be different now, seems to come from something besides Simon. I peer into her wide, terrified eyes and I realize as she presses her hips against me that she seems to have put on weight and become more tired recently, and I think of how late and how often Simon has been staying at the megachurch, and I remember the way she looked at Addie in the car, and in a moment of horror I know what it is.

"No." I grasp her so tightly that my fingers leave marks in the skin around her shoulders. "No. Not you, Mel. You can't be."

She is crying again.

"Not his," I say urgently, shaking her. "Mel. Not his."

Simon moans again, loudly, from the floor.

It takes me fifteen minutes to get a hold of Sweets at the megachurch and to arrange for her to pick up Mel, still sobbing, in the main drop-off area; it takes me another twenty minutes to coax Simon, moaning and clawing at his elbows, down to check-in. It is nearly midnight when I make my way back to Addie and Dorian's room in time to see Addie on her back getting ready to deliver, sweating and pushing as the doctor instructs her, all the while gasping and contorting her face in that strange birth-mask of agony: the twins' bodies invading and eclipsing the woman's and then renouncing it, ravaging it, as snakes knead and ravage the skins they shed. Dorian is beside her, still clutching her hand.

One of the assisting nurses recognizes me and beckons me in. I mask and attire myself like Dorian; I too stand by the bed, out of the way of the doctors, and whisper to her in the calmest way I can.

"Push, Addie," we urge, all of us together: the doctor, the nurses, Dorian, and me.

She pushes, obedient not to us but to the mandates of the bodies inside of her, tortured by the driving will of the unborn.

The first one is born three minutes before the second. Both of the babies are bright pink and underweight, but they are healthy and strong, with a wiry strength that I recognize as Dorian's, and I know when I see them that they will survive. It is not a strength of muscle and sinew so much as a gripping biological will, a ferocity that emerges in the screams and the determined kicks of the legs. Their faces are wrinkled and damp, and when they are placed into Addie's arms, one in each crook, she looks down at them with an expression that is something like bewilderment and something like relief. They both lean in to peer at them, Addie and Dorian: one face to a face, matched sets of eyes staring into eyes just like their own.

"How do you feel, Addie?" I ask her.

"They look different than they did on the screen," she says. She does not take her eyes off their faces, but her voice is listless and detached, as if she were describing a flaw in a product she had just ordered from the internet.

"You mean on the ultrasound?" Dorian says.

I think she means the ultrasound, and then I think she means the television screen, and then all of a sudden I don't know what she means. Maybe she's picturing the fry in the tank and the way they drifted, iridescent and vulnerable, in the water.

"Yes," she says, "they look different from everything."

She sleeps, Dorian dozing beside her in the chair. The babies are in the ICU, sleeping in their isolettes, breathing sweetly into the alarming, quiet night. It is two in the morning and I am on my way to talk to the neonatal nurse again when I hear his voice and stop at the end of the hallway, a sudden fist of anger striking the inside of my chest.

They are standing in front of the ICU window peering in at the sleeping twins and conferring in low voices. He still wears his khakis and polo shirt, and she is standing so close that their thighs graze, her smooth bob swaying a little as she points and gestures with him. In their shared pride and animation, in the little snatches of eager description and possibility that float to me at the end of the hallway, they almost resemble a proud set of grandparents looking in on their newly born grandchildren rather than a set of deranged medical experts forging a new path for research.

Without taking my eyes off them, I pull out my cell phone. He answers on the first ring.

"Hi, Ellie," he says in his slow drawl. Behind him, I can hear the thick din of Railbenders: tipsy laughter, clinking bottles, Aerosmith wailing from the jukebox.

"You're an asshole," I snap.

"I told you, Ellie," he says, and I can hear him smiling on the other end of the line, "I was waiting for you. You never came, did you?"

"You don't know what you've done," I tell him, staring straight ahead.

He begins to say something else, to cajole me, but I hang up without waiting for him to finish.

They are still peering through the window, pointing and conferring, and in that moment I see the twins' lifetimes shrinking into a single point, concentrating as a sun ray begins to slowly disappear behind a shutting door. For them there is only the ward and, beyond it, the cure. And beyond that, endless generations of the disordered.

Chapter 11

Addie

The nurses bring them to me when they are stable. They are both placed in my arms, the small shriveled babies, each wrapped in a little pink blanket, each sleeping with her eyes screwed up against the light as if the world is already too much. Their cheeks are pudgy like the cheeks of the pugs on *Domestic Dogs of America* and their skin is a bright, flaming pink. Faces already bathed in a flush of emotion. Their bodies yanked out of safety and thrust into loud noises and fluctuating temperatures and crowding, warm bodies.

Looking at them I think of their long gestation in the ward, that period of thinking, planning, waiting. This is not like the birth of the seahorses, that triumphant exultant explosion of new life in the tank, that vibrant culmination. Inside that place in my body where they used to be is a new feeling of lacerating hollowness. I am cured. Yet part of me is empty. They have made it to where I do not want to strike but also to where I do not want to feel, I think, looking at the tiny faces slumbering. Dr. Lark's children, or Simon's children, the seed does not matter: they are only the frailest versions of people who are already frail, and they will only grow frailer with time.

I look at Dorian leaning over me and I see that she sees the same thing I see, a future stretching forward into nothing, that desperate shutting of the eyelids against the ravages of the world. Their eyes are closed but Dorian's are alive, with that same look we shared right before she raised the poker to strike and strike again, in that instant when I reached out and covered his mouth.

"No," she says, reading my thoughts. She reaches out and takes them from me, one after the other, and lays them in the little bassinette the way the nurse showed us. They wring and unwring their tiny limbs restlessly. They are like a plastic sandwich wrapping when you squeeze it and then watch it expand and loosen back out, slowly.

"The time for that is gone now," Dorian says. "It's time to dress."

With a slow, deliberate gentleness, a new habit of patience and attention, she slips the needle out of my arm, unhooks the IVs, and helps me out of bed and into the old scrubs I wore before the twins were torn out of me, the scrubs with their distended waistband that the babies used to fill. She takes my hand and leads me out of the room. It is five in the morning and the hallways are empty as we creep past the hordes of sleeping mothers and their crumpling and uncrumpling children. We are nearly to the exit doors when one of them, one of mine, sets up a long, curdling wail. I pause and Dorian pauses, standing still in a listening pose, before she pulls me through the side exit and out into the parking lot, which is blank and bare and spread out under the winking gaze of a million stars.

Dorian shrugs.

"They'll get to have them, but they won't get to have us," she says. "Sometimes you have to fail before you can make it work."

"But it did work," I say. "Didn't it?"

I clutch her hand and follow her across the empty lot, toward the woods behind the hospital, toward the ring of mountains that cast their bland, indifferent shadows over the well and the sick.

Acknowledgments

This novel was inspired by a September 15, 2006, episode of *This American Life* called "Unconditional Love." Additional sources consulted include Colby Pearce's *A Short Introduction to Attachment and Attachment Disorder* (2009) and Mark Chaffin, Rochelle Hanson, Benjamin Saunders, et. al., "Report of the APSAC Task Force on Attachment Therapy, Reactive Attachment Disorder, and Attachment Problems," *Child Maltreatment* 11.1 (2006): 76–89. I also consulted coverage of the trial of Connell Watkins and Julie Ponder and their deadly "rebirthing" technique in the *Denver Post*, *The Telegraph*, and *The New York Times*, and on the Advocates for Children in Therapy website.

Inspiration for the nature program scenes in this book came from the Public Broadcasting System's show *Nature*, especially "The Mystery Monkeys of Shangri-La," "Meet the Coywolf," and "A Murder of Crows."

I couldn't have written a word without the support of friends, family, and fellow writers. Sean Murphy offered advice and encouragement for an early version of the manuscript. Amy Barclay, Jesse Hausler, Perry Barrow, Jessica Hutchins,

Alexander Wille, J.P. Murray, Meghan Kuckelman Beverage, and Ryan Lowe (a.k.a. "The Demon Bunnies") all gave me rigorous and helpful feedback on the short story that became the germ of this novel. Special thanks go to Kevin Beverage, who read countless drafts of this project in both early and late stages and offered thoughtful and astute comments. He is as much this book's author as I am.

It has been a tremendous pleasure to work with Lanternfish Press. Christine Neulieb's incisive, wise edits greatly improved this book. I'm very grateful to Christine, Amanda Thomas, Feliza Casano, and everyone at the press.

My generous, talented colleagues in the Literary Arts department at Point Park University are an endless source of wisdom and good-humored advice about the writing life. Special thanks go to Kirstin Hanley, Chris Girman, Jess McCort, Karen Dwyer, Sarah Perrier, P.K. Weston, Kim Bell, and Kris Julian.

I am also grateful to Lisa Smith, Jake Smith, Shirley Korwek, and Barbara Smith for love, support, and many gifts of books. Thank you for believing in me.

My father, Bill Smith, read the opening pages long ago and encouraged me to keep going. I wish he could have lived to see the end of it. I miss him every day and will always remember his ardent love for the creative life.

John Zeller has been unfailingly encouraging and deeply honest about my work; I couldn't ask for a more supportive partner or a better home to write in.

Photo credit: John Zeller

About the Author

Barbara Barrow is a fiction writer and literary critic who adores all things feminist, fabulist, and surreal. Her short fiction has appeared or is forthcoming in *The Forge Literary Magazine*, *Cease, Cows*, *Folio*, *Zahir*, *NANO Fiction*, and elsewhere, and her journal articles have appeared in *Victorian Poetry*, *Journal of Victorian Culture*, *Victorian Periodicals Review*, and *Nineteenth-Century Contexts*. She is Assistant Professor of English at Point Park University in Pittsburgh. Follow her online at barbarabarrow.com or on Twitter and Facebook.